I0638655

# The Last Atlantean Prince

## In The World Of Hyboria

Lawrence BoarerPitchford

Published by Lawrence BoarerPitchford, 2022.

THE LAST ATLANTEAN PRINCE

**First edition. February 17, 2022.**

Copyright © 2022 Lawrence BoarerPitchford.

ISBN: 978-1736509692

Written by Lawrence BoarerPitchford.

# Table of Contents

# DEDICATION

This story is dedicated to the memory of the late Robert E. Howard, a gifted author lost to the world before his time. Howard created the barbarian fantasy genre, and from his creative mind came one of the most iconic barbarian characters of all time - Conan the Barbarian. While later media entities and authors have taken Conan and re-shaped him into what he is seen as today, the original incarnation of the character is worth revisiting. If you grew up reading the pulp fiction works, and comic books, you know the primal and pragmatic grip that the stories can have on the imagination. Long live the memory of Robert E. Howard, and may his soul be at peace..

# ACKNOWLEDGEMENTS

SENIOR EDITOR - Wendy Schimer
Copy Editor - Roselyn Pitchford
Cover Art - The Book Nymph PR

# CHAPTER 1

## Re-acquaintance

The Captain of the Frontier Rangers was explicit: no one was to attack until he ordered breath given to the war-horn. It was a standard order, and under most circumstances, none would disobey. But often the gods play havoc with convention, and those of savage nature can run off with high spirits.

Benhargan was not one for flights-of-fancy, but even the most disciplined of warriors could at times forget themselves. He remained crouched, hidden within a large leafy bush. Every muscle in his body was tight; a coiled spring ready to be sprung. The foe who released that energy would find a hero's fight.

From across the glade a host of Pict warriors emerged. They approached, following some unseen trail. Each scoured the ground for any sign of interlopers.

The anticipation of battle pumped through Benhargan's veins, as he waited for the signal to engage the enemy. Then, one Pict caught his eye. One savage of the group made Benhargan rethink his adherence to convention, and think of his own glory.

The warrior was large, with a painted face, pierced nose and lip. Around his neck hung a lace of ears, and up and down his arms were black-ash tattoos of skulls.

His headdress of iridescent blue and red feathers glistened in the morning sun— a sight intended to strike terror in his victims. This Pict was the Managan...the Lord of Skulls...a very powerful warrior possessing an elevated position in the Pict clans. To kill such an adversary, the victor's purse would hang heavy.

The enemy came close, picking through the tall reeds, and checking for dented sod and broken blades of grass. He was not more than a few feet away when the savage focused on the bush.

Stopping a few inches from Benhargan, the Pict lifted his loincloth and proceeded to urinate into the shrub. The Barbarian remained as still as a stalking panther.

A foul stench of urine perfumed the air. The steaming stream ran from side to side, hitting Benhargan's rawhide boots with each pass.

The Pict looked confused as he took note of the change in pitch of his flow striking the ground. He moved it away, then back; the sound of liquid on leather was unmistakable. His eyes grew wide with surprise, then just as quickly rage.

Benhargan's meaty hand latched onto the Managan and pulled him into the bush. Three quick thrusts of his dagger produced an outpouring of blood, but did not slow or quiet the enemy.

Giving a warning shout to his party, the Pict attacked, plunging his flint knife into Benhargan, cutting through his leather shirt, and into the muscle of his waist.

The barbarian stepped back, pulling the Pict with him, then rammed him into a nearby tree, again and again. The knife flew from the Pict's hand. The warrior's face turned grim as he latched his fingers around Benhargan's bull-like neck, and with all his strength tried to strangle the life from him.

Benhargan glared back, an expression of battle-lust written across his crooked smile. The Pict's eyes bore into the Cimmerian like red hot brass spikes. About the bush they thrashed – the Pict kicking and squeezing – Benhargan holding firm like a metal vice cinched tight. After a moment the Pict's grip loosened, then became limp; the crimson fluid that filled his body was all but gone. Benhargan let the body slump to the leafy soil.

In the distance, the screams of the Pict tribesmen shook the leaves. They poured out from the far woods into the meadow. It was much more than just a host.

Benhargan looked to his right, and Bulvife nodded his head.

"I'm glad you did that," Bulvife said. "I was beginning to wonder if we'd enjoy any battle this day."

Benhargan replaced his dagger in its sheath.

"Yes, that fool of a captain was trying my patience. Why does he pine so long to signal the attack? How could I let a trophy such as the Managan walk away unchallenged?"

"Small matter," Bulvife said. "The enemy comes, and now we let our arrows seek blood, and our blades gorge upon the flesh of our foe!"

Through the brush the two barbarians charged. In the glade, the Managan's men whooped and ran at them headlong from the edge of the far forest. Bulvife let loose arrow after arrow until his quiver was empty, then drew his brass sword and flew into the enemy ranks.

The bulk of the war party was upon them. Blades of metal and stone smashed into one another. Bits of flesh, blood, hair and bile splashed about - the foul bits landed upon the indiscriminate cheek and chest.

From all around emerged the Cimmerian's brethren – the Frontier Rangers; their weapons ready, and lust for battle in their eyes. The hard fighting was now at hand as more Picts came, and the rangers formed up to full strength – all eager to collect bones for brass.

As the fighting stretched on, the line to enter the afterlife grew longer, and the gods welcomed many a soul as the sun was chased behind the world by the moon.

BULVIFE'S BOOTS MADE a sickly sucking sound as he walked across the crimson soil. He was covered in the horrors of war, and longed for more fight as his veins throbbed with battle-fervor.

Benhargan approached, in his hand the head of the Managan. "This one, and sixty others I've sent to the nine hells makes me the lord of this battle! Their souls will bring a pretty price. How did you fare?"

Bulvife surveyed the many bodies around him. He spied a wounded Pict crawling toward the thicket. Strolling over he drove his sword into the man's back. "Sixty-three," he said.

"Boast!" Benhargan accused. "I see only two score dead by your hand at best."

"Yes, but you do not count the one's yet to be killed. There are more," Bulvife said.

"Where? Are they hidden under your tunic?" Benhargan sarcastically asked.

"It is said that the wise man anticipates what he cannot see. There..." Bulvife pointed at twenty Picts less than fifty yards and closing.

"Crom is generous this day!" Benhargan called to the sky. "Come forth and meet your end!" he shouted at the Picts, then charged holding his sword high and the severed head low.

When there were no more Picts, the drums of retreat rumbled and the tally made. Benhargan and Bulvife returned to the rangers' camp deep in the forest. There, they would drink, eat, and tell tales of their fighting.

A crimson hue colored the sky, as Banhargan knelt by the brook. He splashed the crystal water over his face and muscular chest.

The Cimmerian washed off the gore and trappings of death, though it was not typical for him to do so. He preferred to wear the spatter a little while, and watch the expressions of those green rangers new to the wildlands. But this time he had other duties to attend to.

One such duty was to present himself to the captain, who was surely going to dress him down for disobeying an order. Second, the caravan of consorts had arrived, and he and Bulvife were awarded first lot since their bounty was the largest of all the rangers.

Bulvife came from the opposite bank, waded into the brook and washed his honey-colored skin with a brown root frothing with white foam.

"You make yourself ready for pleasuring the captain?" Benhargan jibed.

"Only after he's had you like a Kush prince enjoys his eunuchs," Bulvife retorted.

Benhargan grunted, said nothing, and continued to scrape off the dirt and gore. Bulvife tossed the root to him.

"Make use of this soap-root," said Bulvife. "I'm sure the consorts would appreciate it."

"It makes me uncomfortable to see how much the walled cities have influenced you," Benhargan added.

Bulvife laughed and shook his head.

After a few minutes both men were clean and the water no longer carried away the exploits of the day. Bulvife left the stream, dried and dressed, then moved up toward the camp.

Benhargan did the same and followed his comrade – striding up the embankment. He followed the twisted path to the tents, through ferns, and past moss-covered logs. The scent of moisture and fungus was heavy and rich, stimulating memories that dwelled within him.

Many rangers were about. There were Vanir, and men from Kush, and even Valkyries from Valk, the city-state in the northwest by the sea, populated exclusively by powerful warrior women.

By the fire pit were a group of rangers - some small and wiry, and others powerful and large. There were some Cimmerians, like himself, playing dice, or competing in athletic games such as boulder throwing, flying-fists, wrestling, and archery.

Meat was roasting over cook-fires, and beer and wine flowed down many a chin and from many a cup. Benhargan walked through the throng and approached a long tan tent flying the banners of the Frontier Rangers.

He entered and stood in front of a rough fashioned wooden table. The captain looked up, then back down at some papers. A moment passed, then he sat back and observed Benhargan.

"Do you know why I summoned you?" the captain asked.

"There is little doubt. The many kills that I've made have lightened your strongbox. Upon my tent pole sits the Managan's head, and before you can take your pleasure with the newly arrived consorts, I will have already had them all.

The captain briefly looked on the verge of outrage, but then chuckled sardonically.

"That is of no concern to me, though I should have you quartered for disobeying my orders. Nonetheless, this map has come into my possession."

The captain handed Benhargan a rolled parchment tied with a red string.

"I need you and Bulvife to seek out the place marked on it, and report on what you find." He narrowed his gaze. "And if your god Crom is waiting at the end, and he rings your ape-neck, I'll be all the more pleased. If he lets you live and you return, you'd better bring to me what you've found. Now, get hence from my sight and sate your lust with the bawdy women."

Benhargan nodded solemnly, turned, and left the tent.

That corn-eater thinks to send me to my death, he thought. He chuckled. Not a plan he could have formed himself, so who fed him the idea?

He walked to where the caravan of consorts had erected tents. Perfume filled the air, and soft voices of the kinder sex chimed about.

Entering the main tent, he saw Bulvife. The man was as insatiable in battle as he was with women. Some might even say he had no shame, for he took one woman, then another, then another, all the while guzzling mead and blood-wine with abandon.

Benhargan grunted and removed his loincloth. He grabbed a beautiful courtesan. "Tonight, I shall temper my lust with you," he said to her.

She giggled, fluttered her eyelids, and swooned into his arms.

Sounds of merriment and pleasure echoed into the early hours. The stars of fate spun overhead, and the moon goddess made sport with the lustful mortals she watched over. Long did these sounds fill the night, until at last the sun came to fill the world with its warm caress.

As Bulvife woke, a hint of sunlight was painting a yellowish glow through the tent walls. He moved to the flap, parted the two pieces of fabric, and stepped out into the cool morning air.

"Why do you leave the comfort of the women?" Benhargan asked.

The corner of Bulvife's mouth twisted up. "There is an ember that burns within my mind."

"Like when we were traveling with the wizard? I'd say the rotten magician still lives," Benhargan said.

"How?" Bulvife shook his head. "None could have survived such destruction. A whole island was blasted into the sky. The seas rose in rage and devastated the coasts of many a land. No man could have lived through that."

"Grimface is not a man, remember?" Benhargan paused for a moment while he poked at the fire with a stick. "The captain has given me this." He handed Bulvife the map.

"For what purpose?"

"He wishes us to travel to the end marked on that map, then report back."

"Did you look to where that mark is?" Bulvife asked.

"Yes, of course."

"It ends at the ruins of Valmalia along the Black River. The area is deep within the Pict lands."

It was Benhargan's turn to foster a smile. "That bastard of a captain thinks this is a good opportunity to be rid of us." He paused. "Look closer at that map. Do you not see the tabulation of wealth, now faded with age?"

"Yes... a thousand stones of silver and gold. Many chests of jewels and jars of spices."

"This map is no accident. There is something else afoot. The faint marks look old, but watch." Benhargan wetted his finger and rubbed it across the faded scrawling. When he held up the digit, there was black on it. "It's an old forger's trick to make the ink appear aged." He looked up at the sky. "I fear those gods that Grimface follows are not done with us. Deceit is the trade-work of wizards, as we both know. This map stinks of Grimface."

Bulvife shrugged his shoulders. "Grimface or not, this is a chance to do what rangers do best. After all, no man should live forever."

"Now that's the attitude the gods look for in fools and heroes!" Benhargan said. He stood by the fire, then nodded toward the barracks tents. "Let's gather our things and be off. I've grown weary of this place. It's time we were back on our terms, free in the greenwood and living by our wits."

"Well, if fear does not stay your feet, lead on," Bulvife said.

They made straight for the Black River. The terrain was rugged, and in places cloaked by shadow over the high hills. Many times, they found frost and snow clinging to broken stone and scrub. The going was tough, and the predators of the mountains stalked their heels with every step.

By the time they descended into the next valley, jagged black rocks were turning to brown grasslands, and vast dark forests rose like cliffs in the distance. And, like a foreboding purple scar, the heathen river the Picts worshiped - the Black River - carved its course through those realms.

At the very limit of Benhargan's vision, he saw the ruined, stone towers of Valmalia—the cursed city.

"Once we get close, the Picts will be of no concern, for even they won't go near that crumbling heath," Bulvife said.

"We're not there yet, and those things that lurk in the forests are not to be dismissed," Benhargan warned.

Bulvife nodded. "You're slow footed and slow witted; I'll out pace you and have little to worry about, as the beasts feast upon your bones."

"Run?" Benhargan looked incredulous. "I will face my foes as Crom intended—blade in hand and ferocious contempt in my teeth! As you've said, you will run..." He put his finger to his chin as if deep in thought. "Cowards run, don't they?"

Bulvife shook his head. "I have seen you run many a time. You know as well as I, that running means one lives to reassess the battle. So perhaps you should consider a run."

"What sort of run do you mean? Run like a tavern wench for her drink? Run like a king for his gold chamber-pot? What sort of running do you speak of?"

"Sport," Bulvife replied. "Let the faster of us reap the most of what we find." He broke into a run, moving swiftly and silently through the trees and brush. Benhargan followed as stealthily and rapidly as a young wolf in pursuit of a stag.

They ran for several hours, passing bubbling springs, and fast-moving brooks. The trees and thick bushes grew in both size and abundance. The high branches, filled with dark green leaves, blocked the sunlight and produced a smothering shade.

Many a terrible thing lay hidden along their path. Ghastly things that lurked in shadows – things that burrowed into the realm of man from the feral lands of death. Things which mortal men feared more than the threat of torture.

Coming around a large white boulder, the two Cimmerians stopped short of a long drop off. They'd followed the pulsing flow of a creek, and now stood poised at the edge of a churning waterfall. Bulvife looked down and saw a hundred foot drop into a glistening depression of green water.

"Look," Bulvife whispered pointing down by the pool. "Picts."

A score of females formed a semicircle around a burly fair-haired Pict shaman. The crowd of women parted, and a young man dressed in frontier leather was brought forth. The savage chanted and waved feathered items in the air. He reached his hands high into the sky, then bowed low to the water at the edge of the pool.

Bulvife removed his bow, but Benhargan shook his head. The two men watched as the shaman took his obsidian blade, approached the sacrifice, grabbed him by the hair, and neatly cut the fellow's throat.

Blood pumped onto the rocky ground as the body of the man convulsed, then went limp. The shaman stood back and chanted.

The sound of the savage's voice made the ground vibrate. Fire erupted where the blood pooled. A stench filled the air - rot and brimstone. From the flaming ground emerged a crimson beast, its body glistening as if new-born from the fiery pools.

# CHAPTER 2
# Wayward Friends

THE MONSTER SLUGGISHLY moved about the circle of worshipers. A sound like ripping fabric filled the air as wings spawned from its back. The creature's eyes opened—orange and black with slitted pupils. It sniffed at the air, then turned and snapped its fanged jaws at a few of the assembled. Fear griped all the worshipers, all less the shaman.

It turned on the crowd, ripping off the arm of one of the unlucky. Its jaws tore into the flesh of another, as its wings cut through meat and bone of several more. Those trying to flee didn't make it halfway to the forest before the horror claimed their lives.

Below, all but the shaman lay dead. The horror flexed its wings as it turned on the remaining Pict. The savage stood atop the bolder and held a staff with a black crystal at the end. The beast froze, its eyes never straying from the end.

Speaking, the shaman addressed the monster; the guttural language smacked of dark magic, and both Benhargan and Bulvife felt a pain in their ears by that foreign tongue.

The demon spread its red wings and shot into the air, circled once, then flew down the river. The shaman danced upon the rock for a moment. He stopped and gazed at the treeline. From the woods, a black and twisted shape shambled forth. It appeared to have a man-like form. Stringy black tendrils extended from it, as if substituting for arms and legs. It approached the native sorcerer.

"It is good. Your powers are suitable for my purposes." The voice rippled the very air as it echoed across the estuary.

The shaman nodded. "Let that magician do his worst," he snapped in Aqualonian. "He's not as powerful as I. You will witness such!"

"You will be rewarded, when your incarnation renders the wizard dead. Do not fail me, for the fiery bowels of Oberscour will be your home forevermore."

The shadowy thing wavered like a banner in the breeze, then vanished. A moment passed and the shaman got down from the stone. He looked at the sacrificial remains of his followers, laughed menacingly, then walked back into the forest.

Bulvife looked over at Benhargan and shrugged. "What was that?"

"None of our concern," Benhargan whispered. "Let's get down and cross the water. The ruins are not more than two leagues away."

Both men scrambled down the cliff and set foot on the cold, rounded river stones. Bulvife moved toward the forest fence, listened, then came back.

"The Pict is gone," he confirmed.

"Good. Let's be on our way," Benhargan said, as he led the way across the rushing green waters.

Once on the other side, the two rangers moved swiftly into the forest and toward the ancient ruins. Here the moving was easier, for a neglected ancient road cut through the forest, and at regular intervals springs of fresh water flowed into carved stone basins.

That night they slept nested in the trees. The vines and foliage allowed for easy bedding and a comfortable sleep. From their respective leather sacks, they ate hardened meal-bread, dried meat, and sipped wine from their skins. When the light of dawn came forth, they traveled up rubble-covered hills and stayed the night in the ruins of an ancient graystone tower that rose above the treetops.

Upon the next dawn, they slipped back into the greenwood, and continued the hard traveling. There were signs of Pict war parties, old camps, and some fresh. About were all the hallmarks of conflict— heads on poles, fields of bones strung up on wooden frames, and burnt corpses festering in the patches of sunlight.

In their lands, the Picts often preyed upon each other. Many clan disputes and skirmishes happened wantonly. Deep within these forests, death stalked every corner, ever present and searching for victims to be claimed.

Benhargan froze. Bulvife withdrew his bow and three arrows. Neither man spoke, but knew there was something amiss. Slowly the two rangers picked their way forward. There was a subtle scent in the air.

Bulvife drew in the vibrant smell. "Perfume," he whispered to Benhargan.

Picts did not wear perfume, only city dwellers did. But those of civilization would never venture so deep into these forests. Only a madman might dare to mingle with such savages.

Making their way forward, Benhargan stopped and motioned to Bulvife. There was movement ahead. Both men remained quiet.

In the wind was the sound of clumsy tromping - definitely not the surefooted movement of Picts. Murmuring came to Benhargan's ears. Aqualonian was being spoken. The Cimmerians moved forward again.

He stopped at a briar-bordered ledge overlooking a wide meadow and many Pict dwellings. Abundant cook-fires and drying lodges were erected. Just beyond he saw a waving black banner with three gold triangles upon it. Picts did not use banners.

The two barbarians skulked along the edge looking for a silent way down. Moments later, Benhargan set foot on the level sod of the meadow. It took only a few minutes more to crawl through the tall grass and into the forest. A dozen yards away, they made their way toward the foreigners' tents.

There were soldiers in black armor standing watch. Long poles with curved blades were at the ready. Other guards patrolled around the tent, looking toward the forest, then toward the Pict village.

Benhargan took a large platter-leaf and rolled it into a cone. He put the small end to his ear and the other toward the tent.

"You, oh great clan-lord of the Valmal, will command all the lands of Cimmeria, Zingara, Aqualonia, Ophir, and Nemedia, as long as you enforce the king's will."

"Why do you serve this dark lord from the ancient lands?" The voice and accent was Pictish.

"He will grant great liberty to those who help him build a new Atlantis. Your race has the fighting spirit of the Atlantians. He likes that. Gather to you as many of the clans as you can, then move them to the sea. Ships will be waiting there three cycles of the full moon from today."

"I shall do as asked. But if your master betrays us, I will stretch his living guts to shade me from the sun," the Pict said.

A large Pict emerged from the tent, his brightly colored headdress falling askew as it bumped agains the V-line of the tent opening. Following him, came a second man, dressed in black armor like the guards, but upon his shoulders were blood-red epaulets.

"No need for threats, he will keep his word," said the man with red shoulders.

The Pict clan-lord looked about and sniffed the air.

"That stench about you masks much in these forests that spells danger. You are lucky to have my warriors to give you safe passage back."

"When we have won, you may take a different view upon the scents that the civilized indulge in," said the man in armor.

The Pict looked bemused by the very thought. "The other clans will be hard to sway."

"Look to the Archillian Clan. There is a shaman who is sympathetic to our cause. For many generations his people have suffered at the hands of the Aqualonian mercenaries – those Frontier Rangers. He is our ally, and a powerful magician."

"I will seek him out. Now stay for our festival. A feast is prepared in your honor, and the full moon will sing to us."

The man with the red epaulets nodded. "We will stay to enjoy."

The two parted company.

Benhargan motioned with his hand to melt deeper into the forest.

After several miles, the two stopped near a brook. They refilled their skins with water and chose the path that would lead them to the ruins.

"What was said back there?" Bulvife asked.

"Those with the triangles have made a deal with the Picts to help wage war," said Benhargan.

"Dealing with Picts?" Bulvife was clearly confused by the idea.

Benhargan shrugged his mighty shoulders. "There is something wrong here. I fear the wizard has again involved us in a fight we'd choose to avoid if our own will was enforced. Come, to the ancient city – it awaits our arrival."

When dawn broke, they approached Valmalia and the black stones of the outer walls. They easily scaled the fifty-foot-high defenses, and clambered down the other side.

Bulvife stopped and motioned for Benhargan to approach. Stuck in the ground was a spear, and tied to it was a bamboo tube with a parchment hanging from it. On the parchment in large, clear black Aqualonian letters was written the words, For Benhargan and Bulvife.

# CHAPTER 3
## Wizard Ways

BENHARGAN CAUTIOUSLY looked about. He grunted loudly. "The wizard!"

The high grass and shrubs of the open area waved in the gentle breeze.

"Then he's not dead," Bulvife said.

"Unless he planted this long ago."

Benhargan examined the parchment. "These letters have not weathered. It is recent. He must still live."

"Open it," Bulvife suggested.

Benhargan took the tube and tore off the end. Inside was a rolled-up document. He unrolled and examined it. The corners of his mouth turned upward.

"Such arrogance," Benhargan said. "How... never mind. This is what he says to us." He drew in a deep breath.

"Beasts, know that I have not been far from you for the past few years. It has come to my attention that there is something at work that the gods wish me to attend, but it is not clear what it is yet. The clues have led me to these ruins, and the legend of a very odd relic.

"I am sure you have guessed that it was I who supplied Captain Rottigur of the Frontier Rangers with the map. I suspected his vanity would guide his hand in sending you to your deaths, knowing what bitter roots you can be for those in authority. Now that you are here, I have a task for you. Seek the crypt of Morgal Bahl located deep below these temple ruins.

"He is the last king to have more than half Atlantean blood run through his veins. In his crypt is a golden torc. Take it and anything else you wish, but bring the torc to me at the Harbor Roost Inn located in the port of Charm on the coast of Zingara. Above all, do not get yourselves killed – for I have use of you still. Grimface."

Benhargan handed the note to Bulvife, then looked about the overgrown grounds of the inner wall. "He still has use for us?" He shook this head. "When I see him, I'll peel the skin from his long-lived bones!"

Bulvife chuckled. "I will wager that you'll be as glad to see him as I will." He spun around and put his bow in hand. "There's something that lurks there." He pointed at some brush fifty yards away.

Benhargan sniffed the air. "Smells like wolves."

A dire wolf emerged from a thick stand of saplings. Large as a cave bear, the creature seemed oblivious to their existence - for the wind blew against the two Cimmerians. Six more came forth.

A mighty howl filled the air as the leader raised its muzzle and cried into the sky. It stopped and looked surprised to see the two barbarians.

The dark black and gray fur on its back stood on end. Growling, the creature's lips stretched back to show yellow fangs, and it roared so loudly that the two barbarians felt the vibration.

Pawing at the ground, the alpha-wolf shook its mane and charged. The other beasts fanned out to thwart any chance of their prey escaping.

Only too late, did the wild dogs realize their mistake. Unlike most, Cimmerians tended to advance when others would retreat, and so it was with Benhargan and Bulvife. The two Cimmerians launched arrows that struck and killed several of the vicious creatures.

Years of training in the greenwoods and savannas of the north had prepared them for this sort of predator attack. Both men moved in perfect concert— the kind of movement forged from years spent with each other suffering, fighting, drinking, and battling.

Bulvife sped forward, his sword in hand. As he closed on the master-wolf, he let out a mighty battle yell, drew his dagger, and leapt.

The barbarian and wolf collided with such force as to cause the two bodies to spin twice in midair before landing hard in the dry brown grass. The two tumbled over, and over – vicious gnawing, by both, Bulvife cursing, and blood slinging into the air.

Bulvife's blade bit deeply into the flesh of the wolf, but did not stop the animal. The wolf gnashed its powerful jaws upon the Cimmerian's bracer and slashed his flesh with dirty claws. Bulvife fought hard - stabbing, driving his blade into the creature's ribs.

The wolf yelped, then broke with a howl. It raced from the grounds followed by a trail of blood. Behind, its companions broke and followed their leader. As fast as the fighting began, it was done, and the foe vanished into the ruins.

The two men backed up to each other. Benhargan's sword was low, his skin scratched in places. He looked over at Bulvife and bellowed a tremendous laugh.

"That was a happy outcome!"

Bulvife removed his crushed bracer and examined two puncture marks in his arm.

"We need to find some pico fungus and crab-moss to dress these wounds," he said.

"I'm disappointed that the wizard failed to warn us of these wolves," Benhargan growled. "His sight is gifted, but fickle."

"He has learned that we Cimmerians can do much without a wizard's help," Bulvife retorted.

"Of course, Cimmerians don't need wizards!" Benhargan looked over at some large stone buildings. "That temple will do nicely for our night's rest. We can make a fire and roast some wolf meat. With our bellies full, we will be mostly healed by morn," Benhargan added.

They scavenged the needed medical supplies and dressed their wounds. Healing would take place, and in a few days, only scars would remain.

The legends of the ruins were well known to them. A hundred lifetimes had passed since a despotic and ruthless race dwelt within. The legends of Valmalia lurked as foreboding laments to those who lived in the lands of Aqilonia, Nemedia, and Gunderland.

Within the crumbling walls and bare stone edifices of the temple complex, the two barbarians made camp. They found an ancient fire pit not far from a long worn and stained statue. There they piled wood for the long night ahead.

A warm yellow glow reflected from the statue's legs, torso, chest and face as the flames licked the wood in the pit. Up into the high roof the gray smoke rose, swirled around, then vanished.

Benhargan put a hunk of red meat over the flames, and several tubers into the coals. Bulvife strung his bow and did a patrol. By the time the meat was cooked, and the fat sizzled in the coals, he'd returned.

"No interlopers," Bulvife stated as he sat. "No sign of Picts or... other things."

"That's good," Benhargan told him. "Now let's feast, though we have no beer or wine to slack our parched throats."

"Water will do little to quench my thirst," Bulvife added. "If only we had some libations."

"And being alone with you will do little to satisfy my lustful inclinations!" Benhargan said.

Both men laughed.

They ate and swapped tales from their past adventures. Darkness came, and the beams of sunlight that poured through the holes in the roof faded. Eventually, beyond the fire, the room became black as a tomb.

They fell quiet, knowing the terrors that lurked in ruins such as these; each man had seen firsthand the horrors summoned by those practicing the dark arts. The dangers were quite real.

The fire burned down to red coals. Bulvife was late into the first watch - the sound of wind outside made mournful echoes in the great hall.

For a few hours he worked at making some torches to be used in the tombs the coming day. Sounds, unnatural, began to penetrate his mind. From atop the walkways that bordered the second floor lurked something.

From time to time an iridescent white glow would advance out onto the high walkways, only to retreat again. Down the connecting halls something was coming.

Voices mumbled over the drafty cool air, so close at times that it seemed an entity was standing directly behind Bulvife. More than once he thought he heard his name whispered, followed by laughter. When Banhargan took the watch, Bulvife told him of his experience.

"What?" Benhargan whispered. "Your imagination is ripe."

"Unnatural things," Bulvife reaffirmed. "They are here, and have some agenda you and I could not understand."

"Sleep, for you have Benhargan to watch over your fearful soul," Benhargan said, his eyes narrowing slightly.

"It is not fear that grips my soul," Bulvife replied.

"Sleep, and don't let curiosity lead your head from its shoulders."

Bulvife took up a spot by the fire, and lay with his sword by his side. He sank into sleep, his ears alert to any indication of attack.

A scent of sweet lilac and jasmine wafted over him. Bulvife quickly opened his eyes to a visage of a woman surrounded in white light. A flowing white dress fluttered in every direction as if immersed in a pool of crystal clear water. Her pale features appeared the ashen color of death. He sat up. Other spectral beings floated about, making ready a table for feasting.

From the corridors came carts loaded with kegs, amphora, and jars of drink. The woman floated away from Bulvife, then back. In her hand was a jeweled chalice that glowed like red embers.

"Drink, living soul from the Dale-lands; drink and know what it is to be a god," she bade.

He took the cup and drank deeply. The liquid filled his veins with fire, and his soul with nourishment. Looking over he saw Benhargan hoisting a tankard to his lips and drank, guffawing, and boasting of his prowess.

Bulvife stood and went to the table. He feasted and drank until his belly stretched tight like the hide on a war drum, then came spectral women – clothes absent and celestial charms vivid and defined.

It was clear they were courtesans. They surrounded the two barbarians and danced in provocative ways. And, though each man tried to grab at them, their hands slipped through the white misty flesh. But when the women laid hands on them, they became entwined in a sticky ectoplasm. Bulvife tried to pull away, but several spectral beings held him fast. As he looked up, a horror appeared. A monstrous face looked down on him—fangs, horns, and blazing fire-red eyes.

In the creature's hand was a glowing orange crucible. Bulvife struggled, rocking left and then right. His muscles bulged under the strain, and his blood pumped powerfully through his veins. He lashed out with his fists, but hit only air.

"Open the creature's mouth," the monster said.

The women clawed at Bulvife's face pulling his jaws wide.

"Now, drink the nectar of the immortals! When it has set, and the time is right, you will be untouchable in battle!"

A rictus grin formed on the creature's face as it poured a flaming orange liquid into Bulvife's mouth.

Bulvife shot to his feet, his blade swinging with deadly purpose. Benhargan fended off several savage blows before he wrestled the man to the ground.

"What possesses you?" Benhargan shouted. "What is it that you fight so?"

The wild Cimmerian slowed. He came to realize the sun filled the room forming shafts of gold. Benhargan let Bulvife up.

"A creature was here... tables set for feasting, and drink. It tried to pour melted gold down my throat..." Bulvife's eyes narrowed as he calmed further. "All a dream... a dream it must have been."

"No, it was no dream. They came, and indeed we feasted on spectral dishes—mead of the gods, wine and beer. They brought forth the elixir of heroes – or so they said. I drank mine without worry. You, had a different experience?"

"Yes," Bulvife said.

"I have heard tell of a substance called mana... a drink, or food of the gods. I think the contents of the cups were mana, and you and I were given leave to share it with them. I do not fear the dead, or the horrors fleshed by wizards. You shouldn't either. Take stock of yourself. You are a powerful Cimmerain! Look upon your limbs – neither wounds nor breaks you suffer from. "

Bulvife looked at his arms and legs.

"It is as you say... but, who can know what damage my soul has suffered?

"Take heed, for only Crom knows the purity of a man's soul. Stay alert, there are dangers afoot still. We have to go down in the crypt. I'll wager you that unnatural things lurk there."

"Let's retrieve that torc and be gone from here," Bulvife stated with a shiver. "These spirits are trying on a man's mind."

Benhargan nodded. "To the under-halls then."

It took an hour for the two Cimmerians to find the partially collapsed ceiling and shattered door of the crypt. Written on the wall above the hole with a large black arrow pointing down, were the words in Aqualonian, 'barbarian's look here'.

The space to crawl into the depths was almost too tight for Benhargan, but with some wriggling, he penetrated the dark and earthy tunnel. An abhorrent scent of death filled both men's nostrils, and a feeling of being buried alive stalked them from the shadows.

Bulvife struck flint to tinder and made a fire, and Benhargan lit the torches. They had to duck down, for the height of the tunnel was clearly not made for Cimmerians. So they went, stooped...coiled like troubled snakes ready to strike with lethal fierceness.

Dark black smoke from the torches hovered along the roof, and the air was stale and musty. Roots protruded from between the stones and hung down from the ceiling waiting to cajole them, forcing them from side to side to avoid their damp embrace.

As the two men descended deeper into the tomb, the roots thinned out, and the height of the tunnel grew more accommodating. Soon they passed an antechamber filled with stacked bones and skulls. The empty sockets of those de-fleshed heads stared blankly out, as the light from the flames shimmered past them.

Finally, a sheet of pure white stone, marked in the middle with a strange carved symbol, bared their path. Bulvife tapped it with the hilt of his sword.

"Sounds solid," Bulvife said.

"Now what?" Benhargan mused.

Bulvife laid hands on the stone and pushed. "It's immovable."

Benhargan threw himself at it, and with all his might attempted to heave the stone, but to no avail.

"It is mighty," he added. "The wizard must know that we can get in, but how?"

Bulvife chuckled. "Perhaps we need to think like a wizard."

Benhargan examined the walls around the door, then along the tunnel. He stopped at the room with the bones.

"Come – why did we not dig through these bones?"

"They are worthless to us." Bulvife's eyes went wide with understanding. "Of course, why would anyone wish to consider a room that has no value?"

"Exactly. Oh, that wizard is crafty," Benhargan said. "Now, help me pull the dead from their rest and see if there is a door behind."

They pulled the yellowed bones from the side chamber and tossed them into the tunnel. When all were out, Benhargan thrust his torch into the cavity.

The outline of a door was apparent. He entered, and took his dagger and found the seams. Ancient dust filled the air as he pried at the joints. His dagger broke at the tip, and he drove the rest in up to the cross-guard.

Prying, he heard a gasp of air sucked into the chamber.

"Grab on and pull!" Benhargan commanded.

Bulvife did, and the stone-door opened - pivoting from the middle.

"Now," Benhargan said, "let's see what splendors await us."

He pushed his torch inside. The darkness abated, and the glitter of gold reflected his light.

As he entered, he saw gems overflowing from bowls, cups filled with gold, and chests and urns filled with tablets and strange metal objects. A corridor led into further darkness.

"This way." Benhargan moved down the hall.

At the end was a bigger chamber. This one had a long, gilded boat, a chariot fitted with bronze horses, and stacks of furniture. Dried foods were laid out as if a feast were planned. Jars of dried grapes, plums, apples, as well as almonds, walnuts, and pecans overflowed from amphorae. Large jars of wheat and rye were there, their bounty spilling out onto the ground.

"Through here, another hallway," Benhargan stated. Again, he moved forward.

His torch illuminated a large chamber. The air was most stale. In the middle of the room was a raised platform with a sarcophagus made of cut yellow marble. Skulls were carved into the sides, and at both ends bronze bulls - poised as if about the do battle.

"Quickly, let's shatter this lid, grab the torc, and be off!" said Benhargan.

The two men wrenched the lid from atop the sarcophagus and let it fall to the stone floor. Inside was a wooden coffin shaped like a falcon with its wings folded over its chest. For only a moment the colors were spectacular, then they faded and peeled, filling the bottom of the container with pastel-colored dust.

Pulling off the top of the coffin, they stared down at a body wrapped in dusty gray linen.

Bulvife took his dagger and cut away the wrapping around the head. The torc was visible— a simple golden decoration that glowed gently with a white light. He reached down and removed it.

The corpse sat up, and the gray, wrinkled, sallow head tuned its empty eye sockets to Bulvife.

The man sprang back like a cat, unloosed his sword and made ready to fight. Benhargan did not move, but studied the thing for a second, then his blade flew from its scabbard cleaving the mummy's head from its shoulders.

The blade clacked against something metallic and did not move further. The hulking barbarian sighed, keeping his arm extended and the blade resting where it stopped.

"Curious," he exclaimed.

"What?" Bulvife approached.

"Look inside that sarcophagus and tell me what you see," Benhargan suggested.

Bulvife stepped up on the platform and looked in. "There are metal rods, some attached to gears and metal cables."

"Again, the wizard's ways are telling. Merely tricks to scare away the casual thief."

Bulvife chuckled. "It's worthy of a cunning magician. Those ancient souls laid this king to rest with thought." He held up the torc. The metal was warm and the subtle glow of white light grew in intensity. "Do you think it's made of star-metal?" Bulvife asked.

"It possesses some sort of magic that the wizard wishes to use, but what it is made from I could not say."

"Let's get clear of these ruins. My gut tells me that we've overstayed our time here," Bulvife said.

"Don't forget to take what we can from the other chambers. Why should we leave a pauper when such wealth lays abandoned?"

The two Cimmerians found a chest large enough to stack most of the brass, gold, and gems in. For good measure, Bulvife tossed in two jeweled daggers and several metal spear tips.

Using two sturdy polearms, they secured the chest and hefted the load onto their shoulders, and carried it like a sedan car all the way to the opening.

They took extra care working the spoils through the collapsed entrance. Once in the open air, they moved out through a side door and down a long hall bordered by tall white colonnades. At the end of the hall, they descended a steep staircase and onto a broad, grass-covered concourse.

Saplings and full-grown trees bordered the plane on all sides. A bubbling brook ran down the middle and into a large pool of dark water.

Beyond the reservoir lay the gates, once epic guardians of the city, now just rotted wood, and loose green brass straps.

On the other side, they made for the forest. Once in that shadowed landscape, where light fell through the leafy canopy in rare dust glittering shafts, they would be on equal footing with any enemy.

Day turned to night, and night to day. As they ran along a worn deer path, Benhargan suddenly stopped. "There are Picts about," he said sniffing the air.

"Quickly, this way to the mountain and over to Zingara," Bulvife added.

The two men doubled their efforts, and as they moved, the burden they carried began to shift. A rattling in the chest rang out like the sound of a thousand gold coins in a box...which was not far from the truth.

Behind them a whooping sound erupted, and several dozen hearty Pict warriors fell in along their path. The various painted faces held grim expressions, and from their mouths exploded murderous cries.

"This may not end well," Bulvife huffed.

Atlatl bolts flew past them; several were so close they shaved hair from skin. The two Cimmerians drove on hard as the path inclined along a bush covered, and boulder strewn, hillside.

The slope of the mountain was growing. Rain fell from the gathering gray clouds. Up the muddy hillside they climbed until they landed onto a level path. Over-ripe droplets fell hard from the dark sky, as the Picts closed on the barbarians.

The path cut diagonally up the hillside, then switched back just below a host of large white granite boulders. Small animals scurried from their wake, as the Cimmerians doubled their efforts.

"We have to fight," Benhargan said, as he stopped and lowered his end of the treasure to the ground.

The chest tipped and some of the contents spilled out.

Bulvife scooped up the golden torc. "I'll hold on to this in the event we have to abandon our bounty," he said.

"I'm not abandoning this loot!" Benhargan growled. "We can take them easily. Loose your blade and prepare to make our pursuers seek fairer game!"

The Picts were nearly upon them as the lead savage gave a battle cry and charged at them.

Bulvife looked around for a place to secure the torc. Seeing none, he slipped it around his neck and bent it into place.

A stinging fire spread down through his limbs. He crouched down as the pain hit his groin like a hammer blow. He buckled at the knees and fell to the ground.

The sky was a vibrant purple mixed with a murky pinkish hue. A haze of white was around the edges of his vision - like an aura of a torch through a distant morning mist.

Ahead he saw the approaching Picts; they seemed frozen. Benhargan's muscles were flexed, and a grimace of battle rage forged upon his lips. He was in mid charge.

A buzzing sound, like a thousand angry hornets entered Bulvife's ears. The pain subsided. He stood, walked past his Cimmerian brethren, loosed his sword, and proceeded to lay decimation upon his foes.

A strange sensation filled his veins. With each slash, cleaving flesh and bone, he felt a powerful charge of energy run through his body. A feeling almost like a massive, crippling orgasm washed over him. Once completed, he strolled back to where he had begun and removed the torc.

Benhargan let out a mighty war bellow and charged into the fray, only to see all the Picts collapse; arms, legs, and heads fell away, and the quivering corpses bleeding out. Not one Pict yelled.

Benhargan skidded to a halt, his swinging blade cutting only air, and looked shocked at the carnage at his feet. "What happened? he shouted in rage. They are all dead! Cowards!"

Bulvife's vision grew narrow, and his sight faded to gray. He felt the bonds of life slipping, and his mortal soul falling into darkness. For how long he lingered in the black he did not know. Was he dead or alive? He could not tell.

When his eyes came open, Benhargan was there. The barbarian was lying across from him near a modest fire.

"What happened?" Bulvife asked.

"You were so overpowered by my display of might that you collapsed like a harem girl after coitus," Benhargan explained. "Such weakness could only lead you to an early meeting with a disappointed Crom."

"It was not weakness," Bulvife protested, "but the torc. I placed it around my neck and all things around me stopped. I strolled over and killed every Pict, then returned and took off the torc. I watched you make a fool of yourself, then some force drained me of life."

Bulvife got to a sitting position. He found his water skin and quaffed down the contents.

"I find your story dubious at best. I am more inclined to believe that they killed themselves, or that I killed them in a berserk rampage," Benhargan suggested. "On the other hand, you have little cause to lie to me, and we have seen many feats of powerful magic done by that creature Grimface. So, I suppose it is possible," he added.

"As you lay helpless, I scouted the area. There are no other Picts about. When you've regained your strength, we will move on." Benhargan stood up and looked into the night sky. "If we travel toward the star in middle of the camel's hump, we will be in line with Charm."

It took only a short while before Bulvife regained his feet. They padded the chest with grass, hefted the treasure again upon their shoulders and moved up the hill.

The two Cimmerians moved swift and silently in parallel to the Aqualonian border, and down toward the Zingaran lands. They followed the valley of the Black River for many miles. At Hyrokein Pass, they broke southwest, down the Teragata mountains and into the open plains of Zingara.

For the most part, the land was flat grassy patches surrounded by thin forests, but when they got twenty miles from the mountain, the landscape changed to treeless rolling hills.

Antelope, deer, and oxen roved in great herds, feeding upon the plenty that grew all around. Hamlets began popping up along their path, and even a few villages. Herd animals appeared, as did the herdsmen who tended them. All the while Benhargan and Bulvife kept on the move.

After five days and nights, Benhargan sighted the high, mud-brick walls of Charm and its surrounding settlements.

Gray smoke hung in the azure sky as the two men and their burden, arrived at the main gates. Soldiers were thick in this part of the world, protecting the brass, gold, silver, and gems of the great Zingaran Empire.

Port cities like Charm were valuable real estate, for the heavy trade from Kush, Argos, Shem, and Stygia, passed though it to get to Aqualonia and Nemedia.

Even as Benhargan and Bulvife passed under the lentil of the massive gate, a long caravan of horses, camels, elephants, oxen, all ladened with trade goods, were heading out. Dust was thick and the two barbarians forced their way inside despite the attempt of the caravan to push them back out.

Very quickly they made their way to a tavern by the docks. The rife stench of fish and waste hung in the air as the two men barged into the public house—pole-arms, chest, and all.

"Clear a table!" Benhargan barked.

Bulvife let the two poles rest on his shoulders as he swung his meaty fists at some burly sailors at the nearest table.

The first two men tried to defend themselves, but were smashed like old jars of beer on a cobbled street. The other four hastily cleared away, and Benhargan and Bulvife set their burden down on the rough-cut, wooden, long-table.

Opening the top of the chest, Benhargan pulled out a hand full of gems. A Stygian seaman in a traditional long black robe approached, his eyes boggled by the loot. Bulvife growled loudly. The man realized how close to death he was getting and stepped back.

Benhargan approached the barkeep and put many colorful gems down on the counter.

"You! Cook meat and make ready a feast. Much beer and wine to sate me and my brother's hunger and thirst. Then seek us a haram of women to sate the other appetites that will surely follow."

"If I were you, I'd make it quick," Bulvife added.

The barkeep looked at the gems with such greed, that many in the bar became afraid that he'd sell them for the pleasures of these barbarians, and made a hasty exit. But those who stayed were treated to food, drink, and womanly companionship the likes only a king would know.

For several days, the harmonic strumming of the minstrels assailed the streets and alleys with bawdy songs and string-plucked melodies. Occasionally, brawls would erupt and spill out onto the streets.

On the fourth day, the two Cimmerians abruptly left the tavern, and in the darkness of the damp morning, they sought out the place the wizard had mentioned.

In Bulvife's hand he carried, wrapped in a silken cloth, the golden torc. They wandered for only an hour before Bulvife halted in front of a mud-brick and timber building.

"Here it is," Bulvife said, "the Harbor Roost Inn."

The inn served as a resting place for those Aqualonains and wealthy Zingarans who traveled abroad. So it was a bit of a surprise when two rough and crudely dressed rangers entered the dwelling, sacks over their shoulders, and smelling of rawhide, sweat, and wilderness. The refined and finely dressed patrons moved quickly away from them.

Bulvife casually walked over to a small Zingaran man dressed in a blue robe.

"There is a man here, bronze of skin, with a dark black mustache. We wish to speak to him."

It was clear that the man was amazed that the barbarian spoke the Zingaran language so well.

"He is not here," the innkeeper said.

Benhargan's fists clenched. "What is this you say?" His tone was such that several of the patrons nearby fled the inn.

"What I mean is that he has left, but instructed me to give you this." He handed a wax-sealed note made of papyrus to Bulvife.

"What does the wizard say?" Benharagn asked Bulvife

"He says that there are those who will try and stop us. The risk is high, but reward is great. He goes on to say that he's left Zingara and traveled to the Bharachen Islands to seek a document that once dwelt in a ruin there. He wants us to travel to Cho Impah in Argos. He says we need to meet a man named Vill of Cho Impah. He will give us more information."

The innkeeper spoke, "Please don't turn my inn into rubble." He held up a jar of beer as an offering.

Benhargan took the jar and then turned back to Bulvife. "This chasing of the wizard's banner is growing wearisome!" he declared.

He tipped up the jar and emptied it in front of the astonished eyes of the innkeeper, then dashed it to pieces against the inn's stone floor. "Another!" he barked at the frightened man, then turned back to Bulvife. "So, it is now to Impah? There had better be much wealth and glory at the end of all this!" He pointed at the cloth bundle in Bulvife's hand. "Keep that torc well, for it looks as if we'll not be getting rid of this cursed thing any time soon."

They drank the innkeeper's beer and sated their hunger with the large joint of mutton. When they'd finished, Bulvife took a handful of coins and slammed them down onto a wooden table. Without further comment, the two Cimmerians left the inn, and the city.

# CHAPTER 4
# A Wink and a Nod

AS FAR AS ONE COULD see, from horizon to coast, the dark blue waters of the Western Sea chopped away at the hull of the small cargo ship. Benhargan watched as sea beasts emerged from the foamy water, and descended back below. In his hand was a jar of wine and he lifted the container up to his lips and gulped down the rich, red contents. The fluid splashed down upon his chest as he reposed and wiped his mouth with the back of his hand.

"It is another few days to Argos," Benhargan said. "This lack of battle is making me restless." He lifted the jar again and drank.

Bulvife nodded, and chugged down some wine. He stood looking out over the railing, then let the empty container plummet into the sea.

"I have a feeling that something is not right with all this. I'll be glad when the wizard makes clear our purpose," Bulvife said.

"His purpose is to play us like dice. He rolls us this way, and that way, then when we come up in his favor he praises us like dogs. When we come up contrary to his will, he admonishes us like slaves. I'd like to see his head on a lodge pole one day," Benhargan grumbled.

"You two," called a sailor, "come and speak with the captain. He wishes that you be aware of our next landing."

The two barbarians went around the rigging and toward the tiller at the aft. There, standing half as tall as either Cimmerian, was a dark-skinned man with powerful muscles—the captain. He looked up at the two men and then back out to sea.

"You barbarians should know that we are going to dock at Volinius to take on some cargo. If you have issues with those that dwell within the city, you may want to stay below in the hold."

"It is they who should hide in their cellars in fear of us!" Bulvife boldly stated.

Benhargan grunted a chuckle. "But, they should leave their daughters at the docks; easier for us to find them."

The captain looked disgusted by the barbarians' comments. "Stay on the boat. We'll only be there for an hour or two."

The day wore on as the small ship cut through the choppy waves. As it came around a tall pillar of stone, great, black, stacks of smoke rose from a city under seige. To the east was a vast army. In the cove, and harbor, war ships lay at anchor. Several turned as the trade ship rounded the point, each prow fitted with a large metal ram, and crewed with hundreds of oarsmen who drove their trade-implements deep into the blue sea.

"Debris in the waters – captain!" shouted a sailor on the prow.

The small ship hit some wood in the water. All around was wreckage and bodies. Upon the sun-roasted sands of the beach, all saw a carpeting of dead men, their bodies bloated in the heat of the sun.

Sailors looked to the captain with trepidation in their eyes and quaking limbs.

For a moment, the swarthy captain appeared shocked by the sight, then he cleared his throat. "They've seen us! To your posts. Archers string bows – and men of arms gather your spears and shields." He leaned against the rudder, then turned to the barbarians. "We'll sail around to the Aber Sand Cove two leagues from here. There we can take on fresh supplies." He looked to a man atop the main mast. "Kirkirk! What banners do they fly?"

"Black and gold," Kirkirk reported.

The captain nodded. "I've not heard of such a livery. Very well," he said loudly. "Make a tight sail! Lookouts, keep an eye on those approaching ships!" He turned to Benhargan and Bulvife. "Black and gold livery? – What lord flies those colors?"

"One ship has broken away, and one still comes!" shouted Kirkirk .

Benhargan grunted his frustration. "Battle is before me, and I am trapped upon this boat!" he angrily stated. "That force is not a raiding party, but a full army. I'll wager that Aber Sand Cove will be occupied. They'll have it secured for supplies. Cho Impah is not far from the city of Messantia. Head north to Messantia; it is only two more leagues than Aber beyond the Argos border. We will leave you there, and you can resupply and find merchants to buy your cargo and help fill your hold."

The captain looked deep in thought, then nodded his agreement. "It shall be so." He adjusted the rudder, came north and a bit west, heading out to sea and away from the conflict.

"Ship off the starboard side," called down Kirkirk.

Bulvife glanced over. "One trireme, fully stocked for hunting," he said.

"Let out the sail," the captain commanded. "Now would be a good time to pray to whatever heathen god you claim," he said to Bulvife and Benhargan.

"He'll do nothing to interfere in this," Benhargan told him.

"Then what good is your god?" replied the captain.

"He is not here to amuse us; we are on this world to amuse him. So, for his entertainment, he'll let us take care of this issue ourselves."

"What cargo do you carry?" Bulvife asked.

"Silk and wool rugs, papyrus leaves, fifty amphorae or wine, a hundred jars of beer, sixty jars of wheat, ten bales of cotton, two crates of hives, a hundred and ten bolts of cloth, sixty-two jars of spices, and five barrels of pickled fish." The captain looked at the two barbarians with great skepticism. "Why must you know?"

"That is quite a lot of treasure." Benhargan thought for a moment. "You said two hives? Termites or bees?"

"Bees," the captain stated.

Benhargan chuckled cruelly. "We'll send our pursuer's a present – some visitors to draw away the attention of their rowers, and busy their officers."

"What are you suggesting?" The captain's curiosity was piqued.

"We'll take some of your goods and put them over the side. The pursuing ship will think we're lightening our load, and want the booty we discharge. No doubt they will bring it aboard. One will be wine, and another a crate of cloth, then a barrel of bees," Benhargan told him. Take a hive and seal it in an empty keg. Cover the edges with wax, then put it over the side on my command.

"If it will get us free, then I have no problem with your plan," the captain stated.

First over the side went two jars of wine tied to sturdy cork-logs. Bulvife watched from the aft as the military ship lowered men over the side, latched grappling hooks onto the jars, and hauled them onboard. Next, over the railing plummeted a large crate - and again, the other ship pulled the container aboard.

A few minutes passed, and the enemy ship began to close. The crate with the bees went over the side. Seamen on the other ship pulled the crate aboard. The trireme came within ballista distance. A large, white stone twanged into the air and smashed into the aft of the ship.

"Your plan has failed. We will be boarded," the captain cried out.

"Steady your nerve!" sternly commanded Bulvife.

The oars on the pursuing ship halted, then the craft began falling back. No sound could be heard, but it was clear that pandemonium had broken out. Some sailors flew from the railing and into the sea, all the while waving their arms about wildly. There was little doubt that the bees were doing their job.

Benhargan watched as the trireme grew smaller and smaller in the distance. The captain barked some orders to his men, as he turned the ship further out into the deep sea. He looked down from the rudder on the two barbarians.

"I do not know how you savages could come up with such a plan, but I thank you for saving my ship!"

Benhargan grunted, then walked forward and sat on the deck. "Bring me five jars of beer," he demanded.

Bulvife joined him and they sat, talked, and laughed for quite some time, until the sky grew dark, and the sun waned and melted into the horizon.

The ship entered the port of Missantia on noon of the fourth day. Many ships were anchored in the harbor, and many more lined the docks and marinas. The small cargo ship found a berth and tied up. The captain went to the aft and inspected the damage done by the ballista ball.

"Curse those black-hearted fiends who bashed in a quarter of my aft," he stated.

"They'd done so to your skull too, if we'd not saved your ship, your lives, and most of your cargo," Bulvife reminded him.

"I shall accept the loss of some of my cargo; the tradeoff is a fair one. Let us part company and not take up arms against one another if we shall meet again," the captain said.

"It shall be so," Benhargan added. He climbed down onto the dock and followed a group of six longshoremen carrying large earthen jars.

He and Bulvife went directly to the local herald and inquired about the banner they'd seen.

The dark and dank hall was lit by many candles and lamps. At the far end, a long table lined with several scribes blocked access to the back of the building.

"We've just disembarked at the docks, and come to tell of an invading force to the south. They fly a mysterious banner that I have never seen before," Benhargan said.

"We have heard that there are three armies on the move recently. One is a Stygian army who is running amuk and sacking towns along the Shem border. Next is Koth, in a border dispute with Ophir. Third is a mercenary force that carries the black and gold banner of some unknown royal house. In all our records, we have no name to place with that banner," the herald said.

"That army is moving this direction. They even now lay siege to Volinius," Benhargan added. "You would be wise to pack all your worldly belongings and head for the hinterlands." He turned to Bulvife. "Come, let us make for Cho Impah." He exited the stone building and into the street.

The crowds were thick, and as he and Bulvife moved along the busy street, they were buffeted and jostled. Finally, Benhargan put his elbows out and began plowing through the many citizens of Missantia. Near the northern gate, the throng grew thin where the two men found a tavern.

For several hours, the barbarians drank and feasted. They also gambled and fought, leaving no doubt that they were not to be conned or cheated.

Benhargan stood, and turned to leave. As he did, he stepped right into a bronzed-skin, raven haired woman—knocking her to the ground. He grunted, and stepped over her on his way to the door.

"You, with the ox-anus breath!" she said.

Benhargan stopped and glanced back. "Ox anus pie is one of my favorites," he told her, then made for the door again.

"I'll have your hands for your impudence, barbarian!" she swore, and out came a sword from a scabbard at her side.

Bulvife sat down again and waved over the barkeep. "Bring me two more jars of wine. I can't leave with such a drama unfolding." He laughed.

"Your rudeness belies your ineptitude for battle. I'm sure that you are best suited to please Aquilonian house boys, rather than women," she insulted.

"And why does a whore keep a sword? Is it that you've tired of being a scabbard for the many swords you've taken?"

She ground her teeth. "I'm going to take pleasure in teaching you a lesson." She took two steps forward. "I doubt that you will make much of a challenge."

"A challenge is it? How about a wager?" Benhargan asked.

"Fine, what are your terms?" she said coming to a halt.

"If I win, I get to teach you the ways of Cimmerian love. If I don't win, my fellow ranger here will pay you your weight in gold." Benhargan fostered a toothy smile.

"Agreed!" she replied, took up a fighting stance and prepared to do battle.

Benhargan turned and made for the door again.

"Hey," she called, "where do you think you're going?"

"I've got business elsewhere," he stated.

"Then you lose this wager," she said.

"There were no terms of time placed on this bet. I'll take you in my own good time, and it is not today." He reached the door, flipped up the latch and exited.

Bulvife drank down his last jar, and stuffed a hunk of goat cheese into his mouth. He stood, swallowed, then laughed nearly uncontrollably as he side-stepped the woman and followed Benhargan out.

"Hey...hey!" the woman called behind them.

Outside, the two men left through the northern gate and along the dirt road leading toward Cho Impah. Carts and pedestrians were in abundance, but as they reached the Kepesh Bridge over the Khorotas River, fewer and fewer people began to appear. Once on the northern side of the river Bulvife stopped.

"You do know that that woman is following us," he told Benhargan.

"Of course, I know. It will take two days for her intentions to be known to us, when curiosity gets the better of her."

"Could she be a spy?"

"It is possible, but if she is, she's a very reckless spy. No, I think her to be a headstrong Zingaran woman who seeks battle with any, and all around her. If nothing else, she will keep this lesson fresh for all her days to come," he said and chuckled.

"You mean that she'll not know when your tutorial will come? I wondered why you toyed with her."

"Wonder no more." Benhargan winked.

# CHAPTER 5
# Vill of Cho Impah

THE WALLS OF CHO IMPAH loomed out of the rainy mist. Grey stones were stacked to the height of twenty cubits, and at fifty paced intervals, high five story towers stood watch over the hilly terrain. In the treeless fields roamed cattle, sheep, goats, and along the terraced hillsides grew various corns, such as barley, wheat, and oats.

A large number of people milled about outside the gates, some selling wares from carts, and others selling bread, beer, slaves, and black lotus.

Benhargan lingered for a moment looking down at the dried, black leafy plant.

"The smell," he said, then shook himself free of the beguiling scent and walked in through the gate.

Bulvife followed closely behind, and only gave the large pot of leaves a passing glance. Once inside, he exhaled loudly.

Benhargan chuckled. "You should know better than to try and hide your weakness from Crom. It is the more powerful warrior who can inhale the black lotus, and turn away. It is the weaker that cringes from its fragrant scent by holding his breath."

Bulvife looked at Benhargan with a disapproving expression. "And in that moment your wits were held by the leaf, a thief could have cut your purse, or an assassin could have let some air into your liver."

"Nonsense." Benhargan dismissed the comment. "That person would have regretted such an act immediately, and I would still have had the pleasure of sniffing in the black lotus."

"I'd like to have seen that," Bulvife said.

"Look!" Benhargan pointed at a roughly fashioned building made of mud-brick, wood members, and thatched roof. Smoke came from within, as did the smell of meat, drink, sweat, and other questionable odors. "A tavern!".

The wooden door opened inward and a cacophony of voices radiated outward. Benhargan pushed his way in, followed closely by Bulvife. They found a set of long benches by the fire pit, sat down, and waved over a slave girl toting pitchers of libation. She set down a container of beer, turned and went through a doorway into a darkened room.

A plump man sitting at one end of the room stood and looked Bulvife and Benhargan over with a curious eye. The man's brown robe hung down to his knees, and around his tubby stomach, a black belt was tied into a knot at the level of his bellybutton.

The girl returned with two more earthen pitchers, a loaf of bread, and mutton joint.

"The lord said you do not need to pay, once you have accepted the drink and meat, you are welcome into the company," the girl said.

Benhargan looked at Bulvife and both men shrugged.

"Then – we eat!" Benhargan said.

It did not take long for the beer and meat to vanish, and the two barbarians to become discontented.

"More drink, and more meat!" shouted Bulvife. More came, until all around the two fighters lay gnawed bones and empty pitchers by the dozen.

The evening grew late and the two men looked around the room. All about them, the other patrons were bedding down by the fire pit. These men looked hardened, rugged - crafted from some foreign god of war, whose thirst for blood was unsated – thus far.

Some wore bits of armor, and all were armed, and Benhargan thought it odd that they were all contented and not fighting amongst themselves.

"I am Pilinius the Kindlefed. What land do you two warriors hail from?" asked the man with the large belly as he approached.

"Cimmeria," Bulvife said.

"Ah, good..." He pulled out a piece of paper and looked at some scrawling upon it. "I don't seem to have any Cimmerians listed, but you have come, so I am loath to turn you away. The prince will be overjoyed with the turnout. In the morn, you will be led by Hun the Basher to where the army is being outfitted." He looked the two men up and down. "You're quite large...an expensive endeavor to outfit you both. Will one of you consider being an archer, or perhaps man a ballista?"

"We will do whatever tasks need doing," Benhargan craftily stated.

"Good, good. What weapon do you specialize in?" Pilinius asked.

"Any one that kills," Bulvife added.

"No, I mean what weapon will you expect to use in the coming campaign?"

"Sword and shield, bow and arrow, trident and net, sickle-sword and dagger, bare hands, it is all the same to us," Benhargan quipped. "Now, bring us more drink, and more meat!"

"Yes... of course. Childris – come and cater to these warrior's needs!"

The girl returned and with her came two more pitchers and a side of boar haunch. She knelt down and ran her hand along Bulvife's thigh and up under his loincloth.

"Your desire is my wish – Cimmerian," she said.

Benhargan looked up from his cup. "Fair terms you make for hiring mercenaries," he said, as he reached for one of the pitchers and quaffed down the contents. "Who is this prince you speak of?"

"Who?" Pilinius said surprised. "He is the shadow-man, an enigma that pays in gold." He eyed the two men with some suspicion. "How is it that you've come by this tavern?"

Benhargan looked about at the other men. "We are the likes of them – the same – but far fiercer."

Pilinius' narrowed eyes widened. "Not much is known of this man. He calls himself prince, and has promised some very powerful warlords client kingdoms in his new empire. Some say he is from Hatush, and others say he is from Job, but I've heard rumors that his eyes are golden, as is his skin. Whispers in the wind tell me that the last prince of Atlantis has returned."

Benhargan nearly choked on his wine. He grunted as he tore a piece of the boar flesh, letting the grease dribble down his chin. "Prince of Atlantis?" he asked, bits of meat flying from his mouth. "What nonsense is this?"

"It is a rumor, but I have met with those who claim he commands powerful magic... magic that only a true prince of Atlantis could possess."

Bulvife shook his head. "The priests of Mitra say that Atlantis sank ten thousand years ago – or more. How could such a thing be? No man can live for more than a lifetime..." He stopped and looked at Benhargan, who was looking back at him. "The wizard," he whispered.

"More than a thousand winters he's seen," Benhargan furthered. He drank down more wine and looked as if he was deep in thought. "The will of the gods cannot be underestimated," he added.

Bulvife shrugged his shoulders. "If they can keep a man alive for a thousand years after his city was destroyed, and keep him alive after an island has consumed him in fire, they surely could keep a man alive for ten thousand years."

Shrugging his massive shoulders, Benhargan grunted and took a large bite from the shank before handing it to Bulvife.

"Worry not about these things, they are of a small matter to us." He turned to Pilinius, "Where can we find a man called Vill?"

"He is an old goat herder that lives at the other end of the city. Why do you want him?" Pilinius asked.

"It is not for you to know," Benhargan countered.

Pilinius stepped back. "No need for anyone to lose face, barbarian... I only ask to account for risk. If you leave here and get yourself killed, then there are fewer men to send to the prince's army and less wealth for me. That is all I have interest in."

"Bring more food and drink," Bulvife told him.

The man looked quite offended by the disrespect, but said nothing more.

The two barbarians ate, drank until late in the evening. Finally, when all fell still and non-stirred, the two Cimmerians slipped out of the tavern and into the shadow-soaked streets.

Crickets and small tree-frogs chirped in the night, as did the sounds of domestic unrest, dogs barking, and babies crying. From time to time the men would encounter drunks who they kindly knocked to the side. At one point, they were beset upon by street-roughs looking for quick coin, but instead found a savage beating for their troubles.

At a bawdy house Benhargan asked about the man called Vill, and was pointed down a narrow and dark alley.

"He lives down there, at the end of the street, on the second floor. Just go up the steps," the dark-skinned man told the two Cimmerians.

The two barbarians went across the street and down the cobblestone alley. A powerful stench of urine and bile permeated the air. At the end rose a set of stone blocks, one set a bit deeper than the one below it.

Benhargan flew up the steps to the wooden door at the top. He reached for the latch, but the door came open. The crossthatch wrinkles of an old man's face was aglow with shimmering orange light as the person stood with a lamp in his hand. His blue-gray eyes looked up at the hulking Cimmerian, as he brushed back his thinning stark white hair.

"I am Vill. You come at the behest of Grimface. I've expected you. Come inside and sit by the fire," he said.

Benhargan ducked as he entered the dwelling, as did Bulvife. The inside was lit with lamps, and candles. It was a modest size space with a fire pit in the middle, and a smoke hole at the top of the room.

The smell of baking bread was in the air, mingled with the aroma of meat roasting in the fire. Vill walked to the opposite side and took down a small urn, peeled off the wax top and handed the container to Bulvife.

"Drink this, it is mead. Soon the meat and bread will be done," Vill told him.

He sat down by the pit and pulled out a stone tube which he stuffed with some herb-like substance and lit with a match-stick from the fire. Inhaling deeply, he examined the two men closely.

"Grimface said that two Cimmerians would come. He also said that while their wits can be tested, their force in battle couldn't."

"Do you wish to find out what he means by good in a fight?" Benhargan challenged.

"Grimface did warn me not to antagonize you, much. You must be Benhargan, and you are Bulvife. Bulvife, what do you think of my mead?" Vill looked thoughtful.

Taking the urn down from his lips, Bulvife nodded. "Like a fresh cool breeze atop the highest mountain. There is a small fire heating my stomach, and it is good." He handed the urn to Benhargan.

"What trickery does that snake of a wizard have you doing for him?" Benhargan took the urn, tipped it up to his lips and drank long and hard.

"You have something for me. It is powerful magic. You lack the skill and knowledge to use it properly – at least not without dying in the process. Give me the torc and I will tell you what Grimface has need of you next."

"You've not answered my question herdsman; what does Grimface have you doing for him?" Benhargan growled.

"We are united in an effort. A man has come who is enlisting warriors from across Hyboria, and Hyperboria. He is creating an army the likes not seen in our time. But, as a thirsty man who draws water from a well, he's taking too much without thinking." Vill took another drag from the tube and exhaled several smoke rings. "A friend of mine, a thief, stole something that relates to this man, and it is troubling."

He opened a leather bag sitting next to him and handed a metal triangle made of a quicksilver metal to Benhargan.

"It is called a rubell cum took, a relic from the ruins of Tre Hur. It is said that those days of Atlantis, the king exiled his sons to settle the other lands around the sea. Tre Hur is one of those settlements. A god-king rose up from the daughter of each of the exiled sons, and from those god-kings came the reins of ruin that would befall the island kingdom, lost these many thousands of years."

"What of it?" Bulvife asked as he took the urn back from Benhargan.

"There in Tre Hur is a cave called the crystal oblivion. Many have ventured inside, and few have returned. Within the many facets of the giant crystals, loom powers that no mortal can comprehend. That magic pulses like the heartbeat of a god. Five years ago, a man and a girl-child came from the mouth of the cave. He wore the rubell cum took around his neck on a chain. The girl had a tattoo of the same on her back. This man now recruits for an army to seize power over all of Hyboria. I will use the torc and see for myself if this man is an usurper, or a true prince of that ancient island."

Benhargan turned to Bulvife. "This man is mad. Give him the torc." He turned to Vill. "Do whatever crazy thing you must. Tell us of the news that Grimface has for us; what next are we to do?"

"Grimface asked that you make your way to the Sistu Valley and sail to the island of Doom-um-nue. There you will meet him," Vill said.

Bulvife nodded. "We will do as he wishes." He reached into his bag and brought forth the torc and handed it to Vill. "It has very nasty effects when you wear it," he added.

"You have worn it?" Vill chuckled. "And you lived to tell about it? I must say, I am surprised, and impressed."

Benhargan took the urn and finished the contents. "Where's this feast you're responsible for?"

"Nearly done my brutes, nearly done," Vill said. "Take your rest, for tomorrow you must leave, if you are to make it to the island of Doom-um-nue, in good time."

# CHAPTER 6
# Scholes of White

THE PIETRA LOCH WAS in the middle of the Sistu Valley. It looked like a tadpole of dark blue in the middle of a sea of green pines. To reach the chalky shores of the loch, a man on foot would take five days. Benhargan and Bulvife needed to reach the marina of Hollyander Scholes along the shores of Pietra much sooner.

The Koplar Road was one way a traveler could take - a dry and dust choked path that wound its way through lands filled with wild beasts and murderous bandits. Or, one could take the ancient aqueduct that led from the Red River to the high stone walls of Hollyander in one day.

They knew of the routes – any good ranger would, but neither Benhargan nor Bulvife had ever been to the great lake before. There had been no need to do so. Plenty of feuding warlords, unguarded tombs, and courtly intrigue kept them busy elsewhere.

Those who dwelled at Hollyander did a brisk trade of herbs, fish, and rare magic items. Some said that the cloth of Tupek came from there, and still others told tales of giants who built the lakeside city, and still roamed the forest seeking to devour those travelers they found.

The two Cimmerians followed the bank of the Red River to a set of cascading waterfalls. As water flowed from the powerful estuary, a canal broke away from the edge of the falls and led into the dense forest.

The two barbarians climbed to the ground and followed the arched supports of the water way. As night approached, they made camp, and settled in.

"It is of little use skulking around just beyond the firelight. We know you are there," Bulvife said.

"He speaks true – for we've known you've been following us since we left Cho Impah," Benhargan added.

A woman's voice came from the dark. "It is not that I have much interest in you, but you fled without completing our duel. It seemed dishonorable, so I sought you out to make sure I have satisfaction!"

"It is only a matter of time before you get your wish," Benhargan replied. "You might as well come to the fire. Neither of us will harm you. We have fish from the river, and kimpaw meat to fill you."

"And there are several wineskins, unsullied by our barbarian lips," Bulvife added.

She emerged into the sunset-glow of the firelight. "Neither of you get any ideas about coupling – or you'll be crying to your god in a higher octave," she declared.

Benhargan chuckled. "Have no fear of Bulvife, for you are only one women – and his lust, of late, has been for plural female escapades. And I, you shan't fear, for I have no strong interest in a woman-in-arms, whose bull-headed desires border on the suicidal."

"I would not be so quick to speak, if I were a leather-headed ranger whose only quality is his stench that wards off all from coming too close!" she barked.

"Good, then I take it you'll be quiet from now on?" Benhargan quipped.

She growled loudly, harrumphed and sat down on a rock by the fire. Bulvife handed her some meat and a wineskin. She took it and ate and drank in silence.

"Tomorrow we will approach the entrance to the water-highway to Hollyander." Bulvife said.

"Aqueduct?" she asked.

"The quickest way into Hollyander," Benhargan told her.

"Why have you come all the way out here?" she inquired.

"Our friend – if he can be so called – has need of us," Bulvife replied.

"He is no friend!" Benhargan corrected. "Yet, we are strangely compelled to aid him. He is a magician who wields powers no mortal should witness. And he is very good at getting us into serious trouble."

"And himself," Bulvife added.

"Why do it then?" Her voice was light and filled with curiosity.

"Some spell of his, or his gods compel us... it is a gnawing at our thoughts... a calling to us to do his bidding from far," Benhargan said.

"Why don't you just abandon him and travel to some far away lands?" she asked.

"There is no place far enough from his reach. His gods meddle in the affairs of men – unlike our god Crom. With such powers, there is nowhere that his magic cannot reach," said Benhargan.

"It is the way of the gods of my lands, to will those who are faithful to do strange and cunning deeds," she added. "I am called Kaltopia."

"So why did you follow us?" Bulvife asked.

"It was... a gnawing at my guts," she replied.

Bulvife and Benhargan both burst with laughter.

"Ah, the wizard strikes again. You'll fit right in with us nicely," Benhargan said.

As the night wore on, all three drank, and even toasted one another. Late in the night they took shifts keeping watch. When the coals of the fire smoldered, and the supple fragrance of the dew-flowers carried upon the breeze, they broke camp and headed out.

Wooden palisades surrounded a military-like encampment of soldiers. Four gates allowed access or egress, and those men with weapons appeared well trained and disciplined.

Bulvife, Benhargan, and Kaltopia gained entrance and approached a high wooden structure. Bulvife strolled up to the five large men who were standing guard at the aqueduct steps. They in turn regarded Bulvife, Benhargan, and the woman with what could only be described as contempt.

"Why bring you this woman?" the leader asked as he reached to touch her hair.

Kaltopia slapped the guard's hand away and stepped back. "Bring it forth again and own a stump!" she warned.

The guard looked enraged as he stepped toward her, but Benhargan stepped in front.

"She is free-born and will not be handled as a slave," he said. "Now, what payment do you wish for passage to Hollyander Scholes?"

The guard stood back and regarded the three with a new look - almost a bemused expression.

"A brass bar for the three of you," said he.

Bulvife grinned. "Brass bar? You ask a lot for passage."

"It's a brass bar or take the road," the guard stated.

Benhargan pulled out a thin brass ingot from a small leather sack under his loincloth.

"Take it," he said and pushed his way past and up the stairs.

At the top of the stone stairs he heard rushing water. To the side was a wooden platform, and on that small boardwalk were canoes. Two young boys stood ready to help.

The channel was eight cubits across. One of the boys looked at Benhargan and selected a canoe that was just a bit bigger than the others.

"Here sir, this will fit you better than most," said the boy.

"You will ride between us," Benhargan told Kaltopia.

"You can address me by my common name – it's Kaltopia - remember," she said.

"Very well – if I must," Benhargan said.

"Kaltopia - it means avenger," she said, smiling broadly.

"Kaltopia," Benhargan repeated, "You will ride between Bulvife and I, so if we are attacked, you will be protected."

Kaltopia looked angry for a moment, then she smiled again. "I'll give plenty of warning before I let loose my blade. Just make sure you both keep your distance; I'll not take kindly to being tripped up by your awkward barbarian fighting ways."

Bulvife chuckled as he picked out a boat, put it in the channel and sat in it. "She is a firebrand!" he laughed. Letting go of the side of the canal, the boat began to leisurely drift down the aqueduct.

It didn't take long before the aqueduct-canoes were sailing along at the equivalent pace of a man in headlong flight. At first, they were fifteen cubits from the ground, but as the terrain changed, they found themselves much higher.

Kaltopia watched the scenery go by. "Look there," she said pointing toward a clearing in the forest.

A road curved, then vanished into the dark foliage. White smoke rose in the distance from many different points. They were now more than thirty cubits in the air, passing above the trees.

Up along the edges of the canal, birds' nests appeared. From time to time small statues of stone or clay would loomed from niches and cracks.

They traveled for some time. Thick white clouds passed overhead, and every so often a gust of wind would cut across the channel cooling each of them. Far ahead, they saw the top of a square tower.

"The gatehouse of Hollyander," Bulvife called out.

"They say giants built it," Benhargan added.

Kaltopia looked over her shoulder at him betraying her apprehension. "That is just a legend, isn't it?" she asked.

Benhargan smiled. "I've seen many legends alive and eager to kill me."

"There was the Kraken we stood before," Bulvife said loudly.

"You two saw a Kracken?" Kaltopia's voice was filled with surprise.

"We've witnessed many a horror, mostly at the hands of that demon, Grimface," Benhargan replied.

The tower was growing larger, and the sun was arching toward the west. As they got closer to the abutments, Bulivfe saw the aqueduct going into a large opening in the side of the tower. On top of the structure were guards armed with bow and blade.

"Three coming in!" shouted one guard who looked out over the tower battlements.

Bulvife came into cool darkness. The ever so subtle smell of mold and mildew was in the air. Large oil lamps were hung from black iron chains inside, and a dozen men with shields and swords at their command stood by.

The water flowed within the tower, but there was a wedge of stone just below the water level that the canoe floated up on, and guards pulled the conveyance onto the wooden floor of the tower. The water continued under the floor and into places unknown.

"Why have you come to Hollyander Scholes?" a large man wearing a polished brass breastplate asked.

"Traveling to Doom-um-nue," Bulvife said.

"The island?" The guard looked concerned. "What business do you have there?"

"We seek a companion who is there," Bulvife replied.

The guard examined each of them. "No pox, and they look healthy enough. Very well, you may descend into the city. Mind your actions, and learn the city laws. Harsh penalties are laid upon those who break rules here." He motioned for them to move toward a set of stairs.

"Where do we find your best house for drink and meat?" Benhargan more demanded than asked.

"There are many places throughout the city. Follow your nose," the guard told him with a dismissing wave of his hand. "Leave now by the stairs, or go by the window back out into the forest, I care not how you get down, or what side of the wall you find yourself."

Benhargan almost grinned at the careless way in which the man spoke to him. "Then, I shall follow my nose," he stated, as he made it to the stone stairwell and proceeded down and into the city.

Only a dozen steps outside the tower, Bulvife held up his hand and stopped. "Do you smell that?"

"I smell mint, bezel, thyme, and some meat. There's beer nearby, and wine too..." Kaltopia replied.

"The absence of urine and dung," Benhargan said. "No stench of livestock or sweat, or quim. This is a strange city."

"Come on," Bulvife said, as he proceeded down an alley and onto a flagstone street.

All around them were structures made of smooth, white stone. Windows were framed in wood or brick, and fitted with glass. Doorways were secured with brass doors, and each dwelling seemed to be uniformly three cubits from one another.

Wide streets branched off at right angles to one another forming perfect rectangular blocks, and on each block five story villas basked in the late-day sun.

After passing several groups of homes, they came to a large market square that had many vendors with push-carts hocking wares. Men and women shouted for attention, holding up silk, pottery, and produce.

Benhargan took a sniff of the air and pointed at one of the structures. "There's the place we want!" He strode toward it, took hold of the latch and pushed the door inward.

Darkness met his eyes, then as his vision adjusted, many candles illuminated tables and benches, and earthen pitchers and horn cups. The scent of beer, wine, and something else he couldn't place, filled his nose.

A man approached them and asked if they would feast. Benhargan went to a long wooden table and sat. "Bring much beer, wine and meat to fill our bellies. We have traveled a weary distance of many leagues to get here."

The man nodded and went away, only to return with serving women and boys who brought platters of meat, cheese, fowl, and drink.

Without delay, Benhargan and Bulvife dove into the food, drinking from the stone pitchers and savagely attacking the roasted meats. Kaltopia took food upon a plate and poured beer into her cup. She watched bemused at the table manners of her companions.

The feasting went on for several hours, until the sun set, and the shadows of the night prowled the city streets. A man sitting behind the barbarians said that the full moon was out, and the watch would be doubled. A woman passed, and Benhargan eyed her lustily. She halted and came back, setting a pitcher on the table. Bulvife sat back and took up the container sniffed it, then looked confused.

"What manner of drink is this?" Bulvife asked.

The woman glanced in the pitcher and shook her head. "It is hydraroot, boiled, left out to ferment, then boiled again. The steam is captured and cooled, and the liquid is set to age in wooden barrels sealed by fire and wax. After two years the barrel is opened, and the liquid is removed and drank. It is called lemerow, after the ancient word for heavenly sight." She chuckled. "You'll understand the name when you consume it – if you be man enough to do so."

Bulvife took it up to his lips and quaffed, then set down the pitcher. He wiped his mouth, leaned back against the wall and thought about Grimface and his mad schemes.

Across from him was Benhargan and Kaltopia, as opposite a sight as anyone could find. Benhargan – massive, muscles bulging, with a voracious appetite. Kaltopia – proper, her features soft and beguiling, eating as any civilized person would, or should.

For a moment, Bulvife's vision was clear, but slowly it became foggy – a mist was rising within the tavern, and he was not able to see those around him. A chill washed over him, as the stoic expression of Grimface formed clearly in his mind's eye – the man's dark black mustache and hair, his squinting eyes, and brown skin. Through a blurry lens, the man was sitting at a table, but he suddenly rose up – shocked for some reason.

"By the goddess!" Grimface shouted. There was a flash of light, the scent of brimstone, and debris showering down. A horror stood there, its claws poised to do evil.

Bulvife fell into a dark tunnel, his mind spinning like a maple seed falling from the heist mountain top. As he regained his symmetry, he looked up into the face of a grinning horror – its dripping fangs and slathering mouth ripe with human flesh and bone.

Someone shouted into Bulvife's ear. He sat up. The tavern was nearly empty, and the embers in the fire pit were glowing relics of the once ample fire. He looked around the room and saw Benhargan and Kaltopia looking at him from across the table.

"What draws you from slumber?" Kaltopia asked Bulvife.

"Two nights hence, we will need to rally to the wizard," Bulvife said. "His very life will hang in the balance."

"Two nights?" Benhargan asked. "Then, there is no hurry."

# CHAPTER 7
# A Wet Doom

GRIMFACE ATE AND DRANK. He sat comfortably in a wooden chair covered in soft cloth that was stuffed with down. A servant approached - a young man lanky of build, dressed in a gray tunic, and sporting dark hair.

"As you requested my good lord," said the young man as he handed a brown leather sack to the wizard.

Grimface opened it and rummaged around inside. Bowing, the servant turned and left the room. The magician was just about to close the sack, when the front door opened and slammed shut. A wave of hot air as if from a forge washed over Grimface. He shot to his feet. A man appeared from blue simmering air.

"Vill!" Grimface said surprised.

The man staggered toward the magician, blood dripped from his eyes, ears, and nose.

"You should've waited for me to come to you!" Grimface rushed to the man's side just as the other collapsed.

"There is no time. Vill stammered out. "He has come. He is a prince from the Bygone Lands. His power is great. It is as we feared – and even now he makes plans to forge Atlantis anew. In his mad-addled mind... he hopes to use the power of a god-king to carve a piece of Hyboria away, and make it an abhorrent."

"What of the girl?" Grimface pressed.

"She... his daughter... she is the vessel to be mated with a dark god..." Vill's eyes closed and the torc fell from his hand. "They call to me, the kuribu..." His body convulsed once, then he lay still.

"Where is he plotting? Where is his army?" Grimface pleaded.

No answer came from the dead man. Grimface took up the torc, stood, and set it on the table. The servant returned with a pitcher of wine, saw the body and looked at Grimface with surprise.

"Poor fellow," Grimface said while shaking his head. "See that he is cremated atop a birch-wood pyre." He handed the servant a gold coin. "Have it done by tomorrow night—the cycle of the full moon. It was the way of his people."

The servant left, then returned with two others. They removed the body, and vanished into the inn.

Sitting back down, Grimface looked at the torc and touched it gently, then took the pitcher, poured his cup full, and drank.

It will be up to those cunning beasts to ferret out this prince. He will not be an easy quarry, he thought.

For many hours he sat, thought, and drank. The fire in the pit, in the corner of the room, burned down to glowing orange embers. Just as he was thinking of seeking out his bed, a sound roused his attention.

The sound was akin to a flapping sound, as if a large bird were descending to the ground just outside the inn. A wave of dread fell over him just as the servant rushed into the room.

"A monster sir, a monster has come to this place!" he screamed in panic.

The wall bent inward, burst into flames and turned to black ash. Charred beams were torn out and part of the second floor fell away.

As the dust settled, the outline of a foul horror appeared. Tall as five men – feet upon shoulders, stout as several Cimmerians, and sporting two roughhewn horns - the living terror looked down upon the wizard.

Grimfaced staggered back. The servant screamed once, defiled himself, then fell to the ground unconscious. The demon locked its eyes on the servant, reached down and took up the limp body, bit off the man's head, then tossed the corps back to the ground.

It bellowed at Grimface and stepped forward, tearing more wood from the inn and lurching in with snapping fangs. Grimface fell back - then the creature shrieked and reeled back as if hit by some unseen force. It turned from side to side roaring in outrage and surprise.

From either side of the monster, two large ragdolls hung from handles buried deeply into the creature's sides. Every now and again, arrows appeared sticking out of the back of the horror.

Hesitation faded from Grimface's mind and he mustered every ounce of dark magic he had and sang out in a harmonic falsetto.

The ground cracked open, flames shot into the air, and another horror crawled forth. From the darkest realms of oblivion came a blackened nightmare. Without a lost moment, it raced forward taking the belligerent demon by the throat and crashing out into the night air. Two man-like figures were flung from the sides of the beast and into the night.

In the grassy glade that surrounded the inn, the monsters grappled. Lightning shot off in all directions, flames consumed the grass and moved over the surrounding vegetation burning it to ash.

Clouds of dust rose as the invader flapped large red wings, but the guardian held on to the creature's throat grounding it as it tried to take flight. The belligerent clawed and struggled, but grew weak, as it's life-force faded. Soon, the red beast lay motionless in the glade. The great wings fell still, the long, barbed tail flaccid, and the body motionless.

The guardian turned to Grimface, and raised its clawed hands to the sky. The ground cracked again; flames, smoke, and embers rose into the air, and it crawled back into the earth dragging the dead demon with it. In a departing flash of light, the air cooled, and the night became quiet as a tomb.

Benhargan, Bulvife, and a woman clutching a bow came forth.

"What was that thing?" yelled Kaltopia.

Grimface staggered, and caught himself at the edge of the blackened tabletop. "A demon..." he said with labored breath, "drawn forth from the underworld by blood-sacrifice."

He struggled back into the chair as the two barbarians, and Kaltopia approached.

"Inferior magic," Grimface added. He looked upon the woman. "Probably conjured by a Pict." The hint of a smile crossed his lips. "Your name would not be Kaltopia, would it?"

She approached and stood, the bow at her side. "I am Kaltopia, daughter of Kaltopus, lord of Fingara, King of Zingara," she stated.

Exhaling as if he'd run many miles, Grimface reached with shaking hand for the pitcher of wine, still upright on the table, and drank from it. "Good," he began, "just as the goddess revealed. I am sorry that I have no servant left to offer you respite for your travel, but perhaps this inn is no longer the haven I hoped it would be." He looked at Benhargan. "Come, help me to travel to the other side of the island and the Inn of the Slaughtered Boar. There I will seek some rest, and I shall tell you of my need for your skills."

As Benhargan helped Grimface up, patrons who'd been rudely awakened by the commotion filtered from the rubble and down the wooden stairs - their eyes wide with shock, and limbs shaking from terror.

"Yes," Bulvife added. "It would seem your stay here will not be appreciated when nerves calm, and money becomes the talk for compensation."

"No truer words were ever spoken, my young beast," Grimface said. "Let's take our leave now."

It took several hours to reach the Slaughtered Boar. The path through the thick island rainforest was fraught with many twists and turns, ups and downs.

Once at the Slaughtered Boar, the innkeeper was very personable and seemed quite open to providing accommodations to all Grimface's company. The building was not common by any means. It was sprawling, covering several acres. Unlike the previous inn, none of the buildings were two stories.

The innkeeper introduced Grimface to his chamber. He examined the wizard with some concern. "You look as if you have been drained of the very essence of life, my friend. Perhaps I can recommend repast that will bolster your strength and stiffen your sinew."

"Well and good," Grimface labored to say. "I'll partake when I have rested." He turned to Benhargan. "Take me in and see me to my rest. Watch over me for now. I'll be deep in sleep for three days. See that I am woken-not! I would not want another incident such as with Otten'bar." He lay down, his eyes resembled glowing red embers, and his breathing fell shallow.

Benhargan stepped back and thought for a moment.

Would he even know if I so kindly emptied his blood upon this floor with a quick stroke of my blade across his throat? He smiled to himself malevolently, then turned, and with a chuckle stood guard at the door.

The sun rose and fell three times as the barbarians feasted, drank and made the local women swoon due to their antics. To pass the time, two of them roamed the grounds, while one stayed with the wizard.

On the morning of the fourth day, Grimface came awake and demanded food and drink. He sat for a long time consuming copious amounts of wine, fruit, vegetables and meat. Afterward, he turned his attention to the three warriors.

"The full moon has come and gone many times since we set eyes on each other. I summoned you beasts for a single purpose."

"The prince?" Bulvife asked.

Grimface cracked a smile. "You are astute, barbarian. Yes, a prince has come to Hyboria, if one may call him such, and he comes with dread upon his lips and the pounding pulse of a war drum within his breast."

Benhargan harrumphed. "Such men are plenty. They are as common as rain drops in a storm."

"This man is different. He is the Ultha born, from the bloodline of the ancient kings of Atlantis - when Atlantis rested upon the sea. The last king sent his latter-born sons to explore the Infliar Lands. These lands you know as Hyboria and Hyperboria, which your feet are firmly planted upon. The king's magician, Pomogoth, led an expedition into the crystal caves, and there discovered the Unfiliar Lands - for which you cannot see with your mortal eyes."

Grimface took a drink from his glass. "For many generations the subjugation of the two lands occurred, then, as you know, the island called Atlantis vanished beneath the waves. Those Atlantians who had been scouring the continent became locked in a bitter war to rule what is now called Hyboria."

Grimface got to his feet and walked over to the fire pit, knelt down and poked at the embers with a wrought iron prod.

"It must have been a heavenly decision to wipe the Hyborian lands clean of that vile brood. The gods fell upon them with pox, war, and decimation. In the end, there was little extra the gods needed to do to purify the world of them. Then, only shadows of those beings stalked the lands. But, unknown to many, one of the princes was in the Unfiliar Lands with Pomogoth. So, that noble boy grew strong, and practiced his black and evil magic, learning from that powerful wizard. Now he has come to Hyboria – from the cave."

Bulvife tore away some flesh from the wing of a roasted mud-hen. "Where do we find this fiend, and how do we kill this powerful creature?"

"My brother asks a valid question," Benhargan said. "I trust you have an answer, and a plan?"

Grimface smiled. "I do, and this challenge will make our stand against Ottin'bar look like a child's game of hill-king."

Kaltopia looked confused. "Who is Ottin'bar?"

"I fear much more than I thought him to be," Grimface admitted. "And now there is a finality coming. I have been told that a glorious battle lay ahead, and in it, the goddess assures me there will be great reward."

"But, who was Ottin'bar?" Kaltopia repeated.

"A cunning wizard who tricked Benhargan and I – and laid waste to Grimface's lands and family. He paid for his arrogance!" Bulvife stated.

"I care little for your religious tripe," Benhargan said to Grimface. "I crave battle, and much. I desire a battle so big, and so spectacular that Crom will recognize it as one worthy of himself, but will burn with envy that I have stolen the glory. This, he will respect!"

# CHAPTER 8
# The Waking of Graygarius

THE DEAD-CALM MADE the surface of the lake like a mirror. Heaven and fathom were one, as dark blue waters reflected the sky upon its face. Gliding easily across, the oarsmen worked together in perfect precision. In the distance the mud-brick walls of Dorio grew larger.

Wooden planks on wooden piles jutted out into the lake, and small sailing boats and rowboats swarmed in abundance.

"The marina is full this time of year," said one of the boatmen.

The craft bumped against the wooden marina. A boatman tied off the boat. Benhargan jumped to the boardwalk. Grimface, Bulvife, and Kaltopia followed.

They walked to the end and up a gentle embankment to a stone wall. The stench of fish was ripe, and many a grizzled fisherman heaved baskets of fish and eel onto long wooden tables, where the unlucky creatures were gutted by old women in bloody aprons.

Grimface led the way into the town and along a dirt road between reed woven walls and mud-covered wicker buildings.

The magician came to a long-house and stood at the opening. A moment passed, and a young girl appeared.

"I am here to see Graygarius." Grimface told her.

The girl looked confused. "Graygarius? One moment, let me fetch Damascuse." She vanished inside.

"Who is it that wishes to see Graygarius?" An old woman appeared.

She was stooped, hands dirty, and she looked upon them with a weathered face and stern eyes. "Is it you who desires words with our master?" she asked.

Grimface looked back at Benhargan and the others, then back to woman. "Yes. Is he here?"

"He is not here," she said.

"Where is he?" Grimface furthered.

"He's dead," she said. "The mistress that dwells here is ill too, and will soon join him. I suggest that if you wish to speak to Graygarius, you visit his tomb, it is the only way he will hear you now – though, I am sure he will not reply." She chuckled, turned and went back inside.

"Most distressing," Grimface said as he turned back to the party. "His death is no coincidence I'm sure. Factions are forming, and the promises of power is being brokered. Come," he said, and led the way down the road to a stone and mud-brick tavern.

Inside he went to the man at the counter and spoke with him. A few moments later, pitchers of drink, and rounds of flatbread were on the table. They ate and drank, then Grimface spoke.

"The tavern-keeper has told me Graygarius has only been dead a few days. I think I can wake him."

"Wake?" Bulvife asked surprised.

"Talk with the dead. It is no easy task, but I think I can do it with the right things. The Graygarius family entombs their dead. If he's as fresh as the tavern-keeper has indicated, I have a good chance to find out what he knows before any are the wiser. When night comes we'll steal away to the tombs." He looked at Benhargan and Bulvife. "You two, seek me a bucket, a jar of honey, a lock of flaxen hair, a dozen torches, and some crow feathers."

Grimface turned to Kaltopia. "You will help me during the ceremony, I will need some of your essence. You will have to stay by my side no matter what happens. If you stray, the shadow-lerds will take your soul. When Graygarius comes awake he will be very angry that we pulled him back into his body." He again looked at the two barbarians. "You will have to restrain him, if he tries to run. It would not be good for his shambling corpse to be found wandering about in the town."

Benhargan and Bulvife left and made for the market. Grimface explained to Kaltopia exactly what would happen in the ceremony. As the sun hovered, suspended at the center of the sky, the barbarians returned with some ill-gotten goods. Grimface began scrawling strange arcane symbols upon red pottery shards. When he'd finished, he put the runes into the bucket.

Hours passed as day gave way to night. The empty pitchers and plates piled up on the rough-cut wooden table. As the dark-hour approached, they gathered up all the items into the bucket and left for the tombs.

They went one at a time into the filthy streets. Grimface led the party, and it took a half hour to reach the graveyard that lay beyond the east wall and gate.

Many of the stone structures glowed an eerie silvery light under the rising moon - pyramids, octagonal buildings, and rectangular mausoleums with brass-bared windows and marble effigies of brooding gods.

They searched for some time, then Grimface called out, "It's here. Come and bring the metal pry-bar!"

Bulvife came and rammed the bar into the crack of the cap-stone. Both barbarians pried the lid off and set the stone to the side. A dark hole appeared, and a vile stench came from within. Into the blackness they descended.

The hole was not too deep - the height of a Cimmerian, and the area was recently swept clean. In the antechamber Grimface took a torch and ignited it. An orange glow filled the room, as dark swirling smoke charged out the stone hole above their heads.

They moved down a narrow hall. A set of stairs carved into the limestone came into view. Down into the living rock they went. At the bottom, there was a long shaft with openings every twenty paces leading to rooms. In each compartment lay defleshed yellow bones or a body desiccating.

"Here he is," Grimface announced.

Lying along one of the slots was a fresh corpse wrapped in white linen with a bowl of figs and dates at one end, and beer and wine at the other.

"At last someone who thinks ahead," Benhargan said as he reached for the jar of wine.

Grimface intercepted his hand, and the barbarian looked on the verge of homicide.

"You and your foolish lusts shall not desecrate this grave. It would cause undue harm to our efforts, and delay our waking. Now you two, leave the bucket. Get hence out into the hall. Stay there until I command you to enter.

"If Graygarius tries to run away, stop him and bring him back. He will have to be returned to the dead after we're done. We can't risk enraging the gods – for they may set curses upon us for this act."

Benhargan and Bulvife did as they were told. Grimface thought he heard Benhargan say something about entrails and strangulation as he went. Kaltopia waited next to the magician, who took the bucket and set it at the edge of the body.

From a small leather case attached at his belt, Grimface produced two vials of some strange liquid that stunk worse than the decay around them. He poured both into the container. On top of that he put the crow feathers, a dollop of wild honey, and over that a sheet of papyrus with writing on it. Lastly, he produced a gray wax candle, lit it, and set the contents of the bucket on fire.

"Keep the torch to the side. You'll see things begin to appear; close your eyes tightly, or they will get inside you. Speak only when spoken to, and then only when I speak to you. If something familiar calls to you, like a family member or lost lover, ignore it; it is a demon trying to decouple your soul from your body." He inhaled deeply, then began to chant in a soft voice that sounded a lot like singing. Slowly it built in tempo, as static snapped and sparked with baleful light that crawled up the walls like deadly snakes.

Kaltopia watched as black tendrils of smoke rose from the bucket and fanned out like the arms of an octopus. An ever-consuming vale of darkness clung to the corpse. Then, something spoke to her.

"Kaltopia, my darling granddaughter, come to me, I have missed you. Do you not remember the nights that I read to you from the scroll of Timberliers' Odyssey?" The voice took a somber tone. "And when you came to stay with us, did I not teach you the ways of Morlengoth and sing to you about the warrior princess Helnorod? Only I would know these things. It is I, your gorm-pa..."

She shut her eyes tightly, but tears fell from her cheeks to the floor.

Grimface's song changed, and a menacing sound came from the man. The walls shook slightly and cracks along the stone shown with white light. He reached into the bucket and pulled forth the pottery shards covered in ash.

He carefully laid out one on Graygarius' head, one at his feet, and one on either side of him. A pulsating red light seemed to surround the body. Things moved within that unworldly shine.

Graygarius sat up. There was a moment where he struggled to get out from the linens. Slowly he shed the cloth like a snake does its skin.

The ashen gray face of a man in his thirties appeared, clean shaven and wide eyed. The mouth opened, and a terrible scream emitted as the corpse looked upon Grimface.

The wizard's song faded, as man-like shadow-shapes with red eyes peered from all around.

"You can look now," Grimface told Kaltopia.

"What am I doing here?" Graygarius demanded to know.

"I am called Grimface, and I have pulled you from the afterlife. You possessed something I need, but only you know where it is."

Graygarius looked as if he would bolt for the door, but then calmed.

"The stench – you've made a mess of my place of death. And I see the dark-lerds have come to see what all this is about. You have created horror by coming here. Grimface, you have done what few still know how to do, so tell me of what you seek?"

"There comes a man who was born of Atlantis who will lay siege to the many lands of Hyboria. I will face him, but I need to know the location of the jar. Where is the jar of Mur?"

"It even now is waiting for you. The goddess made it and fired it in the kilns of Kaydor. In my hands I strove to do good with it, but now the hag who murdered me searches for it to make an offering to a dark prince.

"Return to my home. The witch will appear as an aged homely creature. Be warned, she is much more, and commands a horned vidak who is bound to protect her. Even as we speak she plies her evil trade to torment my wife into betraying me. If you hurry back, you might rescue my love. The jar is below the house submerged in a box. Know ye who woke this spirit, the hour grows short for you and your kind." Graygarius shook, then lay back becoming still.

Grimface extinguished the candle, and the dark specters that lurked along the walls vanished. "It is done. You may enter," Grimface called to Benhargan and Bulvife. Kaltopia staggered suddenly and Benhargan caught her. "I used her life-force to help me break the barrier between this world and the next. She will be weak for several days, but she will be fine."

"It was my grandfather's voice I heard," she mumbled.

"Those who dwell in the darkness will say anything, and sound like anyone to get you to allow them to steal your soul. If they do, your soul can be lost—sold into slavery for pleasures of things you would not want to know of," Grimface told her. "Now, we must fly to the house of Graygarius. His wife is in mortal danger, and what I seek is hidden there."

Grimface raced from the tomb, leading them to the house of Graygarius. The opening was illuminated by a lamp, and just outside was an old man with a basket of fruit on his lap.

The wizard stopped and stepped back. "Wait!" he shouted. Behnargan and Bulvife immediately produced swords and charged in front.

Standing, the old man transformed into a hellish creature with scales, horns and claws. It rose up until it was more than ten hands above the height of Benhargan.

Kaltopia stumbled back and fumbled with her bow, notched an arrow, steadied herself, and fired. Grimface fell back behind them all and called to the sky in words unearthly.

Fire emitted from the beast, as it flexed its scaly muscles and cried out a terrible roar that shook the boardwalk. From behind came Damascuse and in her hand, was a glowing ember of red and orange. She held it up and sang in a foul and guttural tone. The creature immediately stormed into the Cimmerians.

# CHAPTER 9
# The Jar of Making

BENHARGAN CROUCHED, then launched himself at the monster. The demon and barbarian collided as the skilled ranger blocked the monster's claws with his sword and delivered a withering elbow strike to the creature's chin.

It fell back, grunted and came again. A thrust of the sword forced the monster back, then it knocked the barbarian to the side and sliced through his rough leather tunic drawing blood.

Benhargan staggered back, dodged, then drove his sword upward into the demon cutting its neck and skull. It roared and smashed into him driving the hulking barbarian back a dozen feet in the process.

Bulvife drove hard past the demon, his blade in hand. He sidestepped the melee and came at the sorceress. The woman saw him and directed her attention in kind. Fire flew up from the wooden slats. Bulvife protected this face, dove through the flames, rolled once, and came up ready to strike. The witch flung herself out of the way...the ember fell from her hand onto the ground.

"The stone!" shouted Grimface. "Kick it into the waters!"

Without hesitation, Bulivfe struck the ember with his boot, and sent it hissing into the cool waters of the lake.

Grimface resumed his song and the sky grew dark. Fire fell from the clouds as hungry flames feasted upon the boardwalk and surrounding reed-houses.

"Protect your master!" shouted the witch, just as a massive glob of black, sticky, fluid fell from the sky and covered her completely. The demon rushed back to protect her.

"No, you fool, I'm covered in pitch!" she screamed.

It was too late - the demon threw its arms around her and both burst into flames. Damascuse screamed, then grew as black as charcoal. In a moment, she crumpled to ash.

The demon looked confused, then turned back to Grimface who stopped singing. "Your keeper is gone now, be on your way," he told it with a wave of his hand.

The monster looked at Grimface, narrowed its flaming yellow eyes, then leapt from the burning house and raced from the boardwalk into the woods.

"Quickly!" called Grimface, as the flames exploded up all around them.

"Do something," Kaltopia shouted.

"No time! Into the lake," ordered Grimface.

They all flung themselves from the blaze and into the chilled blue waters. Burnt debris fell all about them like a hellish snowstorm.

The wizard plunged into the water. Around him were the muffled plunk of the others. White bubbles raced past him. The orange glow of the fire above illuminated the lakebed. His clothes were now saturated and pulling him deeper toward the stony bottom.

He struggled for a moment, then saw a metal box with a rope and chain just below the piles supporting Graygarius' home. In his mind he saw the urn – a glow in the middle of the metal container.

His lungs were beginning to burn, but he knew he had to secure the relic. Dipping down he latched onto the rope and chain and wrapped it around his arm. Darkness swallowed him as his air failed.

"Where is the wizard?" shouted Bulvife, as he broke the surface.

"He is still below," called Benhargan.

Bulvife took in several quick deep breaths, held the last one, and dove down. The wizard was easy to see; his robes flowed like a rainbow of smoke. He was snagged on something, and Bulvife grabbed onto the man and pulled hard for the surface. Once above the water, he called to Benhargan.

"Come and help. The magician is caught by something. Help get him to the shore."

Benhargan latched onto the wizard, and both men swam with the power of two sturdy dolphins. It took only a moment before they reached the rocky beach.

They hauled the wizard out and laid him down, as ash and smoke swirled about them. Kaltopia pulled herself from the water and fell to her knees next to Grimface. She looked down at him and realized he was not breathing.

"Step aside, you brutes!" she commanded, and proceeded to put Grimface on his side and slapped him on the back. She rolled him over and looked at his face.

"He's still not breathing," she said. "I'll wake him with a kiss!"

She put her lips to his and breathed into his mouth.

His chest rose, then a column of water shot out of his mouth... he choked, and more water came forth. For a few minutes, he coughed until the color had returned to his face and he was able to speak.

"Which one of you creatures brought me back?"

"It was the woman," Benhargan said. "She possesses some form of strange resurrection magic."

"She merely filled my lungs with air," Grimface said. "Thank you, Kaltopia. Your company on this expedition is a blessing."

Kaltopia blushed. "It is a Zingarian technique that we learn as warriors—the practice of the healing arts," she said.

"We will remember this thing you have shown us," Bulivfe said. "It is a very useful technique."

"I know much more, and can teach you both," she offered.

Benhargan pulled on the rope attached to Grimface's arm. "Look at what the wizard has caught," Benhargan said, while hauling the metal box from the water.

"Yes!" said Grimface as he got to his feet. "But first I have a message from Graygaruis. He spoke to me as I lay dead. It is a warning, that we are the cause of his wife's death... just now." He pointed at the flaming debris sliding into the lake – all that was left of the reed-house. "The fire has consumed his wife as it did the witch."

The wizard went to the box, but stopped and looked along the shore. "Look you three, in the surf." He went down the shore and pulled from the waters a strange black stone. "The witch's arcane-stone," he said. "What divine help! We are truly unworthy," he told them while looking up at the sky.

All three of the warriors looked up and then at each other.

"A blessing by the goddess is upon us." He turned to Bulvife and Benhargan. "Let's get this box somewhere I can open it. We have finally something of use to aid us in our tasks ahead."

"What of Graygarius?" Kaltopia reminded Grimface.

"Oh, yes, he was a bit angry at our clumsy way of dealing with the witch. He may make trouble for all of us, when we cross over. Calling back souls and murder tend to make the celestial judges dour."

"It's of little concern to we rangers," Benhargan said. "Between war, and our less legitimate exploits, such judges will be judging us until the stars fall from the sky." He laughed. "Now, tell us more of this stone and box."

In the distance the loud clang of a bell was ringing. Men and boys were running to the fire. Buckets were filling with lake water, and brave souls doused spreading flames.

From across the lake, the hint of sunlight was caressing the night sky.

"Come, bring the box and let's go to the closest tavern," Grimface said, as the Dorio citizens frantically fought the fire.

The four made their way along the shore until they found a place where the bank formed an incline leading up toward the town-proper. They moved along several of the paved paths to a round building with a hanging copper shingle that showed a pig and a hen on it.

Inside was a wood floor, many long tables and benches, and several patrons. Benhargan put the metal box on the table. A simple wooden peg held the latch and Grimface spared no time in opening it.

He looked down at an urn, which he pulled out and set on the table next to the box. "We have the torc, the jar, and soon we will have the third item."

"What third item?" Kaltopia asked.

"The holy water from the sacred spring of Kahal Mora. Once the urn is filled with that ancient liquid, I will command the power of the river Acheron. Our enemy will be incapable of escaping its current of death!"

Benhargan scoffed. "Kahal Mora? That old story? There is no place of that name that I've seen along these roads."

"That is because you know it by another name, a name that your kind have lent it," Grimface told him. "You would call it Hode, the dwellings beyond the crag."

"Is it near or far?" Bulvife asked.

"Far. Many leagues travel by both boat and land. There will also be many trials and labors we will have to endure along the way. We will have to travel to the south, and when we arrive we will need to be cunning. Many eyes will be watching for us— to undermine our efforts, and murder us."

"How many eyes?" Bulvife asked.

"Thousands. By the time we come to the end of our lives, maybe hundreds of thousands. All of them seeking power, and some who are already powerful will be seeking immortality, all gotten if they bring our heads to he who calls himself prince."

"You waste time with all this talk," Benhargan chided. "It is time for action. Let us take to the south road today, for the sooner my blade drinks in the blood of our enemies, the better it will be for me and my kind." He looked over at Bulvife and nodded.

Bulvife nodded back. "True, we are men of action and battle is the hot lust that runs in our veins."

"Very well," Grimface said, as he put the urn back in the box. "Take this container and guard it with your lives. There will be things out to get this treasure – things that you have not encountered yet that may bend your simple minds. But first, we must find horses and a cart. Then, we will keep to the roads for speed is our goal."

"Those abominations that you and your kind conjure kindle not my fear! You warn of fearful things?" He brandished his sword. "Men fear this in the hands of a Cimmerian!" Benhargan boasted.

"You say that you have not been struck dumb with fear yet? Soon you will - I assure you," Grimface said, as he led the three outside and to the local stable master.

They purchased horses and a cart. Loading the box on the cart, they padded it with some blankets and other supplies.

The cart trundled along the rutted street, passing the area of Dorio blackened by fire. The souls that still plied water to the smoldering wood looked upon them with weary eyes.

At the marina, they loaded their cart and horses onto a flat-bottomed ferry, and began the trek across the lake. As they rounded the tip of the island, the smell of cooking fires grew thick, and from time to time, flocks of black birds blanketed the sky - diving this way and that.

The ferry made its way along a curved spit of land and docked at a wooden pier. All disembarked.

"We'll make our way along the Kopler Road through the valley. Once on the other side, we will go south," Grimface stated.

"Do you not worry about the bandits and monsters that lurk in these woods?" Kaltopia asked.

"If you fear such, then why don't you take up a place as a handmaid here in Hollyander?" Benhargan jibbed.

She gave Benhargan a withering look, then shook her head with a smile. "I do not enquire for myself, for I fear nothing," she boldly said.

"Wait a while. When you travel with us, you'll learn what fear is, especially when we encounter more of those things Grimface attracts," Bulvife suggested.

The start of the road was bumpy, and as the worn cobblestones vanished and the rutted dirt road appeared, the going became a lot worse. They were bounced, jostled, and even buffeted about as the road turned and straightened, and then turned again.

They crossed creeks and brooks, and even over a stone bridge that spanned a dark green river. The night came and went, and their traveling became routine. As the pines began to thin, and the forest gave way to birch, maple, and beech, the crossroad of the southern highway appeared.

# CHAPTER 10
# Divine Rule

THE BUBBLING AND CHURNING of a rushing brook drew Benhargan's attention. They followed upstream a few hundred yards to a pool of crystal clear water. A dozen massive gray stones were positioned around it. The barbarians unharnessed the pony from the cart, and hobbled it with their other horses near fresh grass.

"Those who are following us are skulking about these woods," Benhargan whispered to Grimface.

"I know. There are several of them. Perhaps you and Bulvife should go and see who, or what they are. Be quick and leave no trace in footfall, broken grass, or branch. Look around for others of your kind; you are not the only rangers in the world."

"We shall be as untraceable as a shadow on a moonless night," Benhargan replied.

"Who is following us?" Katlopia asked in a hushed voice.

"We've been followed since we left Dorio. You didn't notice it?" asked Benhargan.

Kaltopia looked annoyed. "No, but how could you have known?"

"A deaf man, feeble in vision and weak of mind could tell three followed us. How is it you didn't know?" Benhargan retorted.

"I'm not deaf, feeble, or weak of mind," Kaltopia said, offended. "I'm as deadly a warrior as you three!"

Benhargan whispered in Katopia's ear as the shadow of night was falling. "Control your anger, for the enemy is even now watching us. Make a fire, and cook a meal." He then approached Bulvife, and in a very normal tone stated,

"That grouse-root we ate yesterday has fouled my bowels - I go to perfume the forest!" He stormed off into the woods and out of sight.

Bulvife took a few moments to gather all the wood in the immediate area, then he wandered off into the forest looking down and collecting limbs. He too melded away with the ferns and shrubs.

Kaltopia made a fire, and began dressing a half dozen, gray hares they'd killed earlier along the road. She stoked the immature blaze in the pit, and spitted the rabbits, then washed the congealed blood from her hands. After she returned to the fire, she put the carcasses near the bright orange coals to cook.

"Come hither," Grimface commanded her. He smiled as if being playful, and whispered in her ear. "There is a big problem. There's a wizard among those who followed us. He is to my right, moving to come out of the woods in front of me. I've blocked his sight and hearing for the moment, but he will come for us in due course. Do as I say, and we may take these fiends by surprise. When I give you the command, come stand by me, and await my next instruction."

Grimface retrieved his brown bag and lay it by the fire, then moved away from the flames. Taking a stick, he made a large circle, ten paces from side to side, then sat in the middle. He reclined back on his elbow, then smiled. "Now woman, strip and dance for my pleasure!" In a very low voice he added, "Put your armor and clothes within the circle. Be ready to act when I call upon you." He laughed a bawdy chuckle then said, "Now dance for me, woman!"

Kaltopia began to dance about the fire. She loosened her metal breastplate and took it off. She came close to Grimface and put it in the circle next to him. Next came off her leather vambrace, then she dropped off her chainmail tasset, her greaves came next, and lastly her boots. She stood naked to the world to see.

"Now, my lovely dear," Grimface calmly said. "Come here to me, so I might stroke your hair."

From across the camp stepped a man dressed in leather armor sheened in lacquer with an emblem of three large golden triangles over the breast. The patterns produced a soft glow and shimmered with power. From behind and the sides came three men with swords, who gawked at Kaltopia's splendor.

"Grimeface," the man said with authority. "I've come bearing a message from my lord and master."

Kaltopia stood behind Grimface with her hands on his shoulders.

"Shall I act now?" she whispered.

"Soon," Grimface replied out of the corner of his mouth. "Speak your peace," he said to the man.

"I've sent your Cimmerians on a merry chase so we can speak alone, and not be bothered by their rash behavior. I come with an offer that is worthy a mighty priest who commands the power. My master says for you to come and join his efforts, bathe in the spoils, and know an eternity without death."

"Or?" Grimface asked.

The man looked surprised at Grimface's response. "Or fall into darkness. Be sent to oblivion by his word. For he says to tell you, he has power over you. Align against him, and he will undo you. Join with him and..."

The man's eyes went wide as blood frothed from his mouth. A brass sword blade punched through the man's leather armor as he came off the ground, and was suspended in the air. He shook violently with his feet dangling down, then was tossed to the ground. Benhargan stood there.

"You fool!" Grimface shouted at the barbarian. "There was more to learn from that creature!"

Arrows drove deep into the body of each of the armed men around them. Bulvife stepped forth from behind the tall standing stones.

"Win the battle, and lose the war, you fools! We needed the information he was about to give!" Grimface said angrily.

"Why don't you wake him!" Benhargan growled. "All three warriors are finished as well."

A flash of light illuminated the sky, as a column of black smoke shot straight up from the fire. A dark black figure formed in the smoke and looked about.

"Such monsters these Cimmerians are!" the smoke creature said. "You have murdered my envoy. This does not bode well for you, Grimface."

The figure gazed down upon Grimface and Kaltopia. "My offer was good; take it or I shall smite you here!"

Lightning flashed, and for one brief moment the spaces between the trees of the forest shown filled with men in armor - blades loosed, and at the ready.

Benhargan looked upon the large force of enemy soldiers. "Time for talk is over! Our enemies have come in force!" Benhargan said loudly. "To me," he shouted to Bulvife

Bulvife rushed to his brethren's side. "If we are meant to fall here, let it be by drowning in our enemy's blood!"

A torrent of wind swirled dust and debris into the air around the fire, then shot it all about. The enemy was obscured for a moment.

"Kaltopia," said Grimface, as he handed her a small stone figure. "Take this and throw it into the fire. Rush back here to me, and dress quickly, for your sword and bow will be needed."

She rushed to the pit and tossed the talisman into the fire. The ground quaked, and a blob of golden light bubbled up from ground. An unearthly scream emitted from the smoke-figure as the light grew, encapsulating all. White light filled the sky, and a blast of air rippled out into the forest.

The apparition was gone, but the soldiers remained. Grimface jumped to his feet, just as Kaltopia reached him.

"Dress as fast as you can!" he ordered her, as he began to sing.

The battle cry of hundreds of men roared from the trees – then the enemy fell upon them.

Grimface gave the barbarians a little extra speed, a little extra luck - all the prayers he knew to have the goddess steal victory from the enemy.

Arrow after arrow flew from the barbarian's bows. The enemy fell by a cool dozen, causing others to trip, installing fear into their ranks. Some of the soldiers reached Benhargan and Bulvife, and the two men threw bows aside, and unleashed their thirsting blades.

With haste, Kaltopia got her cuirass and sword belt on. A villain was nearly to Grimface. She dodged left, scooped up her buckler and deflected a fatal sword blow meant for the wizard.

Her blade sang out as it collided with her enemy's brass sword, wooden shield, and leather armor. Two more came for them. One at a time she took the enemy to task. Small wounds appeared on her arms, legs and breast, but she drove hard into the foe, leaving the coiled bowels of her enemy a tangle upon the ground.

Grimface raised his arms and sang out ever louder; his tune changed rapidly as the ground vibrated, and dark, terrifying figures rose up from the musky soil. The horrors grabbed at the belligerent's feet and legs, pulling some screaming into the leafy sod. Things climbed from the fresh humus and smashed into the enemy – claws slicing through armor and shields.

Benhargan and Bulvife burst with bawdy laughter. The two men were taken with the blood lust as they cleaved arms from torsos, and painted the forest in hot blood.

The enemy wavered, then the tide reversed as the bodies piled up. A horn roared from someplace in the woods filling the air, and the enemy fell back receding into the forest.

Grimface's song changed, as plant roots and vines slithered out of the forest, entangled those left behind, and pulled the dying and dead into the woods to a fate unknown.

The dark creatures withered and vanished. Fire shot into the air from all the cracks in the ground, as Grimface collapsed.

Bulvife ran up to the wizard and knelt down. He checked the man for signs of life, then called out to Benhargan, "He still lives!"

"And, we'll be the worst for that news!" Benhargan shouted back.

Kaltopia sheathed her sword, then spun around to face Benhargan. Blood and gore covered her face and body. A wild look was in her eye.

"It's good to see this in you - battle lust," Benhargan said coming up to her.

She looked at him. For a moment it seemed as if she'd attack, but she did not.

"You are about to lose that wager," Benhargan said, as he took her in his powerful arms.

Their lips smashed together, as their hands tore at each other's armor and clothes. To call it lovemaking would be an error – for even in the act of coitus, battle-lust fueled their passion – a sight that could not be called pretty. They rolled about in the sticky red mud - their bodies locked in an embrace of lustful rage.

After quite some time she lay prostrate, her body quaking. Benhargan picked her up and laid her by the fire and rose to the bemused expression on Bulvife's face.

"Why so mirthful?" Benhargan asked.

Shaking his head Bulvife said, "Even Crom has never seen such a display. I think he would approve."

Benhargan grunted. "Crom's amusement is of no concern of mine," he said. "Now, gather the wizard and bring him to the fire. At first light, we will find our way through the forest to Pishtun. There we will shelter until the wizard has his legs about him."

Bulvife grabbed Benhargan by the arm. "You and I both know that these woods did not at first have so many warriors. There were only three scouts that followed us, and that other. Where did that force of soldiers come from?" Bulvife asked.

"It is the way of wizards, to deceive, or conjure. In this case, I think it was both powerful magic and cunning. So powerful was our enemy's magic, that it hid the multitude. I know that my skills would have easily picked out such a force – but since I didn't – it must have been strong magic. Look at the wizard; he was nearly killed by our enemy's magic. That's something we've never encountered before."

Kaltopia stood and began reassembling her armor. "Whatever happened, it was unnatural to be sure. If Grimface had not been here, we'd all be dead."

Benhargan chuckled. "If Grimface had not been here, those murderous villains would not have been so eager for our blood."

"His magic is powerful, but I fear there are those whose magic is more powerful. They'll be coming to find us," Bulvife added.

"We're in this fight as deep as our wizard now. There will be no getting clear of it." Benhargan lamented. "So, let us find pleasure in what battles we come upon."

"Then let us to Pishtun and wait not for first light. There we will rest, feast, and," Bulvife eyed Kaltopia, "sate our baser desires."

They found the pony wandering in the woods – he'd broken his rope in a panic. One of the other horses stood dumbfounded, drunk with shock from the battle. The other two horses were gone. It took a few minutes to gather up Grimface and check the contents of the wagon, hitch the pony, and find a path back through the woods. They would now be at a walking pace until more horses could be acquired.

Bulvife played scout, while Benhargan led the pony by hand around briars and across dark river fords. By daybreak, they had made a dozen miles. As the days passed, they stayed clear of the roads, and avoided the villages and farms that littered the valley.

On the fifth day, they came to a high-gate which offered access to the walled town of Pishtun. The guards seemed uninterested in the four of them, and only bothered to ask for a bribe before letting them pass.

Once inside, the two barbarians shoved unsavory pedestrians out of the way as they led the cart down a stinking narrow street toward the southern gate. Several inns were there, waiting to entreat those with brass, or copper in their purse.

Bulvife made his way to a three-story stone building fronted with gray colonnades supporting a second-floor balcony. Patrons, some dressed in colorful togas, watched with disgust as Bulvife went inside.

A few minutes later the barbarian exited with a tall thin man whose long red hair was woven into a ponytail.

"Three nights will cost you two brass ingots, plus two silver for the stabling of your beasts and storage of the cart."

"How about we sell you the horse, pony, and cart?" Bulvife suggested.

The man stopped and considered this.

"I'll take them. Do you have the brass to pay?" asked the innkeeper.

"Yes," Benhargan said.

"When you leave, you can find fresh mounts at a farm just outside the city. If you are traveling to Hode, you might consider staying at Hugh the Bowright's inn. I'm sure he'll be happy to put you all up."

Benhargan nodded. "We will consider such as we travel on from here."

For several days they stayed there, rarely leaving the room except for food and drink. At last, Grimface woke. His skin was pale, and he looked about the room somewhat confused.

"We're in Pishtun at an inn near the southern gates," Bulvife told him.

"What happened?" Grimface asked.

"We won," Benhargan stated.

"I see that. I remember a burning ember in my mind. There was a... face... a voice in my ear singing with such power. Oh, this prince has many tricks. Unfortunately, now he knows some of mine."

"And ours!" said Benhargan.

Grimface poured some water from a pitcher into a basin and washed his face.

"The spring we seek is not far from here. If we can get the water, we might have a fighting chance to kill this abhorrent creature." He turned to Bulvife. "You were wise to let me sleep undisturbed. I'm nearly at full strength. Come, I must eat, drink, and then we will be off to Hode."

The grease dripped down the wizard's arm as he tore into a chunk of boar haunch. With steady hand he lifted his cup to his mouth until all the contents were drained. He wiped his mouth with his sleeve and stood.

"Come!" Grimface said as he walked to the door and exited. He led the way toward the southern gate and out of the town. "We'll get fresh mounts in Hode."

Benhargan carried the box, and Grimface the torc. Bulvife kept watch from the front, and Kaltopia the flank. They walked until mid-of-the-day.

The cobblestone road stopped, giving way to a rutted dirt version of the highway. From there, they walked for several hours until a side road bifurcated off and up a hill.

Up through the path they went. Midway, they saw a wide and flat space and a stable. Some carts were parked to the side, and in a pen, a group of ten horses stared back at the travelers.

Further along, the road narrowed into a path, and the path led to a jagged crag leading through the mountain face. Benhargan took the front this time, followed by Grimface, Kaltopia, and Bulvife.

The gap was long, four hundred feet or more, but no wider than a large man's shoulders. At the end, Kaltopia gasped with surprise.

"The white stone – it is dazzling," she said.

A large caldera containing a grassy meadow, filled with yellow and purple flowers stretched for a mile. All around were high rocky cliffs. In the middle, a large town made of white stone grew from the very soil.

Bulvife looked up to see a metal grate with spikes pointing down suspended over his head by ropes. A handful of soldiers stood guard. They wore lacquered-leather armor, and carried not only shield, sword, and bow, but also long polearms of varied shapes and lengths.

"What do you want here traveler?" a man in a black armor gilded in blue gems demanded.

"We seek refuge for the night, and fresh horses for a trip on the morrow," Grimface told him.

The man eyed the two barbarians and Kaltopia closely. "People don't come to this city by chance. You have business here – what is it?" the soldier demanded to know.

Grimface smiled. "We seek Hugh the Bowright. It is said he dwells here."

The head-guard nodded and gave a hand signal to his warriors. "Let them pass," he said loudly.

The red and yellow flowers stretched for a hundred yards – the sweet musky scent strong and thick. Paving stones formed a road that led to wide brooks that surrounded the town as does a wreath of laurels upon the head of a priest of Mitra.

They passed over several wooden bridges. The waterways seemed manmade, and they appeared to form concentric rings surrounding the town. As they traversed the final moat, it was clear that much thought was put into defending the settlement – for if an enemy breached the guards at the crag, they would then have distance and water to contend with to reach the treasures of Hode.

The walls of the inner buildings were adorned with gold, brass, and silver. Jewels were used to accent rooftops, eaves, and door-frames. Each person they passed, the ones wearing togas, wore precious stones set in necklaces, wrapped around wrists in bracelets, and mounted on rings. Those men and women walked and talked as if they had no cares of the wicked world. A short man with long blond hair stopped the group and regarded them with some curiosity.

"Cimmerians?" he asked.

Grimface looked bemused. "Yes, they are."

"Fine specimens you have. Do they belong to you, or do you claim them?"

"None possess Benhargan! I am a freeman, capable of inflicting great bodily harm," Benhargan said menacingly.

"No Cimmerian is a slave," Bulvife responded, "for we'd embrace death before being taken into such service!"

"I do not speak of slavery, but of mentorship," the man said.

"These beasts and the woman are with me, and under my tutelage. We seek the inn of Hugh the Bow-right," Grimface said. "Can you point us in that direction?"

"His place is along that street there. Take it to the end, by the third tower-wall. Climb the steps to the roof, there you will find the door. He takes all lodgers. If you ask, he may take you to see the ruins below his inn – they are part of the footings of the ancient wall of the first city." The man looked the party over one more time, smiled and left.

Down the street they went. At the end, Grimface climbed to the top of the stone stairs. A wooden structure covered the door providing shade from the sun, and protection from the rain.

Grimface pulled open the door, and put his left foot on the creaky wooden ladder below. Darkness swallowed his legs as he went slowly down. He felt as if he was descending into an abyss. As his eyes adjusted to the dark, he saw the hint of a hazy orange glow from oil lamps set about the room.

A man in a long robe with golden cuffs was standing there. He approached, and as he entered the light, his swarthy features were apparent.

"What can I do for you?" he asked while bowing slightly.

"We seek respite and news," Grimface said.

"Very well. What is your name and where do you hail from?"

"I am called Grimface, and I am traveling with some companions," Grimface said.

"So, you have come to undo the prince?" he casually asked. "And I see you've brought your beasts with you."

The roof-door slammed shut, the lamplight vanished, darkness swallowed them, and the smell of brimstone filled the air.

"Like flies to carrion," a voice spoke. "And you think the trinkets you've brought can destroy an Atlantean prince? Grimface, your tactical thinking is in question! But wait, I suppose you would like some water from the spring of Acheron before you try and undo me. So, shall it be, and then you can test me. When you come up wanting, what will you do?"

The darkness began to abate. An orange glow appeared – the shimmering of many torches mounted in sconces placed along gray stone walls. Grimface was in a round chamber two hundred cubits in circumference.

In the middle of the stone floor, Grimface saw a perfectly round hole with black water that reflected no light. Near the well stood a tall, muscled man, wearing dark black armor with three golden triangles upon the breast.

"It is there. Take your urn and fill it. Sing your song to bring forth the powers of your magic. I'll wait," said the figure. He removed his helmet to reveal the handsome face of a man in his forties. His golden eyes followed Grimface as he approached the well.

"So, a prince of Atlantis? A bit theatrical wouldn't you say?" Grimface asked.

"Prince? I think that I would prefer the term king! For, my father and all my brethren have perished. I am the only one left – and thus warrant the rank of King of Atlantis... but your lands will do just as well."

"Or, to be anointed a god?" Grimface asked.

"God?" the prince chuckled. "I am not so filled with hubris as to insult those creatures who rule beyond our sight. Not a god, but a king – that is good enough for me – King of all Hyboria, a title I shall retain as I rule for thousands of years," the man said.

Grimface bent down and scooped up some of the black water into the urn. He walked to within twenty feet of the prince and set out the torc, ember and urn. The prince looked unconcerned, and this made Grimface uneasy.

"Any last words before I send you to oblivion, Prince Bailgard?" Grimface asked.

"Do your worst," Bailgard stated and then looked down at his fingernails as if assessing their length and fitness.

Grimface took the torc and put it on. The room spun into a purple haze. An unpleasant buzzing filled his head, and the feeling of pin-pricks covered his body. He picked up the ember, then grabbed the urn and plopped the ember into it. Holding the container out in front of him he began to sing. The notes of his voice vibrated the still air like ripples upon a pond.

Swirling fire engulfed Bailgard. Violent flashes of light illuminated the room. The ground quaked, the air fouled, and tendrils of static cascaded about burning the walls.

Grimface staggered back and fell to his knees. He looked up. The prince stood with an expression of mirth; nothing had happened to him. Grimface got to his feet, mustered the last of his strength, and sang again. The ground opened up, and unworldly horrors emerged. They immediately fell upon the prince in savage fury, only to be brushed aside by the man and as if swatting flies in a tavern.

"This grows wearisome!" Bailgard looked annoyed. "Be gone!" the prince commanded, and those things summoned by Grimface reeled back, and withered like old bean-vines.

Bailgard sang loudly. Pain began to enter Grimface's bones, and he felt a force clawing at his soul.

Tearing the torc from his neck, blood, black and thick, came from his nose, ears, and eyes. The urn tipped, and the ember fell from the jar, rolling out onto the stone floor and to the feet of the prince.

Reaching up, Grimface felt his face, then touched his ears. His fingers were coated in the sticky dark fluid.

Bailgard grew quiet, eyed Grimface, then spoke. "Abandon this foolish fantasy. Listen to reason now. Though I am superior to you in every way, I cannot be everywhere at once. I need powerful lords to administer my new kingdom, and you may join me. Think of it, this land and its contents for the taking. Women, food, power; all to be used as you see fit. In a vision, I saw you in the southern lands. You were upon a mound, your beasts stood high ground and were ready to do battle. I believe the vision is of you and yours taking the southern kingdoms in my name! If you join me, I shall reward you. "This war is going to happen, and you can be a victor in the coming campaign, or suffer the tortures of the damned by being conquered. You will be a great ally. Choose which you will be – ally or enemy? Friend, or foe?" He held out his hand in mock-friendship."

Grimface fell to one knee, but slowly got back to his feet. "Where are my beasts?"

"I cannot believe you have any feelings for such inferior creatures." Bailgard looked disappointed. "They are there behind you, out of the way," said the prince.

A dozen feet away were Benhargan, Bulvife, and Kaltopia - frozen like stone statues. As he approached, a soft female voice came to Grimface's ear. He lifted his head slightly as if to hear it better.

"Take those creatures you claim, and plunge into the pool. I will swaddle you in a glory-light. It is the will of the gods that you live, and fight he who will one day challenge the very throne of heaven!" said the voice.

"Prince?" Grimface asked.

"What is your answer?" Bailgard pressed.

"May I speak with my beasts, just for a moment?"

"I shall grant it, but only for a moment," Bailgard said and waved his hand.

The fighters came alive and drew their blades. The prince laughed heartily, and motioned to Grimface to engage the troupe of warriors.

"At your leisure," the prince added.

Grimface approached, stopped halfway, then yelled. "To the pool and in!" He dashed to the well and plunged into the icy cold water.

A blinding light erupted, and he was buffeted all about. Around him were sharp claws grabbing for him, then the foul breath of death. He hit the ground hard knocking the air from his lungs. Rolling to the side he saw Benhargan, Bulvife, and Kaltopia follow, each hitting the ground. He got to his knees and looked about. In every direction were green fields of grass and grazing animals.

A shepherd looked at the group with surprise, then ran screaming towards the west.

Grimface gasped for a few moments as his lungs pumped like bellows. Standing, he looked down at his shoes, then up at the heavens.

"I see that brute force will not gain us any ground with this prince. The magic that I wielded is subordinate to his. Few could have survived my onslaught with those tools. Where does the answer lay?" he called out.

"Where are we?" Bulvife asked.

"I don't know," said Grimface.

"What trickery has befallen us, wizard?" demanded Benhargan.

"Saved our necks you mean - but it wasn't me who did it. I don't know where we are, but I'm going to find out." He began walking toward the west.

"How do you know to go that way?" Benhargan challenged.

"It's the way the shepherd fled. Surely, he would be running back to his village to tell of our clumsy arrival."

"What happened?" Kaltopia asked, confusion etched upon her face.

Grimface glanced over his shoulder. "A blessing... I think."

# CHAPTER 11
# Unexpected Predicament

THE FIVE BUILDINGS belonged to the Ultravoni clan, and the elder of the group came out to meet them. He apologized; first for his son-in-law's claims that they fell from nowhere, then for not having adequate slaves to offer them carnal delights.

"We have traveled many a weary mile to get here," Grimface told him. "Such things as few slaves do not diminish your hospitality. Right now, a pile of straw, and a warm fire will feel to us like a palace bed chamber, and any food you can spare will be as a royal feast!"

The chief seemed satisfied with Grimface's reaction and did his best to provide the very best of what he had. Wine was taken, and meats eaten, and music and games provided. The Ultravoni were numerous, and the various families that made up the clan were kind and thoughtful.

Late in the night, while the four slept – lightly – a cry from outside broke the peace.

"Lepremore fighters!" someone shouted from afar.

The Ultravoni compound erupted as men grabbed swords and shields, javelins and spears. There were enemy warriors among the buildings, and Grimface saw a dozen in the village square coming toward the villa.

The two Cimmerians were up, weapons at the ready.

"This way," a young woman called to them. "The underground river will lead you to safety!"

They followed her to the door, and into the courtyard of the villa. Not more than sixty feet away was a stone building with a tall bronze door with a lantern dangling from one side.

Arrows flew past, and one struck the girl – who fell hard. There was much chaos all about. The enemy was lying in wait, and sprang the ambush just before they reached the door.

It was close quarters fighting as sword and dagger bit into flesh. Blood cascaded into the air and fell like rain as Bulvife's blade cut arteries and bone.

Benhargan grappled with two men, then kicked one, and slashed the other. In the dim light of the lantern, the barbarian saw one of the dead men wore the gold triangles upon his chest-piece.

"This way!" Bulvife shouted, grabbing the lantern and pulling open the brass doors. In they all went.

Benhargan slammed the doors shut, and set a long metal bar across brackets to lock them in.

They ran for what seemed like hours, until they came from a broken hole in the side of a high cliff where water fell onto jagged rocks and cascading pools.

Dawn swaddled the darkness with pink morning light. With aching muscles from fatigue, Kaltopia and Grimface stopped.

"We have to rest," the magician told the Cimmerians.

"Yes – I've come as far as I can on these two feet," Kaltopia told them.

Benhargan paced like a caged lion. "They will be upon our heels. This is no place to rest!"

"I will scout about," Bulvife told them and slipped over the ledge and down along the pools.

"Ah, look there," Benhargan said pointing at a range of hills in the distance. "That peak is Malamot. We are close to the Sheshash outpost."

"Good – that is good news indeed," Grimface said. "Not more than a league away if we make good time this day."

Bulvife returned. "There is a rumble in the rocks and ground. I fear the enemy is closing."

"Keep out a keen eye – for those jackals will not forfeit our capture or our murder for lack of effort," Benhargan said.

"Look!" Kaltopia said pointing into the sky.

In the distance was a strange sight. A man standing atop a large Hashspursian rug – his golden robe with green trim billowing out about him.

A rumble shook the ground, and below that airborne horror, dust rose into the sky.

"There are men on horseback, and that dog upon the rug is leading them. Tired or not – if you value your skin, we'd better flee now!" Benhargan told them.

"Bulvife, guide the wizard and girl to safety!" Benhargan commanded. "I will lead the foe in another direction! There is a narrow pass south east of here. I can hold them alone there - if they take the bait. By Crom, the stones will run red with their blood!" He nodded to his comrades, then slipped over the side and like a mountain sheep, leapt at full pace down and away.

It was a merry chase. The barbarian left just enough clues to entice the enemy along a different path. With little prodding, even the floating man failed to resist Benhargans ruse.

For several hours the chase went on, until Benhargan came to a narrow gap between two sheer cliffs.

As the first of a score of cavalry came, their squadron was forced to compress to one horse and rider. Here the Cimmerian's sword sang through the air, and like cordwood, the bodies of both man and beast choked the pass.

This went on as the sun dipped, and the shadows of the mountain made the light fade from the coming night. Try as they might, the enemy could not extricate the barbarian from the opening – though spears, and swords slashed at the man in earnest.

"You are clever – you beast of Grimface!" said a voice from behind Benhargan.

Benhargan spun around. It was a man, and his eyes glowed green from within the darkness of his cowl.

"Enough of this foolishness, I see now why you were so easy to follow. You will pay for being clever! Look into my eyes, barbarian," said the man. "You're as a rat to creatures of magic! The great god Set loves to devour rats."

Benhargan's chest was being constricted. He flexed, but to no avail. His breath was being crushed from his lungs. The image of the man was fading, and the stench of snakes was heavy. Darkness followed.

IN THE DISTANCE THERE was a clank. The sound occurred again, and again—a rhythmic tap, tap-tapping.

Benhargan groggily opened his eyes. He was lying down on flagstones. A smith stood over him driving a red-hot rivet into a binding-ring of an iron collar around his neck.

He moved to stand, but found his wrists and ankles bound by shackles, anchored by wrought iron chains, and tied to spikes driven into the ground. The smith stepped away, clearly disturbed by the hulking Cimmerian's movements.

"Worry not, you fool," said a portly man dressed in a brown tunic.

The man approached and stood with his feet planted wide. For a moment, Benhargan thought he recognized him.

"Do you remember me, barbarian? I am Pilinius the Kindlefed, and you partook of my hospitality, then absconded without fulfilling your contract."

Benhargan grunted as he strained against the chains. "There was no contract. Show me the parchment with my mark scrawled upon it!"

Pilinius chuckled loudly. "Such an aristocrat," he said to a soldier holding a pole-arm topped with an axe head. "Did you not stop to read the paper on the door before you entered?"

"There was no paper!" Benhargan challenged.

"You're wrong. The paper made clear that if you were to enter and partake of the food, drink, and women, you'd accept a post in my mercenary army. I was surprised when I found that you and your," he knelt down just out of reach of Benhargan, "companion, were gone. You are both forfeit any payment, and now are my personal property. Oh, what sport we will have with you fighting in the arena!"

"How did I come to be here?" Benhargan demanded.

Pilinius laughed, stood, and turned to walk away. He stopped and turned back. "Don't worry, we'll find your barbarian brethren; his trail is still warm. I'll have him crucified so it will be a reminder that your loyalties lie with me."

He turned again and walked into an alcove and darkness.

The sun was warm, but not hot. Benhargan got into a crouched position—the only position that the chains would allow him once on his feet.

He surveyed the area—a wide courtyard, gray flagstones, a whipping post, four half-walls made of red brick, and seven armed men in armor standing about.

One of the men was throwing dice, while his opponent offered insults about the pedigree of his birth. Both were clearly Argonians, for he saw their plum-covered brass helmets sitting next to them.

The others were a motley bunch of soldiers - men-of-fortune from several northern realms; men who pitted their training and experience against those who would challenge their paymasters.

From across the courtyard came a man in a bright green robe bordered with golden laced cuffs.

"You are the largest Cimmerian that I've seen in many a year. What has brought you down from the Nordheim borders?"

"So I can put my hands about your lily-white neck and squeeze until your eyes burst!" Benhargan growled.

"Feisty. You will surely not disappoint in the arena," the robed man said.

Another man dressed in black armor and wearing a Zamorian helmet approached. Benhargan saw instantly that the man was an experienced soldier - a man not to underestimate.

"Hyro ben Hasmer, the prince wants to know what happened to the enemy sorcerer. Where are the three now?"

"A formidable opponent he is," the man in the robe said. Hasmer became quiet and stared off into the sky. "The other Cimmerian leads the two toward the west, to the walled city of Geragon. They cannot escape my serpent's eye. Set is a mighty god, and though they may think they have eluded me, the coils of my god's power entraps them even as we speak."

The man in the uniform looked down at Benhargan. "I will have your skills tested in the arena, for I have a desire to know your worth. You may be of value to our efforts."

"That is a foolish desire, for I'll kill you and use your skull as a chamber-pot," Benhargan said between clenched teeth.

"I like your optimism, Cimmerian," the soldier said. "If we are meant to meet on the field opposite one another, let Mitra keep our competition free of dishonesty." He turned to the guards. "Prepare him for the arena, and present him to the Master of Games" Turning, he walked away, back from whence he'd come.

The man in the robe sat on one of the half-walls near the two Argonians.

"Look into my eyes, beast! I own your soul! I send the coils of Set to take you, crush you, and drive you into darkness!" He stood and approached.

Benhargan stared at him. A stench filled his nostrils; the stench of a den of snakes. In his ear he heard the hissing of a distant voice speaking a word; a word his soul feared.

Deeper and deeper he fell into those dark glossy orbs. Darkness enveloped his mind, and soul. Around him he felt those binding coils crushing his chest, and making breathing and movement impossible.

When his sight came back, Benhargan was in the middle of an oblong arena, a brass sword in one hand and a shield in the other. He looked down - the ground was stained crimson in large patches.

He shook his shoulders and the ring of iron about his neck clacked loudly against the chains. Raising his shield and sword, the chains connected to his wrist manacles rattled loudly, as did his ankle shackles - allowing full movement, but no hope of escape.

"Let in the competitor!" shouted a man dressed in black robes high above the wall of the arena.

Fifty yards away, a wooden door opened and a wiry fellow with ill-fitting armor came stumbling out. In his left hand, a trident hung down toward the ground, and in the other, a rectangular shield that the man struggled with.

He came toward Benhargan. His helmet slumped forward and covered the man's eyes. He stopped, adjusted it so he could see, then came on again. Benhargan watched with a bemused expression.

Ten feet away, the man lifted the shield and lunged at Benhargan – who sidestepped the attack, and knocked the man's trident aside before ramming his own shield into the other.

The man flew backward off his feet and landed hard on the ground losing the shield, his weapon, and the helmet. He looked up with startled eyes, terror written on his face.

Benhargan stood stock-still staring down at the man. A moment passed, and the man got to his knees and feet, then gathered up his equipment. Again, he came at Benhargan. Again, the barbarian easily blocked the attack, then kicked the trident from his attacker's hand. The three-pronged spear flew into the air and Benhargan plucked it from the sky as it tumbled toward the ground.

Benhargan tucked his sword into the leather strap that was around his waist, looked down on the trembling man and narrowed his eyes.

"Finish him!" called down the man in the black robe.

Quicker than a snake strike, the Cimmerian turned, hurdled the weapon at the man in black, who screamed in pain and shock.

The crowd gasped as the tri-barbed weapon sunk deeply into the man's chest, driving him back off his feet and into the pillowed seats behind. Female screams followed, then the shouts of angry men. Benhargan waited.

From the opposite door came ten armed guards, well-armored. Behind them, came more of the same.

"Now, a worthy challenge for a man such as I," Benhargan said under his breath.

Blood colored Benhargan's eyes. The crowd cheered, clapped, cried in fear, and even laughed at times with nervous guffaws. Man after man fell to the sandy ground— some wounded, some broken, and most never to rise again.

The last thing that Benhargan remembered was felling the coils about him – that crushing weight was about his chest again. Across the arena he saw the robed wizard, the folds of his clothes billowing out behind him... his eyes - those dark and bottomless eyes - the stench of snake, and the emptiness of thought.

A voice spoke his earthly name - Benhargan. His eyes opened, and he looked around - stone walls, flickering torches, and his limbs in chains.

He stood and stepped forward only to find the chains secured behind him to an iron ring embedded in the wall. Directly in front of him was an iron-strapped wood door.

The sound of a metal latch being removed drew his attention, and he saw the fat man in the brown tunic come in.

"Impressive," Pilinius said. "You killed more than twenty-two men before we could... muzzle you." He looked Benhargan over. "What do you remember?"

"You will remember my face as the last thing you see in this world."

Pilinius chuckled. "Such arrogance! I don't fear mercenary barbarians such as you. You can fight, there is little doubt to that. Against my better judgment the prince has authorized me to invite you to fight for his army. He offers you a command with compensation. He needs cohort commanders such as you."

Benhargan spit on the ground. "When I'm done with you, I'll be off to kill that wizard, then on to that prince you speak of."

"So you choose the alternative? Be reduced to my slave? I can easily order Hyro ben Hasmer to do something to your head to make you as docile as a puppy, and as obedient as a harem girl."

Benhargan reached with both of his meaty hands for the man's neck. Pilinius was just out of reach. The mercenary captain chuckled again.

Relenting, Benhargan put his hands down at his sides and stepped back a few feet.

"Now, that's a good doggie," Pilinius added with a smug grin.

Benhargan lunged forward. The chains came to the very limit of the metal's strength. He flexed all his might; the iron links snapped.

His hands latched around Pilinius' neck and he squeezed. A sickly popping sound filled the air as the man's neck snapped and his bulging eyes stared in abject surprise.

Benhargan wore a wicked smile upon his lips. The color of Pilinus eyes fading to gray; his life extinguished without a cry for help ever escaping his lips.

"Perhaps you should have been a bit more wary," Benhargan suggested.

The cell door splintered out into the hallway. Four guards stood dumbfounded as the imposing Cimmerian strode into their midst. Down the hallway he went; the chains connected to his wrists used like Hikarian fighting sticks - right over left, then back again. Blood bathed the cold stone walls as skulls were crushed and limbs snapped like kindling.

Benhargan stopped and looted a sword and dagger from one of the dead men. He tucked them into his belt, then looked around. The mangled corpses lay about the chamber. His brow knitted, and he mumbled a name.

"Hyro ben Hasmer," he said. "You and I will meet, and I will deliver you to whatever dark god you follow."

Down the torch-lit passage Benhargan strode. He smote any he came across; foolish men who thought they might subdue the Cimmerian. Then, he came to another door. He reared back his foot and smashed it in twain. Into another fire lit passage he stepped. From side to side he swung his chains, then came to an abrupt halt. A figure stood in a dark part of the hall surrounded by dead guards.

"I was doing fine without your help," Benhargan said.

"I see that," replied Bulvife. "Now, if you don't mind, follow me. I know where the forge room is."

Both men moved quickly down the hall to an antechamber. Inside was a forge and instruments.

# CHAPTER 12
# From the Wolf's Den

BULVIFE SEIZED A HAMMER and chisel. Benhargan lowered the collar onto an anvil. A few moments later, the shackles and collar were on the floor, and the two barbarians were on their way up the stairs to the Keep.

At the top, Bulvife stepped over two bodies. He peeked around the iron strapped wooden door and into a passage. They crept, making as much noise as falling snowflakes upon a downy field.

After moving through several corridors, they came to a bustling kitchen. A roaring fire was in a stone alcove; many types of meats were roasting upon spits, each turned by youths whose sweaty faces betrayed the intense heat they were slaved to.

A maelstrom of activity masked the Cimmerian's quick and silent movement as they passed. A corridor cut left, then right, then left again.

Bulvife halted. Ahead was a large audience hall. At the far end he saw a group of men, dressed in leathers, heavy capes, and colorful hats. All along the walls, every fifteen paces, were armed guards, polearms held at their sides.

"Follow," Bulvife whispered, and led the way into a side passage that ended at a very wide set of stairs. He looked about, then went down. At the bottom, two tall wooden doors barred their path. No guards were present; the path was unfettered.

"Now, to get clear of this place," Benhargan said, and took up the forward position.

Smashing his shoulder into the mighty portals, he pushed the two impediments outward with such force that they nearly came loose from their hinges.

The two barbarians flew down the stone stairs. Ahead of them was a large ball of green and gold cloth tumbling to the ground. The mass undulated and moved like a sack of wildcats.

The two Cimmerians landed onto the sandy ground and bolted toward an open gate. Benhargan glanced over his shoulder. An arm erupted from the pile of green cloth.

"Guards!" a scream blared out. "Stop those men. Release the dogs!"

Both men charged from the Keep and into the open land beyond. At the other end, a vast field of reeds led into a swampy bog. Several wall guards watched but did little to stop the fleeing men.

That voice, the robe, there was no mistaking it— it was Hyro ben Hasmer, the wizard. As Benhargan made the reeds, he shouted over his shoulder.

"Sorcerer! We shall meet again, and when we do, I will show you the pity a Cimmerian shows his foe!" Then, he and Bulvife vanished into the thick swampy stalks.

At times the water was only ankle deep, and other times it was up to their crotch. The rangers maneuvered this way and that, over spits of land, and back into the stinking black waters. In the distance a blast from a battle-horn filled the air. Dogs barked, and men shouted.

After a while, the sounds of pursuit fell further and further afield.

The water was knee-deep as they came to a rise in the land. Nettle and briars appeared.

"Here!" called Bulvife. He pointed at a cluster of tall willowy plants topped with large red seed-pods.

The men spared no time in cutting the tops and running about in confusing patterns as they crushed the seeds between their palms and spread the dust in their footprints.

"If only we could stay and watch the hounds after they snort this maddening-dust," Bulvife said then laughed.

"I'd like to have a few minutes to trim the chaff from our enemy's ranks," Benhargan added.

"There's no time for games, nor vengeance. Come, Grimface and Kaltopia are this way."

Bulvife dashed through a clump of poisonous weeds and stinging brambles more deftly than a seasoned red deer. Benhargan followed, and the two rangers vanished like swamp gas into the ether.

After traveling through the bog, and two long, cold nights in the rough, the two barbarians were growing anxious to meet up with Grimface. The trundling water of a creek was not far off, and the Cimmerians skulked toward it.

Following the brook, the two rangers searched for any sign of habitation. For many miles they traveled, climbing over white granite boulders, and under low hung branches of stooped willows. Bulvife stopped as did Benhargan. They listened—a waterfall, and something else. A few voices somewhere ahead.

The first voice was that of a woman, and the second, that of a man.

"Grimface?' Bulvife quietly mused to Benhargan.

Benhargan shook his head.

Quite suddenly, there were many female voices as a cacophony of noise grew.

Benhargan took out his dagger and carefully cut away some branches from the thick brush. A bevy of nude nymphs were bathing in a wide pool of dark blue water. Beyond them, a waterfall crashed down, spilling its contents into another wide pool that led to the estuary.

"Women, and a few eunuchs," Benhargan whispered.

"Eunuchs?" Bulvife asked surprised.

"No guards," Benhargan stated. "Come, let's see what this is all about."

The two moved silently through the brush, treading across soft loam and slimy mud along the bank. Benhargan held up his hand. They'd come to the place where the pool emptied into the creek.

"Come ladies, he is waiting and ready for you," a deep masculine voice said.

"That was no eunuch," Bulvife whispered.

"No," Benhargan affirmed.

Bulvife maneuvered around some green ferns. He saw a dozen large men dressed in coif, cuirass, and greaves. All were armed with sword and shield. They looked to be battle-tested men.

"Their shields," Bulivfe said. "Golden triangles are upon a black background."

"Come," was all that Benhargan whispered, as he slipped into the brush on the opposite bank.

They wove their way through the forest. It was clear to Bulvife that his friend was circling the pool. The hulking warrior stopped and pointed.

There, in plain view, was a train of covered wagons, all brightly colored and adorned with golden triangles. Many men-at-arms were about, but none seemed to be worried about attack.

A door in the side of one of the wagons opened, and out came a large man with olive skin and dark black hair. He wore armor that was strange to the barbarians. On his chest were golden triangles, and at his side a dangerous-looking sword of strange origin.

"Send Scout Group Two to clear the way to Black Keep. And instruct Hasmer, I don't want anything to interfere with our gaining more conscripts. Then, notify General Leach that Kush, and Ophir are moving against us. We must get to the citadel before they can mass and engage us at Coldhill Bridge."

"Sire, do you wish to pick your consort for tonight, or wait?" a man in a white robe asked.

"Later. I still have five magicians to entreat. Greedy they are, and hungry for power. They will do my bidding, and those who stand against us will feel the wrath of Atlantis upon their necks. Death will be a welcome reprieve to those who do not yield."

The two men walked down the long line of wagons and vanished from sight. From a distance, dogs started to bark.

"The dogs smell something!" yelled a man in armor. "This way!"

Melting into the forest, the two Cimmerians used the tried-and-true evasion methods they'd learned from years fighting savages.

They traveled for many hours, until the late afternoon was upon them. In the air was the scent of pine, jasmine, and mint. The air was cool, and not far off the sound of running water caressing stone as it made the trek toward the sea.

It was not long until the rangers found civilization. First came the smell, then came the sight of tall walls and battlements.

In the surrounding fields, carrion birds flocked so thick that the ground appeared to undulate in black waves. In fact, the birds hid a grisly sight; thousands of bodies, now ripe from days in the sun.

"There," pointed Bulvife, "smoke. Someone must still live within."

"A sickness, or purge perhaps?" Benhargan guessed. "Or, the enemy of these people now reside in their fort."

"Let's see what's around," Bulvife suggested, then led the way through the greenwoods.

An hour passed as they circumnavigated the wall. The way around was not difficult, only time-consuming as they evaded scant patrols and wandering souls. Between the forest and the wall were fields, and a few huts and stables.

"Let's wait here until dark," Benhargan suggested.

They created a blind, then sat, intently watching the large gate. As the sky turned from bright blue to purple dusk, they saw military men and supplies coming and going. Soon, the two Cimmerians broke cover, and lurked through the fields – over the bloated dead bodies, and up one of the walls.

RUE LEMOD HEARD A KNOCK on his door. He opened it to find Grimface and a woman.

"What are you doing here?" Lemod asked surprised.

Grimface looked with weary eyes at the man. "By any god you hold holy, let us in!"

Lemod stepped back, and the two came inside. As he shut the door and threw the bolt, there came shouts along the street. Someone grabbed ahold of the door and pulled, but the door was securely barred.

"This one is locked. They must have moved down the street," a man declared.

The sound of foot-falls diminished as whomever it was, left quickly.

"What is this all about? You and I have not laid eyes on one another in many years."

Grimface sat down and pointed at a set of cups and several jars. "There will be time enough to hear our story later. Fetch some drink so we might wash this dust from our throats."

Lemod got down three cups and a large jar of wine. He poured some libation into each cup, then sat down.

"Who is after you?" he asked.

"There are several who'd like to see our skins stretched out to dry in the sun," Grimface said. "Now, the brass-soldiers of the Kofur King are trying to intercept us. He is making an alliance with everyone he can. The seeds of war have taken root, and now all of Hyboria is preparing for battle."

"War?" Lemod was surprised.

"Yes," Grimface stated. "I have come for one thing that will make a difference. Let me read the spell."

"Are you mad?" Lemod said, now shocked at the request. "You do not want to make that journey. You will not survive – and you know it!"

"There is that possibility. I must try! For, recent events now drive my heels, and if this foreign prince is more powerful than I, the only thing that will defeat him is sending him to oblivion, Grimface said. "Trust me, his magic is powerful, and his cunning exceptional. He will endeavor to make slaves of us all."

"Really?" Lemod said, then studied Grimface's eyes. "But, there must be another way? The spell will devour you. You'll get lost in the land of the dead." Lemod sounded desperate.

"There is more to life than this ol' sack of bones," Grimface said pounding his fist against his chest. "Nonetheless, I must read from it and travel through the Kingdom of the Dead. There, in the Hall of Souls, I will find our enemy's true name."

"What are you both talking about?" Kaltopia asked, annoyed that she didn't understand anything they were saying.

"E'yarus Detramorus eprium," Lemod said. "The book of the dead."

Grimface glanced over at Kaltopia. "The spell is older than the race of man... older than all races known and unknown. It is a doorway carved into our world by demigods who lived among the stars."

"It was forged in the afterbirth of creation. The magic is not common, nor sedate," Lemod added. "Grimface will be risking his soul, if he uses that spell."

"Don't use it," Kaltopia said.

Grimface poured some more wine into his cup. "I will start the song tonight. By morning, I will have passed into that dark realm. But, before I do, I want to study the map. I'll need to know what is beyond the caves, the rivers, and the desert. I have little time to find my way by wit alone."

Smiling sardonically Lemod shrugged his shoulders. "If you must risk annihilation, then the best I can do is help."

BENHARGAN LAY HIS HAND on the rough surface of the stone wall. It was cold, and a bit slick from the thick mist that grew from the trampled grass and field-crops. He motioned for Bulvife to follow, and the two Cimmerians scaled the outer perimeter. At the top the sound of a man in armor approached. Both men hung by their fingers from the small ledge at the top.

The clacking of armor came and went. Bulvife slipped over and onto a narrow walkway. Benhargan followed. On the top, the two men slunk their way toward a square guard tower.

In the shimmer of torchlight, a deep voice rang out.

"Those black feathered fiends eat their fill upon that field of death, and what do we get? We get to eat the sloppy leftovers from the governor's feast. It's not right."

"Shut yer keg-hole!" another voice scolded. "It is enough to serve and fight! Count yourself lucky to be able to eat and drink, and not a meal for those carrion creatures out there!"

"This prince who comes knows little of what is in the hearts of men," said deep-voice.

"Don't forget your oath. If the governor wants us to hold this position and deny soldiers from Sol passage, and the army from Cree supplies, then we should be content."

Deep-voice grunted. "I will pray to Mitra for those unlucky souls who now reside in the field beyond. For choosing mutiny against the governor and their own comrades, they have paid a heavy price."

Benhargan pointed over the inside ledge and slipped silently over and down. Bulvife followed. Once on the ground they quickly traversed the courtyard.

Both men froze. A torch light appeared at the far end of the Keep; then came two more. The orange light reflected off the stones of the fortress as three men dressed in brass cuirass and greaves escorted a young woman in a flowing white gossamer dress.

The four came to a set of stone stairs. They ascended up to a brass-strapped door and went inside.

"Come," Benhargan whispered.

Great billows of strong lavender wafted across the two Cimmerians. They stopped, looked toward a garden path, from which the smell emanated. Both barbarians followed their noses.

The narrow paving stones wound around to a small arched bridge, then into a garden. A sudden cacophony of sounds behind them made the rangers slip into the dark green foliage bordering the path. The woman in white passed by, her bare feet lightly slapping against the stone path. The three guards followed, but stopped near the place where the rangers were hiding. The woman went on.

Benhargan and Bulvife crept silently through the garden foliage. A heavenly voice sang somewhere near them. They halted. Peaty earth and soft loamy sod allowed them to lie down and quietly crawl forward.

Large leafy ferns lined their path, and the powerful scent of wild roses washed over them. The red-velvet flowers lined a large pool of water. Standing at the edge was the woman, her stark blond hair hanging straight down over her shoulders. She appeared to be praying; her hands were clasped, and her face turned down to the water – her voice like that of a mother cooing her newborn bairn.

She walked into the pool, as the full moon shown overhead causing the water to look like liquid silver. Halting, her voice changed – as did the song.

The tune was direct, the type used to sing of valor or bravery. The lilt coming from her was soft. Both Benhargan and Bulvife felt a moment of complete calm and happiness. This went on for some time – how long neither barbarian could tell, for their minds were a swirl with pleasure and warmth. Within, they saw rich imagery of beautiful nude courtesans, and amphorae of mead, grape wine, and beer; all flowing together in one moment of emotional connection with beast, plant, and heaven.

She stopped singing. Glancing to the exact place where the Cimmerians lay, her features seemed unearthly. An awkward moment passed. Neither ranger moved.

Bulvife's eyes met hers; he could not look away. It was as if he was getting closer and closer to her. Her golden, almond-shaped eyes pierced into his heart; he knew she would be his, this night.

Above the pool some mist formed. The woman turned back and looked up at the fog. From it, loomed a terrifying image. Great glowing red eyes cut through the darkness. A being of horror that no mortal mind can fully comprehend hovered – disembodied as it came forth.

Benhargan and Bulvife felt their muscles cramp, freezing them in place in unending agony. They were forced to view the unholy thing as it came from the dark and lashed its tentacles around the woman.

The creature swarmed around her. She screamed. The sound of wet flesh slapping and slithering over other flesh filled the air. Then, it stopped. The rangers felt all their muscles relax. The girl collapsed and lay at the edge of the pool, both bloody and unconscious.

Bulvife got to his knees and staggered from the foliage. He rushed to her side, knelt and checked to see if she was alive or dead; he was sure she was lifeless. To his surprise, she still lived.

He checked her for wounds as he stripped off his leather vest, and tore his gray tunic into pieces to stem the bleeding.

"We don't' have time for this," Benhargan said coming along side. "Those guards will be here soon."

Bulvife ignored his friend and sopped up the blood, only to find the woman had no wounds. She stirred and looked up into his face. Bulvife could not look away.

She sat up. "Stay," she said, and neither barbarian could move. She entered the pool and washed the blood and tissue from her body. As she stepped from the waters she looked over the two Cimmerians. "You have come to me I see," she said. "I saw your faces in a vision." She turned to Bulvife. "Now, you must fulfill your destiny. I will take you into me."

"What?" Bulvife was surprised.

"The goddess spoke to me of a man who would come. A vision that my master does not share. This night I was mate to the Sarogoth, by my father's behest. But, what he does not know is a man from the north of Hyboria would come too. The prophecy says that a child will come from my union – and a god-king will be forged by both god and mortal. Your essence will complete the spell. From what we sow this night, shall bring forth a new age in the lands of Hyboria, and end my father's claim."

The woman paused. "Do not worry," she added. "The guards will not come. This is a sacred pool. They are forbidden to approach."

# CHAPTER 13
# A Dark Path

GRIMFACE ENTERED THE bedroom at the end of a long hallway, and sat on a straw mattress atop a raised woven-rope bed. In his hand was the ancient scroll.

"You will not want to witness this. Your fragile mind cannot understand what is about to happen," he said to Kaltopia.

Kaltopia looked upon Grimface with compassionate eyes. "I pray that Mitra watch over you," she said.

Grimface smiled under his mustache like a father to a daughter. "You are kind to say such." He pulled out a folded papyrus note sealed with wax and handed it to Lemod. "When my beasts arrive, see that they get this," he added.

"I'll see it is done." Lemod turned to Kaltopia. "Come with me," he said, taking her by the arm and leading her out of the room into the hall. He closed the door and escorted her to the room with the fire-pit. "You may hear some very strange sounds come from that room. Under no circumstances should you open that door. No mortal has ever uttered those words. While Grimface is not like you, he is not a god. This stunt may be the end of him."

She looked down the hallway at the door. A soft sound was drifting from it—a hypnotic sound like that of a minstrel strumming a lyre. A strange glow emanated from under the portal. Kaltopia sat in the far room, her eyes never straying from the door that hid the wizard and his tricks.

The melodic sound changed - an odd chanting began to grow. Kaltopia heard other voices, all creating a harmony – a sort of music – unearthly to behold. A scent of sulfur wafted to her; the rotten egg stench that embalmers and grave robbers know well.

Hours passed as she drank wine, and listened.

Lemod rose. "There are many more hours to go of this. You would do well to sleep if you can. I go to do just that. May you rest soundly and wake well," he said, then left by a doorway hidden by a rough cloth curtain.

She sat there – then in the distance, a war drum was added into the maelstrom of sounds. A voice whispered in her ear.

"Beyond the brittle shell lay all that you desire. Come to me, and I will show you your father, and his court. I will grant you a visit to your grandfather – to hold his hand one last time. Come, I am just beyond the door," said the voice.

For a time, she sat still. Grimface had warned her of things beyond the sight of man that would lure a soul to doom. Still the voice cooed in her ear, speaking of the peach orchards of the gods, and the juicy and sweet fruit that the immortals eat.

"Paradise," said the voice in her ear. "Come, see the green meadows filled with wild flowers and sunshine."

She felt a touch at her elbow—a sense of gentle coaxing, drawing her toward the closed door. "A peek behind the door will not undo you; trust me – have I lied to you yet?" the voice asked her. "Benhargan, he pines for you. I will show you what he is saying about you right now. Could he be forming the word love?"

She could take no more; her curiosity was taxed, and her patience stretched to the limit. As if in a dream, she rose from the table, and approached the door. After all, Grimface was in there – he'd be sure to make it safe for her. He knew that there was love to be had. He must know – for the voice was just behind the door, in the room with him.

From the base, she saw the flickering of an orange hue, like the setting of the sun upon a summer's eve. She put her hand on the door – it was abnormally warm to the touch. Her hand moved to the latch. It clicked open, and she pushed.

Right away she felt dizzy, as if she'd looked down from a great height. There was no room, just an empty expanse of yellow shifting haze. Large leathery wings flapped, and eyes peered out of the mist. Its face was horror incarnate –fangs dripping with murky-orange fluid. The haze cleared, and in the distance circled monstrous creatures, as if hunting a frantic prey.

She felt compelled to step in – pulled as if by an invisible rope secured around her waist. Then, a terrible rumble emitted from the mist that froze her in place.

That sound molested her mind. Her flesh was being peeled away from the muscle! Every fiber of her nerves was ablaze with savage pain. From her toes to the tips of her hair, agony began to twist her into a shapeless mass.

Her soul, thoughts, and hopes faded, and were replaced with oblivion. The voice vibrated her chest, and a heaviness about her heart was crushing her; then it spoke a name.

She screamed – and kept on screaming.

Lemod tackled Kaltopia to the ground, slammed the door shut, and pulled her back, dragging her by the arms toward the far room.

"The voice – the voice!" she shouted as her body went into convulsions, and white foam emitted from her lips.

Several servants came running. He held up his hand to stop them.

"Markanus, run and fetch me the black-lotus oil! Delutche, find some silk ropes for restraints, then go to the far hall and prepare a bed." The two slaves vanished into the darkness of the villa.

Markanus returned with a glass vial filled with an oily pitch-like substance. Lemod removed the glass stopper, grabbed Kaltopia by the back of her hair and pulled down.

"Open her mouth," he said to Markanus, who immediately obeyed.

Kaltopia screamed in frightful horror, clawing at all around her in a fevered attempt to escape. Lemod got control of her arms, and let several drops fall from the vial into her open mouth. She slowly fell calm, as her eyes glazed.

"Help me get her to the bed. Restrain her arms and legs. If she wakes before I can pull back her soul, she may kill any one of us," said Lemod.

Once on the bed, Markanus secured her ankles while Delutche tied her hands. Several straps were placed over her chest and hips, rendering her immobile.

"By blessed Mitra," Lemod said while pulling up a stool and sitting next to the bed. "It will not be easy to reunite this soul with its body." He stood up and clasped his hands together over his head. "Now goddess, hear my prayer...".

THE YOUNG WOMAN LET her torn and bloody garment fall to the grass. She took Bulvife by the arm and led his powerful manhood into her womanly abyss. There, all time stopped. The movement of the heavens stood frozen, as the two fell into a lovers embrace - lusty and passionate.

Benhargan kept looking back toward the path, his sword in hand - but strangely, no soldiers appeared.

Perhaps this happens all the time, Benhargan thought.

The cries of pleasure, groaning, and the odd grunting continued for quite some time, even as the predawn approached.

Bulvife fell prostrate to the ground gasping of air. He was dehydrated, nearly to death. Benhargan sat cross-legged casually watching the morning sky grow purple, then lighten by the moment.

"Has she consumed you, leaving you a flaccid worm for your trouble?" Benhargan asked his brethren.

"Water... water," Bulvife croaked, as he crawled to the pool and drank from the cool spring.

"If you're finished," Benhargan began. "I believe I've been as patient as Ishtar, and as resolute as Mitra sitting here waiting for you to... unburden yourself."

Bulvife sated his thirst and rolled over to find the woman next to him. She cupped some water and brought it up to her mouth. Her full red lips drew in the liquid with poise and elegance. She stood, picked up her dress, washed it in the water, then put it on. Her smile was unnerving – there was a hidden knowing beneath those golden eyes.

She stopped on the grass and looked back. "The guards will not approach," she reaffirmed. "Beneath the pool is a sacred grotto. Find your way from there, but do not follow me. We will meet again." She turned back and vanished up the path. Yet, her scent remained; floral – and musky.

Bulvife drew in the mixture of smells, then he looked at his fellow barbarian, smirked, and shrugged his shoulders.

"So, you've taken liberty at the expense of our lives," Benhargan casually said. "She's probably telling the guards right now about us, and we'll have to fight our way out of here."

Bulvife looked at his friend. "Don't be an idiot," Bulvife said. "There is a way out of here that the guards do not know of."

"The grotto?" Benhargan questioned.

"Yes – so says the princess," Bulvife said.

"Princess?"

"Don't ask me how I know that."

"What was that thing that attacked her?" Benhargan asked.

"How should I know? Perhaps Grimface will know," Bulvife said.

"The sorcerer will only give us double-talk, I'm sure," Benhargan replied.

"Come on," Bulvife told him, as he waded into the pool and dove down.

Benhargan followed without question, diving deep into the quicksilver water.

Through the cold dark they swam until the orange-yellow shimmer of several torches appeared. Both Cimmerians popped up in a large grotto.

Bulvife climbed out. The area was not large. All around were stone and clay idols, some of which were overgrown with moss. A sense of the ancient was present, and both Barbarians searched for any hint of hidden treasure.

"Look here," Benhargan said, as he approached a stone throne where a recently placed flap of parchment lay.

Bulvife shook his head. "The wizard. How in the name of all the gods does he know our path before we've even laid down a foot?"

Benhargan took the document and opened it. "Beasts, the tunnel leads to the under-halls and library of Lord Teribin the Ruthless. Find the map with the Argonian symbol of Gyatrud upon it. Delay not bringing it to me at the city of Phisnor. Seek out the house of Lemod – there it is that I will dwell for a time."

Both Cimmerians were quiet for a few moments as they gazed at a stone throne carved from limestone.

"There is a path leading into the wall," Benhargan pointed. "A fool's path to be sure."

"Grimface often said to discount the foolish may prove a fool's fatal undoing."

Benhargan shrugged his shoulders. "So, now what?"

Bulivfe took the lead. "Follow the tunnel," he said over his shoulder.

The passage led to a chamber, and the chamber to a host of rooms.

Through a brass-strapped wooden door, the two Cimmerians found a room filled with cross-thatched shelves stuffed with scrolls made of parchment. On the wall hung a full cow hide with a map drawn in ink all over the surface.

"Here," Benhargan pointed. "The symbol of Gyatrud." It was scrawled along the bottom. Benhargan's hand was just about to rest upon the map when a voice came from behind.

"Hey, what are you doing there?"

Before the guard said anything else, Bulvife dispatched him. But, the body convulsed, and flopped into a shelf ladened with scrolls. The chain reaction sent the scrolls falling off the ledge, one after another like a hailstorm.

"What in the name of Chiron is going on in there?" shouted an angry voice.

Benhargan grabbed a ball of twine, then the map. He followed Bulvife as he rolled up the map, looped twine around it, and fastened it over his shoulder.

"Something has happened to Olen," called a voice from the scroll room. "He's dead!"

Bulvife heard more voices as a commotion brewed behind the Cimmerians. Many people were now coming to investigate.

The barbarians turned a corner and ran straight into five armored men. Both Cimmerians put out their elbows and drove on like a bull in panicked flight, smashing the soldiers down as they went.

"Intruders!" shouted one of the fallen.

The two rangers turned left, then right, then two more lefts. The door was just ahead. Benhargan threw it open and they dashed headlong into the night-shrouded courtyard of the fortress. More shouts followed.

Guards emerged from hidden doorways, and men appeared on walls and towers - at the ready. In the darkness torch bearers ran alongside the guards, and the barking of war-dogs echoed in the distance.

"This way," called Bulvife.

They ran into a tower and climbed up to the fifth floor. Both barbarians stopped at one of the doorways leading onto the fortification ledge. In the distance, men with torches looked down into the courtyard.

Benhargan exited the opposite way, then stopped at a crenellation along the wall. He made a gesture of going over and down. Bulvife nodded.

The barbarians slipped over the side, and hand-over-hand descended the wall, dropping silently to the peaty ground and skulking into the night.

They moved across the open fields and into the forest. Once in the woods, the barbarians melted into the background.

# CHAPTER 14
## Friend a Drift

AFTER TWO DAYS ON THE run, Benhargan and Bulvife came to a city. Once inside, they wasted no time in searching out the closest wine-house. There, they spent many hours discussing their next step. Long after dark, they staggered out of the wine-house. Bulvife followed Benhargan, as the hulking Cimmerians made their way through the dark streets. Slowly, they became aware that something was just ahead; a shadow that shimmered in the darkness.

"There," whispered Benhargan. "A shapeless horror, as if Grimface summoned it himself."

"Or is another wizard at work?" Bulvife asked.

"Just follow," Benhargan said.

The thing wove its way through the narrow streets until it was in front of a doorway. It shimmered, then vanished.

For a moment the threshold appeared aglow, luminescent in the silver moonlight. Benhargan walked up and drove his thick knuckles against the weathered wood.

"Who pounds so furious upon my door?" came an angry, but curious voice.

"I come seeking Grimface— a wise...man who is often too wise for his own good," Benhargan responded.

The door was thrown open.

"Who are you?" asked a short man with a balding head.

"Benhargan, and this is Bulvife – rangers from on far," Benhargan boldly told him.

"How did you find my home?" the man asked.

"A shadow – a shapeless abomination that hovered in the night," Bulvife responded.

"Grimface was wise to send out a reever to find you in the city," said the man.

Benhargan shoved the door open and barged inside, his hand upon the hilt of his sword. "You know Grimface of which I speak? Say so now, or suffer my blade!" he barked.

"I am Lemod of Shem, a man nearly as ancient as our common friend. Come and sit by the fire. We shall drink and eat, and I will tell you of a perilous journey he makes even now."

The three went to the fire-room and sat around the pit. In the corner of the smoky chamber were amphorae and several spits with meat ready to cook.

Benhargan sat, placed his sword across his lap, and nodded to the wine containers. "Be a man of your word and fetch the drink. Bring me a horn, for I have a wicked thirst that needs to be slaked!"

Bulvife sat like his friend and waited quietly – all the time watching the two doorways.

Lemod fetched cups and jars of wine, and put the meat over the coals. He sat opposite and appeared to be deep in thought.

"Well, out with it. Where is Grimface and Kaltopia? We have news to speak to them about," Bulvife said.

"The one you call Kaltopia is in the far room." Lemod motioned down the hall. "Grimface has left."

"Isn't it like a wizard to abandon his friends in time of need?" Benhargan grunted.

"Where has he gone?" Bulvife asked.

Lemod sighed. "He's traveled far beyond anyplace you could know of, or dream of. Deep within a nightmare he dwells, passing along a road that will deliver him back to the land of the living, or entomb him to damnation until oblivion consumes the stars."

"Blood and bone, blade and axe, these are the things we Cimmerians understand. So keep your riddles for another wizard, and say what you mean in common tongue!" Benhargan demanded.

"He has read from the Scroll of the Dead, and now he dwells there beyond our sight and knowing. In legend there was a being that knew the way, and wrote it down in magic ink upon the living flesh of a god. When the god was slayed, that skin was tanned into a scroll – and upon that document is the map of the afterlife. A thousand men have tried to venture there. None have returned. But it is the only place for a magician to find the true name of an enemy."

"How do you know Grimface?" Bulvife asked.

"I have known him for many a year. We wandered the world after the old floods, when the mountains of ice turned to inland seas, and rivers carved the many valleys you know today."

"What of this place the sorcerer is traveling?" Benhargan asked.

"If he becomes lost in the other realm, your news will not mean much. You will want to return to Cimmeria to live out the last short days of your lives among your own. This Prince of Atlantis comes, and few are safe from his growing army and power."

"Wizard or not, I shall cut down their ranks, and my brethren will shepherd many of them to the underworld. We will die with blade in hand, and blood of our enemies upon our lips!" Benhargan said.

"I admire your courage," Lemod told him.

"What of Kaltopia? You say she is in the back," Bulivife added.

"She is in the back room. Her mind is mad, and her soul broken by the blessed god Gera Gorn – King of the Underworld. It is through his domain that the path of the dead begins; she gazed upon that landscape, and now her mind is tortured by horrors you cannot understand," Lemod told them.

"We will go get her soul back," Benhargan stated.

Lemod laughed hard and long. When he finished, he looked upon two very annoyed barbarians.

"How simple your minds are. Grimface did say you lacked an understanding of the elements of nature."

"Your tone is about to become much higher of you persist in goading me," Benhargan threatened.

"He warned me that you are quick with violence, but not so with wit. No matter. There is no way you can retrieve her soul. You can only hope that her soul can find its way back to her body. In the meantime, you can go see her."

"After we've eaten your bread, meat, and consumed your wine," Bulivfe said.

"Ah, I almost forgot. He provided me with this – to be given to you when you arrived," Lemod said as he handed the note to Bulvife.

"Another note?" Benhargan asked.

"It would appear," said Bulvife.

KALTOPIA WAS FACE UP, hands and feet strapped down to the bed, and her eyes glazed from the black lotus oil. Lemod motioned with his hand for the two barbarians to enter.

Benhargan stared, tension etched along his jaw. "How long has she been like this?"

"Four days," Lemod answered.

"When will she wake?" Bulvife inquired.

"Possibly never, or it could be today. There is no way to know. There are things in the underworld that no man... or woman can comprehend. The human mind falls into chaos when such things come to pass," Lemod said.

Kaltopia suddenly began to writhe against her ropes, and speak in tongues.

Lemod quickly produced a vial from a pocket and opened it. "Hold her head and open her mouth," he commanded.

Benhargan did so, and Lemod let slip a drop of the extract into the woman's mouth. She quickly became calm and silent.

"She will be okay, for now," Lemod stated.

Bulvife turned and left the room. Lemod followed him. In the main chamber, the barbarian kneeled at the fire pit. Lemod sat across from him. There was some crispy fat in the coals, enlarged by the heat. Bulvife took it out, let it cool, then popped it into his mouth.

"Now what? Cut her throat?" Bulvife suggested.

Lemod looked shocked and appalled at the suggestion. "What a barbarous design you fathom," he said.

"She is of little use in the state she is in. It would be mercy to end her life now," Bulivfe suggested.

"I'll not condone such a thing, nor would I allow it to be done under my roof. Believe me when I say there is hope. The gods play havoc with mortals, and often the most unlikely surprises come to pass when we least expect them." Lemod stood and fetched several small jars.

He handed one to Bulvife. "Drink this. It's made from bogolite root; once fermented it will relieve anxiety, and often alleviate one's own wits. You might even be struck by the divine, and have visions."

Benhargan stood over Kaltopia. There was something strange in his heart. He'd taken many a woman, and even cared for a few, but this was something very different. An insatiable longing filled his veins and for a time he stared down at her beautiful features—red full lips, dark hair, and golden-brown eyes.

He looked back at the open door, then down at her again. Bending down, he sniffed her hair, then ran his fingers through it. With his powerful hands he cradled her head, and crushed his lips to hers. Passion ran like fire through his limbs, and just briefly, he wanted to have her there on the bed, though his large form would have made it problematic.

He righted himself, turned and went into the hall, stopped, then looked back. His eyes narrowed and he came about, then went into the main room with the fire pit. Once there, he calmed his breathing and the pounding of his heart.

Bulvife and Lemod were drinking and talking. Benhargan sat down, took the jar from Bulvife, drank deeply, and handed it back.

"Now, tell us of the fate of Grimface," Benhargan said.

"Perhaps you should read the note... if you can read," Lemod stated.

# CHAPTER 15

# Enemy at the Gate

BULVIFE DRANK MORE of the mystic elixir. The note from Grimface lay to the side on the ground next to him

"Travel to the coast? Seek the inlet at the river Buriva? Waste not a moment?" Benhargan said annoyed. "He gives us no good direction." He turned to Lemod. "Where is this River Buriva?"

Lemod took a long drink of wine. "Beyond the westward mountains, past the Tiplon gates. There you will find the high lakes that feed the Buriva river and its path to the sea."

The front door slammed shut, and the bolt thrown into place.

"There is an army at the gate!" shouted a voice.

Lemod stood as the servant entered the room. "What army do you speak of?" he demanded to know.

"They fly the banner of gold triangles. The word is the city fathers will open the gates to them soon."

"Open the gates? Surrender without a fight?" Benhargan was appalled.

Bulvife came to his feet. "A fight you say?" His curiosity was piqued.

"Those fools in the council will doom us all! How many in the enemy host?" Lemod asked.

"Ten thousand they say... maybe more," the slave told them.

"Only ten thousand? Bulvife, you may find a bed for sleeping. Only one Cimmerian will be needed for this battle!" Benhargan told him.

Both barbarians broke out into laughter as Lemod and his slave stared at them with shocked expressions. After a few moments, the chuckles rumbled into silence. The two Cimmerians gathered their items.

"It seems we will take our leave of you," Benhargan said. "Fetch the woman. We are taking her with us."

"You're mad," Lemod said.

"Perhaps. That doesn't change the fact that we're taking her. Give us the black lotus extract. I will use it to keep her in slumber."

"Only give her a drop upon the tongue – any more will make her ill and maybe kill her," Lemod told him. "But, I don't see how you will take good care of her."

"When we finally find Grimface, he will know what to do," Bulvife said.

It looked as if Lemod would argue, then he frowned and motioned to his slave to retrieve Kaltopia.

Benhargan followed, then hoisted the unconscious woman onto his shoulder. Bulvife went to the door, peeked outside, then signaled his companion to come to the threshold.

"No soldiers yet. Where do we go from here?" Bulvife asked.

"Where does every city scoundrel and rogue go when threatened?" Benhargan asked.

"To the underground – but where do we find the 'under' part of this ground?" Bulvife asked.

"The access to the under-halls are not far," Lemod told them. "Go out of my door, then left. Follow the street until you come to a wall fountain, then go right and take the very next left. A door will be in front of you. Open it and you will gain access to the ancient mines. Go deep, and follow your nose. There is a ledge at the far end that overlooks a valley." He handed Bulvife a lamp filled with oil. "Take this, you'll need it."

"Let's go," Bulvife said, and disappeared into the dark streets. Benhagan followed with Kaltopia in tow.

It took only a few moments to reach the ancient tunnel. In the darkness the portal was impressive. Ten qubits in height and five wide – made of layers of wood, brass, and etched stone.

Bulvife latched onto the handle. He pulled, the door swung effortlessly outward. Light beamed out of the opening, causing a dull yellow flickering to wash over them. Sconces lined the inner walls, and fat black candles provided plenty of light. They entered and closed the door behind them.

The room was wide, long, and bare. At the other end, stairs descended. Both men drove deeper into the mines.

Below, on the second level, torchlights illuminated tunnels and rooms. Rows of stone sarcophagus sat in narrow isles. Beyond, stairs vanished into darkness - access to the lower levels. Bulvife ignited the lamp wick at the last torch. Into the darkness the two Cimmerians vanished.

A strange quiet swallowed them. A musty and ancient smell rushed to their nostrils. Much of the walls contained images. On all sides, they saw white plaster decorated with faded colored reliefs of ancient battles. As they moved, dust rose in gray puffy clouds.

After some time, they came to a split. Kaltopia moaned and Benhargan set her down. He pulled out the vial of lotus oil and placed a drop upon her tongue. She sighed, and her glazed orbs focused on some far-off thing.

"This way," Benhargan said pointing to the left. "I can just make out the strong scent of rosemary."

As they quickly moved along the passage, Bulvife came to a skidding halt. A man stood in their path. In his hand was an oil lamp, the wick flickering a dark red. His height was equal to Benhargan's, and he stood there – his robed body, stern face, narrowed eyes.

"I," he began, "was beginning to lose faith in your ability to find your way."

"Yield the path, or face death!" Benhargan hissed.

"I am Bailgard, last Prince of Atlantis!" the man said, as if it meant anything to the barbarians. "I am a man of little patience, and I yield for no man. Where is your companion the wizard? Where is the one you call Grimface?"

From the darkness two creatures emerged. Both stooped to fit in the space, their horns scraping the ceiling and causing debris to fall. One advanced a little further than the other; its barbed tail darting from side to side.

"Wait for my command," Bailgard said to the monster. "There will be time enough for play later."

Benhargan put Kaltopia down and leaned her up against one wall. He drew his blade and stood ready. Bulvife did the same.

"I'm waiting," Bailgard said annoyed.

"It is written here," Benhargan said pulling from under his tunic a brown leather sheet. "All you need to know is here."

Bailgard motioned for one of the monsters to take it. The largest of the two advanced, then with six-inch-long claws, gingerly picked up the leather and brought it back to its master.

Bailgard took it and looked confused by the strange flap of leather. "What is this?"

"Mine loincloth reveals much to the curious - clean the urine and shite off and you can behold a wondrous sight – the clean loin cloth of a Cimmerian," Benhargan said.

Both barbarians broke into a boisterous laughter.

Bailgard dropped the filthy leather to the ground with a look of utter disgust. "You find this jibe funny at my expense? I will make you pay for this slight!"

Bulvife took two steps, rolled between the legs of one of the demons, and came up on his feet. He thrust his sword, cutting into Bailgard. The man was fast, and he darted to the side - yet Bulvife's blade lapped up some of the man's blood.

"Take the other one, I am fine here," yelled Bailgard, as he countered with his own sword. Their clashing blades produced sparks, all the while Bailgard never let drop his blazing red-glowing lamp.

The demons rushed at Benhargan, but due to their enormous size, they wedged in the passage and seemed confounded as to how to get free.

Benhargan attacked driving his sword into one of the horrors. He withdrew the weapon from the hard-callous flesh of the monster. The creature staggered back, then raked Benhargan's face and chest with its claws. The demons broke free, and they both concentrated on carving Benhargan to ribbons.

Blade for blade, Bulvife battled Bailgard. The red light shifted in the dark hall dazzling Bulvife's vision, and making the Atlantean prince difficult to hit. Savage blows were delivered and countered. At one moment they thrusted, parried, and blocked, then circled about and attacked each other again.

The heat was growing in the narrow hall. A great roar was bellowed, and Benhargan had only one monster left to deal with.

A look of miscalculation came over Bailgard's face. He tossed the lamp into the air, reached into a pouch slung at his belt and threw some dust. Bulvife stepped back; a fireball erupted as the powder reached the red flame. Bailgard vanished. The demon appeared confused, then turned, trampled Bulvife as it charged past him and after its master.

Both belligerents were gone.

Bulvife pulled himself up from the dusty ground. Benhargan checked Kaltopia; she seemed no worse for wear. He hoisted her up on his shoulder, and through the hot air that burned their lungs with the stink of brimstone, they again rushed down the passage.

"At least he is without the aid of one unworldly horror," Benhargan said.

"It will make a good song for bards and minstrels," Bulvife responded. "The story of how Benhargan cowered behind the great Bulvife, to only kill one demon, and let the other escape." He chuckled.

Benhargan narrowed his eyes. "And, you – great Bulvife – he who shall be known as the man who let Bailgard live," he countered.

Bulvife chuckled loudly.

They came to another fork in the path.

"This way, the air is much fresher," Benhargan said.

Before long they saw just the pin-prick of white light ahead. Slowly, it grew bigger.

The barbarians walked out onto a wide and isolated ledge. Below was three hundred feet of sheer cliff face.

"How are we going to get her down?" Bulvife asked.

"Why would Lemod direct us here with no means of descent?" Benhagan mused.

"Grimface," Bulvife calmly said. "How would he think this out?"

Benhargan set Kaltopia down. He sat next to her, deep in thought.

Bulvife moved to the opposite corner of the opening. There, he sat atop a large rock... that collapsed shooting dust into the air as he sank down.

"Look here," he said, as he got to his feet.

A large coil of rope was next to the cavern, covered in a tarp camouflaged to look just like a boulder. He pulled the cover away and examined the tightly woven strands.

"It looks sound," Bulvife said. "Of course, a wizard thinks ten steps ahead at all times."

"Okay, we lower Kaltopia down, then climb down ourselves," Benhargan reasoned. "But, what do we anchor to?"

"Come now, my ripe smelling chum – the iron ring of course," Bulvife said pointing at a large black and rust-colored ring fastened to the ledge.

"Now, that's thinking like a wizard," Benhargan quipped.

They tied the rope to the ring, and the other side around Kaltopia's body. After pulling on the rope with all their strength, they decided it was strong enough to hold them, and then some.

Kaltopia descended as the two barbarians let the rope down hand-over-hand. Once she was firmly on the ground, Benhargan went. He latched onto the rope and slipped over the edge. Slowly he made his way to the ground. At the bottom, he signaled for Bulvife to come down.

Bulvife was not more than twenty feet down when a jet of fire shot out of the cave. The ground shook, broken rocks fell, and Bulvife held on tightly to keep from falling.

From over the edge something fell; it was a man - sword and shield was still clasped in his hands.

Bulvife took a vice-like grip on the rope with his left hand, and snatched the falling man from midair. It was Lemod. The shield and sword broke loose and fell away, but Lemod did not slip from Bulvife's grasp.

The barbarian pulled him to the rope. "Hang on!" he shouted.

Lemod did, then looked up to see his savior. "Barbarian?"

"Benhargan is already on the ground," Bulvife said.

"I've sealed the tunnel. Know that the city-fathers let the enemy in, then were executed and the city sacked. We must away for our very lives," Lemod said.

Both men quickly scaled down the rope.

At the bottom, the four refuges dashed into the thick greenwood.

Benhargan stopped and sniffed the air. "Water, fish, lake root... there's a lake ahead."

"I smell it too," Bulvife replied.

They pressed on. After a while Benhargan pushed his way through some thick brush and saw the shimmering splendor of the mountains reflected in the blue waters.

Along the shore they took a rest, filled their skins, and discussed their next move.

Benhargan poured some fresh water into Kaltopia's mouth. She consumed it, but remained mute and immobile.

"How did you come to the ledge?" Bulvife asked.

Lemod drew in a deep breath. "That so-called prince, once inside the walls, gave orders to loot and pillage. His men took those foolish city elders and dashed their brains upon the defensive walls. After that, they began raping and looting. They came for me, and my slave threw himself at them - I narrowly escaped. I ran into several of the enemy soldiers in the market square. I killed five, but others came to their aid. There was only one place for me to go – the under-halls."

Lemod went to the water's edge and splashed the cool liquid over his face. He cupped his hands and drank deeply, then continued. "I thought that I was done for, but somehow I made it to the mines. They followed, but they did not know that I'd boobytrapped the last fifty cubits of the tunnel. That blast took the lives of at least ten more of them."

"The gods are fickle," Bulvife said.

"And Crom cares only that we are bold, valorous, and have a blade in hand when death calls," Benhargan stated.

Lemod's face took on the look of a man concerned. "I hope that Grimface is not lost to us. If anyone can figure a way to defeat a god-like being such as Bailgard, it will be him."

"Bailgard? We met him in the mine – and to his chagrin, nearly took his life," Bulvife said.

"Really?" Lemod was surprised.

"Yes – he will think twice before underestimating Cimmerians again," Bulvife added. He looked up at the sky. "If we're where I think we are, I know a place we might stay the night."

"What place is that?" Lemod asked.

"The ruins of Chur Dol Gohan," Bulvife offered.

"That place is cursed!" Lemod said. "The dead stalk the grounds, and unmentionable horrors lurk in those ancient dungeons.

Benhargan chuckled and looked over at Bulvife. "You are thinking like a wizard. Only fools would tread there – and we can assume Bailgard is no fool."

Bulvife smiled. "Good thing we're just the type of fools who would go there. If we travel hard, we can make it there before tomorrow's dusk."

# CHAPTER 16
# Where Fools Tread

IN THE DISTANCE THEY saw massive temple ruins, crumbling walls, all tilted at unnatural geometric angles.

"There it is, Chur dol Gohan," said Lemod.

As they got closer, glowing shapes high up on the battlements and in ruinous open widows looked down on them.

A deep ditch encircled the mile-wide ruins. A berm was built on the opposite bank - well over twenty feet high.

They came to the fifty-foot-wide moat filled with black, brackish water. In the center of the moat, and directly in front of the collapsed gateway stood a stone column – once the resting place for half a drawbridge.

They lit a torch. Under the darkening sky, the light illuminated the bridge structure. No wood remained, only corroded – large brass brackets covered in green patina.

"There," Lemod said. "A rope on the other side."

Benhargan narrowed his gaze, and saw a thick horse-hair rope hanging from a stone column.

There has been someone here before us," he said.

"Grimface?" Bulvife mused.

"Perhaps," Lemod said. "He is fond of leaving messages." He sat down. "This should not take long. Keep alert – our enemies may be about."

Lemod closed his eyes and began humming. The moon overhead began to arch toward the southwest. Across the moat the rope moved like a snake. It slithered this way, and that. A foul stench filled the air as the rope moved across the ditch. The end dropped into Lemod's lap. The rope fell flaccid, as he pulled up the slack, then stood.

"There!" he said.

The magician looped the end around the tusk and trunk of a stone elephant that sat guard at the water's edge. Pulling on the cord, the two barbarians seemed satisfied the rope would hold.

"Across," Benhargan instructed.

It took a few minutes to traverse the watery expanse. Once on the other side, Lemod and Bulvife found long planks that could be extended across the ditch to allow passage. Benhargan, carried Kaltopia over.

"Let's get inside," Lemod said, and began to lead the way.

A few minutes later, the barbarian laid Kaltopia on a raised altar carved from lapis.

"Where am I?" Kaltopia asked.

"By Mitra!" Lemod said surprised.

She slowly sat up. Benhargan watched her closely. She seemed no worse for wear. She got to her feet. A few times she stumbled as she walked, but caught herself.

Benhargan grunted. "Good to see that you are no longer a prisoner of the dead."

She studied everyone for a moment. "Where am I?" she asked again.

"Your soul was lost," Lemod said.

"We're in the ruins of Chur dol Gohan," Bulvife replied.

She looked on with no comprehension. "I have never heard of such a place."

"Come," Benhargan said to Bulvife. "Let us find some supplies - wood and food."

The two Cimmerians left, moving further into the crumbling city. Lemod sat down and watched Kaltopia.

"What is it you see?" she asked him.

He cracked a smile. "While you were tied to the bed in my home, I took little note of you, but now I see your beauty – such beauty," Lemod said.

Kaltopia blushed, though she did not mean to. "Your words - I do not know how to respond," she said.

"A complement is like a rose – it needs no response for one to suffer its beauty," Lemod stated.

Bulvife and Benhargan returned, their arms full of firewood. They dumped the wood, then ventured off again.

Lemod set to work making a fire. In sort-order the fire blazed, surrounded by broken bits of marble, lapis and granite. He lay back, watching the shadows of the room, as they shimmered, and twisted to the movement of the flames.

"I am a broken woman," Kaltopia began. "My soul is cut through to the marrow."

Lemod looked at her with caring eyes. "It is like a deep wound – it will take time to heal. You will not be yourself for a while. The first part of the battle is won – you've come back to your body. That's something very amazing."

"There are things too horrible to describe that lurk just beyond my sight." She closed her eyes tightly.

"Time – let it heal you," Lemod offered up. "Before you know it, you'll be right in the head, just as you were before."

Benhargan returned and flopped a dead rabbit near the fire. He sat down and did the grisly work to prepare the creature's corporal remains for eating. After a time, Bulvife came back. In his hand he held a string of fish.

"Where did you get that?" Kaltopia asked.

"A brook passes through these ruins. The fish were easy to catch," Bulvife said as he too sat and prepared the creatures for cooking.

Hours passed as the light of day fleeted. Rain fell against the broken roof and puddles formed in places on the ground. A haunting sound echoed throughout the old temple – the low moaning of agony and lament.

Bulvife took the first watch. A white mist rose from the floor of the building. It was not long before shapes moved from room to room. Sometimes the forms were black and man-shaped, other times the dimensions were less comfortable – things inhuman and unworldly.

Benhargan took the next watch. As he moved about with sword in hand, a group of armored spirits approached. They brandished weapons and even stabbed at Benhargan, who in turn just laughed at their attempts.

"You are dead – be gone and find your path to your god. Leave the living to suffer as you did!" Benhargan chided them.

One of the abominations flared into rage, and when it swung its blade, it cut the Cimmerian across the face and shoulder.

"I curse you, you filthy shambling corpses!" Benhargan called after them as the group of spirits fled down a column strewn passage. A moment later, the dead returned and flew into a fit, ransacking the party's goods – and tipping over a severely rotted table and chairs.

Bulvife and Lemod came running with blade and bow.

"What is this?" Bulvife called out.

"Those are the desmond ung - lingering souls whose business upon this world is not resolved," Lemod said, as all three men watched with waning concern.

A bird cried out, a glimmer of light appeared through a high window, then the things wavered, the mist grew thin, and all were gone.

The room fell silent as a tomb. Sunlight cut through a significant crack in the roof. The peril of Chur Dol Gohan was at an end.

"Where is everyone?" Kaltopia called.

"Here!" Benhargan replied.

She looked at them from afar. "What are you three doing there? What happened to your face?"

Benhargan laughed. "Enraged spirits," he said, as they all returned to the fire pit.

It took only a few minutes to pick the remains of the fish and rabbit clean, drink some water, and break camp, before heading back out the way they'd come.

"CHUR DOL GOHAN?" BAILGARD asked surprised. "They think they can escape my sight – but they are wrong. The spirits there won't save them or help them – so why hide there?" He nodded to another area of the map. "That is the place you call Tiplon Gates. They will have to cross there if they intend to go northwest."

A man in a red beard came close. "This is where our trap will be sprung." The man pointed at a narrow space between two tall cliffs.

"These creatures you call Cimmerians – they are not easily bested," Bailgard said.

"No sire, they are fierce, crafty, and brave; we must not underestimate them."

"Then don't! Now, off with you - leave me!" Bailgard said with a wave of his hand.

The prince stood alone in the candlelight, from a dark velvet sack, he took out an item wrapped in white leather.

He set the item on a dais, and removed the leather. A crystal skull shimmered in the firelight.

"From beyond time, by he who forged the elements – I ask that the great old god Dolhotan come forth. You, whose skin formed the world, and blood quenched the land, come by my request. Let me know it is done – that my daughter is with child; a god-king dwells within her womb. Tell me that my true name is safe, hidden from those who seek to undo me."

A shadow formed into an apparition, and rose high into the air. For a moment it wavered, then became flesh. The creature was not human in any way. Slumped at the shoulders, all manner of weeping wounds covered it. Its one eye was open; the mouth fanged, the eye a milky white with a dark blue center.

"The deed is done. The Sarogoth has come forth to plant the seed. It now germinates in her. Such an exquisite belly – a feast if I so desired," the thing said. "Now for you, Bailgard, ancient is your blood. To quench my thirst with it would not be out of the question... but, for that which binds you in this world – your name – it is with me now."

The creature waddled toward Bailgard. The man narrowed his gaze.

"Back whence you came, Dolhotan, until I call upon you again."

The thing quivered, turned back into a shadow, then faded from sight. Bailgard smiled, wrapped the skull up again, then stopped and stared off into the darkness. "Grimface, you will not murder me that way!" He chuckled. "I am beginning to lose some respect for you, and your powers. I will try one more time to entice you – then, if you will not bend as a reed – you will break as the oak!"

# CHAPTER 17
# Pilgrims of Conscience

IT TOOK THREE DAYS to reach the Tiplon gates. The cliff walls that formed the pass were covered in dark green moss. Moisture dribbled and leaked from the cracks in the black stone.

The path was straight, and the walls were coming closer together the further along they went. Benhargan seemed on edge, and Bulivfe's eyes scanned the tops of the cliff and back at their flank.

"Halt!" shouted a red-haired man who approached on horseback.

Benhargan drew his sword.

"If you fight, you will die. Throw down your arms and you will be taken as slaves," said red hair.

"Give me a blade!" demanded Kaltopia.

"Shh..." commanded Benhargan.

Several men stepped from sharp crevasses along the high walls – their bows bent and ready for release. From up the pass came a group of men on horseback. They held lances at the ready, and wore the same heavy, black, armor of those in the service of the prince.

"Who commands you?" Benhargan demanded.

"We are soldiers for Bailgard, the last Prince of Atlantis." one of the men said.

"Show me the triangles," Bulvife ordered.

The soldier pulled away a black cloak to reveal the three golden markings on his chest.

"Now, throw down your arms and surrender to us," the man ordered.

Without any warning, Benhargan crouched and launched himself at the man's horse, felling steed and rider. The other cavalry-men were so shocked at the Cimmerian's movement that they did not move a muscle. Arrows rained down, as those on the ledges fired at the now fast-moving barbarian targets.

Bulvife rolled, came up on bended knee, and put a sturdy gray-goose shaft into each man who stood on those lofty perches – each corpse crumpled, and then plummeted to the jagged stones below.

The felled horseman, climbed from the dirt only to meet Benhargan's blade. Blood painted the walls, as the barbarian separated the man's head from his body. The remaining men on horseback turned and rode back the way they'd come.

A lilting voice rose high. Down the canyon walked a woman dressed in a yellow robe. She wore a sturdy leather glove, which supported a large golden eagle. The creature spread its mighty wings and flew into the sky.

The woman's singing was growing, and a great weight pressed down upon all the warriors. Bulvife was driven to his knees. The song clawed and tore at his mind with each changing pitch.

In that moment, Lemod climbed to his feet and sang out. There were no discernable words, only mutterings as if the wind in the trees spoke in a way that only a woodland spirit would understand.

Benhargan looked up and saw soldiers coming from behind the sorceress. A man halted at Benhargan and raised his blade for a killing blow.

With all his might, Bulvife sprang from the ground and landed upon his friend, rolling hard to the side. The woman stopped, surprised at the Cimmerian's ability to resist her spell. The soldier missed and turned, only to find Benhargan's mighty fist squarely in his face. The soldier slumped like a discarded war banner.

Lemod did not stop, and the woman realized her mistake all too late. She screamed in what sounded like abject horror, then frantically clawed at her own face drawing blood. Her skin turned black and cracked in places, then she doubled over and writhed upon the ground in such pain as to delight Ugoth the Pain Merchant.

Lemod stopped. The woman lay prostrate - dead.

The men on horseback charged, only to find arrow after arrow felling man and beast.

"Look out!" shouted Kaltopia.

Lemod took two steps but was hit hard from behind by something tearing into his flesh. The eagle was on him, and he tried to dislodge its long talons as it forced him to the ground. Bulvife stood and rushed to his aid.

One quick stroke of his sword and the fierce bird quivered and went limp. He pulled the beast away, and blood poured from fatal injuries produced by six-inch talons born through flesh and bone.

There was nothing more that could be done, for the monstrous avian had pierced Lemod's heart and lungs rendering him a dead man.

Kaltopia grabbed Benhargan by his tunic and held him fast.

"Never leave me out of a battle again. I might have saved Lemod if I had bow or blade."

Benhargan grunted, then rolled Lemod onto his back. His eyes were open, but gray. He closed the man's eyes, lifted him, and set him in a niche where neither those coming nor going could see him.

"I'm sure the gods of earth and air will watch over him here," Benhargan said, as he picked up a fallen weapon and handed a sword to Kaltopia. "Next time you fight," he added, as he pushed onward through the high pass.

THE SEVENTH GATE OVER the Tiplon mountains receded in the distance. Ahead, a vast forest appeared. There, a heavy fog lurked – covering both meadows and skulking around the trunks of the greenwood.

If there were enemy soldiers among the heather, moss, and fern of that valley, they would be difficult to detect. On the other hand, and under such conditions, rangers excelled.

It took several hours to reach the forest. The mist was thick. Moisture formed and dripped down Benhargan's dark black hair onto his face.

Bulvife at the lead stopped and crouched. Dark forms moved ahead - the subtle sound of boots denting sod and snapping twigs came to ear.

"The Cimmerians were coming this way, so stay alert," a male voice said.

"They will pay for murdering Bloodlance – and being insolent!" a younger male voice spoke.

"Quiet. Those barbarians have ears like wolves," said yet another one.

Bulvife gave Benhargan several hand gestures, turned slightly and began moving. Benhargan took Kaltopia by the hand, indicated silence, then followed.

From there, they moved down to the rolling grasslands. A few more hours of travel, then the mist lifted. In the distance, there was a strange sound.

A town or hamlet was not far; they heard the moo of a cow, and the crow of a cock. The smell of cooking eggs and meat filled their noses, and the three hungry souls drifted toward the food. The briny smell of the sea filled the cool air, and the three travelers found themselves looking down on a blue, rushing river and an ocean inlet.

Not far from the river was a palisade wall surrounding a large town. Beyond, thundered the sea. From within the settlement, white smoke charged into the sky, just to be blown inland by the ocean's heavy breath.

Kaltopia and Bulvife went up to the wooden gates first. A man in a gray tunic stood guard.

"Welcome traveler," said he.

"Greetings," Bulvife responded.

"There is meat and drink inside. Brass is welcome, as are jewels and silver, honest sweat, and flesh," the man said giving Kaltopia the once-over.

"Mitra be your host," Bulvife replied.

"Ah, pilgrims! We have a shrine also, near the Robber and Rooster tavern," the man told them. "Crimes are punishable by death, so keep your exploits honest."

"Our only goal is to be honest," Bulvife told him.

"May the god keep you well in your visit, and your travels," the guard said after them, as the two travelers entered the town.

Benhargan came a bit later. He had watched the town for a time and made sure they had not been followed. Finally, he approached the gate, and after a brief parley with the guard, entered.

It had taken only a few minutes to find the nearest tavern. Inside, Benhargan found Bulvife and Kaltopia drinking. A short time later, the man tending the bar approached the three.

"Greetings travelers, what brings you to Regulot?" the barkeep asked.

"Ah, Regulot!" Bulvife said. "Now, we know exactly where we are."

"We are pilgrims seeking spiritual comfort and contentment," Benhargan told the barkeep.

The man looked at the three with great skepticism. "Pilgrims?" He shrugged his shoulders. "If you say so. Try our red wine. It is from the Fereshi vineyards outside the city. I also have daisy-beer, and meal-beer, as well as mead."

"Bring us each," Bulvife said.

"Very good," the barkeep stated, turned and left.

"Where do we go from here? Shall we go north, or south?" Kaltopia asked.

"The wizard will show us the way. His gods seem quite willing to keep us wound up in this divine scheme," Bulvife told her.

# CHAPTER 18
# Tomb of Friends

BENHARGAN, BULVIFE, and Kaltopia moved from tavern to wine bar, and beer house to brothel, searching for any sign from the wizard.

The port city of Regulot was crowded. Originally built to contain three thousand inhabitants, it was bursting at the seams with ten times that many.

Camel caravans were coming in from Shem, and boats ladened with spice, dates, and rare herbs came from Zingara. Every sort mingled and cajoled from harbor to market, and market to parts far-flung.

As they wandered the streets, much human and animal waste clogged the avenues and walkways. Thick white smoke choked the alleys and markets.

"Why here?" Bulvife asked.

"The wizard is a strange one. Perhaps we are to make a sea voyage," Benhargan mused.

"There must be another message here. No cause to think he's abandoned you now," Kaltopia reasoned.

It took little time to find the waterfront and a wine-house. In that dark, dank, dive, they took up seats and drank, ate, and argued about their next move.

Two days they spent there. At times Benhargan rolled the bones. Bulvife went about cavorting, and listening for news of the golden triangles. Kaltopia brooded and stared over her horn-cup at the mayhem going on about her. In all this noise and confusion, a man whose head was covered by a blue cowl burst into bawdy song.

"Sit back in your seats, hear what I tell
"A story of old, as jaded as hell
"Of the sailors who sailed the Blue-bottle Sea

"Those lost souls who traveled to Leez
"They traveled to Leez
"They saw the great sea
"In days lost to time
"There at the port, those sailors did cavort
"With desire born of the sea
"They'd tired of Jeb, and Kaleb and Red
"All, those men of the sea
"They traveled to Leez
"They saw the great sea
"In days lost to time
"The girls they were a lot
"In taverns with beer they sought
"To sate such carnal grief
"They traveled to Leez
"They saw the great sea
"In days lost to time
"The lust it was hot
"Gold they had not
"When returning to the ship for the sea
"So they said farewell
"To the beer and the girls
"And, every one of them cried when they peed!" the sailor sang.

"Another!" shouted a burly man in the back of the public house.

The bard looked about the room, then went to the bar. As he walked he sang again.

"It was ole Brama's best that we took the test
"The test of a thousand seas.
"Burning bright as the stars in the night, and wet as rainy delight
She was soft as the girls in Leez.
"There is a scent of musk in the air, a bawdy thing bare.
"The sheets raised, and the tassels soar.
"In the wind the gods would sing, and the wind would ring
The fame of the Leez whores.
"Brave men sail the seas, and women they please

"And the boys all eager to learn.
"But, the seas they are rough, they tumble and are tough
And young boys can be found on their knees.
"Be a smith, or a dyer, or ring-tailed stout
"Pick something that pain mothers not.
"A eunuch in silk, a butcher's meat-bilk
"A royal vizier's fancy-lad to please.
"Pray to the gods, or the devils below
"Take gold for sods, or a wife for show
"But, with the wind at our backs, the sails stretched tight
"I long for the waters we soared!"

Following the singer was a jolly fellow with golden-blond hair strumming a lyre. The songs continued for some time, and before it was all over, all the sailors in the tavern were singing loudly to the lyrical tunes.

Benhargan tossed a brass coin into the man's bucket. The minstrel nodded his pleasure to the hulking Cimmerian.

From across the room a man with dark red hair approached. He looked up at Benhargan. "I am called Vililf the Hearty. I am a Vanier and have traveled to this port from afar. I was told to come here to do a task, and seek out, in the process, two Cimmerians to help me."

Bulvife sat forward and put his elbows on the table, and took a drink from his wine cup. "Who told you, and what task?"

Vililf narrowed his gaze. "Several moons ago, I found a man dying upon the side of the road. He gave me a small clay tablet. On the tablet were directions to a treasure. He instructed me to come to this tavern and seek the help of two large north-men."

Benhargan grunted. "What is the treasure?"

"There is an ancient war chest locked in a tomb in Kush. I know where it is, but cannot get it myself. You look as the man described you – filthy Cimmerian rangers from the frontier, fond of drink and dice. Am I right?"

"It's a sign," Kaltopia whispered.

"Indeed," Bulvife whispered back to her. "A sign of the wizard's trade and handiwork."

"Tell us more, and then we'll decide to join you or cut your throat," Benhargan said.

The Vanier was a head shorter than the two Cimmerians. Though threatened, Vililf seemed quite confident and bold. He sat down on the bench opposite the three warriors.

"Not far from Tresh Helotat, in the Flaming Desert, there is a tomb. It is dug into the side of an ancient river bank and overlooks the valley of Pen. There are two tricks to entering the tomb; I will only tell you when we are there," Vililf said.

"What is said to be in the war chest?" Benhargan asked.

"Rubies, emeralds, and blue sapphires," said Vililf. "They say that in the chest are also rare weapons made of enduring metal, some of which are imbued with dark magic. In clay pots are gold chains, silver, bronze bars, and coins. That is where you come in. You both are strong like oxen. You can carry the treasure out. I could not do it alone, and my agents in Kush could not carry such wealth quickly to liberation."

Benhargan looked at Kaltopia and Bulvife. "While we wait for that carbuncle – the wizard, why should we not fill our coffers with such? We will take half of what is in that chest, and split it between us. Are we agreed?"

"I will be a part to this endeavor," said Bulvife.

Kaltoipa nodded. "I'm in."

Vililf nodded. "Then good – you three will divide half the booty, and me and my cohorts will do the same to the other half."

"It is agreed," Benhargan said.

"We must go south along the coast," Vililf said.

"By foot, or by sea?" Benhargan asked.

"Let us away to my boat," Vililf stated, then stood and led the way to the door.

They sailed with the setting sun upon their right cheek for several days. Once arrived, they tied off the ship at the Kush port of Prion, and were introduced to a swarthy fellow from Kush named Kihim ben Ali ben Shehad. It was clear the Kushman and the Vanier were well acquainted, and they wasted no time in getting camels, donkeys, and horses for the trip. Vililf handed Benhargan, Bulvife, and Kaltopia white robes and turbans; garments that could be loosened and the extra cloth pulled across one's face to protect from sand and sun.

They crossed dry and desolate plateaus and ventured down barren rock-strewn wadis. The tan desert wastes stretched to the horizon, and beyond. By the time they made the first oasis, all were exhausted - taxed by the sun's beastly heat.

Hundreds of palm trees surrounded a body of water more than six hundred feet wide and twice that long. A small civilization flourished there in the middle of nowhere.

Many tents were set up - some red, some yellow, and some white. Clans gathered at their own tents and eyed suspiciously the newcomers. As night fell, the secluded clansmen began making the rounds, introducing themselves and offering drink and meat – grand hospitality was on display.

Food was eaten, and much libations drank as the night wore on. Dancing slave girls jiggled and bent in provocative ways, all to the tune of each clan's musicians. The little-bear in the sky was overhead when Bulvife, Benhargan, and Kaltopia retired. The next day, hard traveling would be their mantra, and waking before the dawn a necessity.

As morning began, all prepared to leave and depart into the hellish lands. In the distance, a strange, and unearthly sound of a base horn rose in tempo, then vanished.

Large sandstone hills and mountains dominated the westward way. Two camel trains followed the barbarians, but at a fork in the desert path, just at the edge of a dry riverbed, the train took the fork toward the setting sun, and the barbarians went in the direction of the north star.

They cut through a narrow estuary – gouged out stone polished smooth from years of flashfloods. Vililf seemed to know exactly where he was going, choosing path after twisting path.

As the midday sun cut down through the channels, Vililf stopped and pointed.

"It is there – the entrance to the tomb." He looked back at Bulvife and Benhargan. "I know the secret word to open it. Once open, you two go in, find the chest, and bring it hence."

"What are the two tricks?" Bulvife asked.

"Ah... beware of the sconces. If you put a torch in one, you will be killed – so says the map. Also, stay to the left when entering, for the right side will spell death - a pit, deep and filled with spikes."

Vililf walked up to the carved stone door, laid his hands on it, and said some arcane words. The portal shook, dust fell from a growing seam around it, then it opened. A ghastly moan came from within.

Benhargan took a torch and lit it. He stooped a bit to fit, then went in. Bulvife gathered half a dozen fresh torches and followed. Kaltopia entered next. They stayed to the left.

The shimmering orange and yellow of the torch posed skulking shadows against relief frescos along the walls. At times the images appeared animated, and other times they seemed to change form – horrors, twisted in agony and writhing to the pulsing light.

"Here," Benhargan said. "The main chamber."

Much gold and gems lay piled - displayed for the mummified king who sat at the far end overlooking his spoils.

"Look here," Bulvife said, pointing at an array of unblemished swords and daggers.

There were several chains with a heavy ball on the end. They appeared to be made of some strange glowing metal. One of the balls had sharp blades, the other spikes, and the third smooth.

Kaltopia found a curved sickle-sword, a dagger and some golden chainmail. None of the armor fit the large Cimmerians, but the weapons were not a problem, so they tossed aside their worn implements and took new ones. Sword, mace, chain-ball, and mighty bows came to the barbarian's powerful hands.

In the far back, covered by a disassembled bronze chariot, was a locked chest five feet by three wide by three high. On each side were loops for poles.

Bulvife spared no time finding two spears to insert into the brackets. Benhargan got on one side and Bulivife on the other. With all their strength, they lifted and slowly moved it toward the entrance. Just as they were leaving the main chamber, something glinted in the torch light.

"Wait a moment," Bulvife said, and set down his end and went back into the room.

"What is it?" demanded Benhargan.

"A reflection of such splendor that I cannot forsake it."

Benhargan growled loudly. "We've no time for such nonsense. The wealth in this chest will supplant any other treasure."

Bulvife strode into the darkness, save for a bright gleam from some metallic object.

"It is a blade across the lap of the king – let us not leave that behind."

Bulivfe grabbed the sword. A clicking sound echoed in the air. The ground shook and dust fell from the roof.

"It's a trap, you fool!" shouted the mighty Benhargan, as he dropped the end of the box and rushed toward tomb doorway.

A thick wall of granite crashed down; sand and dust choked the air. The entrance was sealed, and the chamber lost to escape.

Beating on the wall, Benhargan called out, "Bulvife, can you hear me!"

There was no answer. Benhargan took the looted dager from his side and pounded the pomel upon the stone. From the other side came a tapping sound.

"He still lives," Kaltopia said.

"Yes, for now. Unless there's another way out, he will be keeping that ancient king eternal company – all for want of a blade."

"What do we do now?" Kaltopia said.

"We drag this chest to the end of this hall, and divide up the riches. If there is a way out, Bulvife will find it and meet us at the entrance."

"You're going to abandon him?" Kaltopia was shocked.

"There is not much more that can be done. Bulvife is skilled. If there is a way out, he will find it."

Benhargan pushed and Kaltopia pulled the chest to the opening. Once there, the Vanir and Kushman spared no time in picking the lock and opening the lid. Indeed, there were gems and gold the likes of which only a mighty king would have known. They took two hours to sort the wealth and divide it.

"It is bad that your companion lost his life in the tomb," the Vanir said.

"Bad for him, good for us," the Kushman said.

"Bulvife will find a way out. We will wait here for him," Benhargan said.

"As you wish," said Vililf. "When you leave here, keep to the right until you find the wide channel. From there, follow down the grade and head straight west. You'll find the oasis."

The two foreigners took their treasure, packed it into leather sacks and bore them onto camels and donkeys. Off down the wadi they went.

Benhargan and Kaltopia waited seven days at the tomb door, but Bulvife did not come forth.

"He is dead," Benhargan declared. "Non – not even the mighty Bulvife could live without water for this many days."

Kaltopia nodded. "Let's take the treasure and be gone. I fear my sadness too heavy to bear waiting here further."

They packed and traveled down the dry estuary toward the desert. It took more than a day to reach the oasis. As they approached, in the distance near the edge of the oasis, a black flag with gold triangles rose along a pole tied to a red tent.

GRIMFACE TUMBLED IN darkness. Falling hard into the slushy green open field shadows of light twisted his mind and all his senses. The palms of his hands and knees were covered in mud. All was quiet – not even the wind sung in the trees – then, a shrill scream broke the silence.

He turned. Not more than a hundred feet away, twenty Picts had taken notice of him. He turned running for all his worth toward a grove of trees in the thick greenwood. His heart was now pumping savagely within his chest. Those behind him, his pursuers, they would be fleet of foot, and if he failed to reach the forest, they would be on him with savage rage.

He tumbled over some old broken branches, and came up running. Ducking limbs, he dashed through a bramble patch, pushing himself forward though a vale of green ivy.

Through the dark mass of leaves he saw a set of boulders covered in moss. Quickly, he climbed, took a step, then tumbled down into some dark hole. He put his hand over his mouth to control his breathing. Sounds of scurrying followed, then silence. He waited.

After quite some time, the light that barely penetrated the forest canopy began to fade. No other sounds of pursuit came to his ears.

Feeling around, he noted the narrow hole leading deeper into the darkness. His hands dipped into finely ground dirt. The scent of animal dung assaulted his senses, as the rotted leaves and decaying wood compressed under him.

He waited some time, then he hummed and fire licked the bark of a dry branch. A shimmering light bathed the colored walls. He was in an ancient tomb. Animal spirit figures were painted all along the stones and ceiling.

He found many sealed vases and many weapons and armor. Snooping about, he discovered a lamp and ignited the wick. To his surprise, it was still full of oil.

Deeper into the cavern he ventured. At the far end sat the lord whose tomb he was in. A regal and majestic mummified corpse, sitting upright, fully clothed in chain armor with a helmet of tarnished bronze, looked upon him with empty sockets. Beside the dead man were a shield and sword, and all around at his feet were laid an array of fine bows, arrows, battle axes, and jeweled daggers with blades made from cut crystal.

Grimface spared little time looting the corpse of its protection and weapons. After putting on the accouterments, he sat next to the stone throne and rested.

In his mind he saw the landscape he'd fallen into. He knew he was somewhere in the Pictlands. This would not bode well, for the cruelty of the Picts was legendary. And those native creatures, skilled in the dark arts, were not to be underestimated.

Sudden fatigue filled his bones and he sat there, closed his eyes. He'd traveled upon the roads of the dead, and into the place of names. It was not easy, and took him to his limit of magic to remain there, and search.

"What now, you sod?" he asked himself. "There was no name for Bailgard. The man, if he could be called such, was without celestial weakness.

Opening his eyes, he turned to the mummified remains sitting only a few paces away. "Any ideas, old king?" he asked. The silence was suffocating. "I guess I'll have to think this one through myself," he added.

"MY PRINCE! A PICT MESSENGER has reported a man fitting the description of Grimface the magician has been seen just west of Aqualonia.

The Headsmen Clan pursued him, but lost him somewhere in the rocky Bayout region," said a man wearing a captain's helmet.

"Small matter," said Bailgard. "He will be found. By now he knows his venture in the land of the dead was useless." Bailgard laughed in a sinister way. "Return to fortress Gravacon and gather more conscripts, then send word of your strength and readiness."

"Yes, my Lord." The captain bowed slightly, then left the hall.

Bailgard turned to his generals. "The forces of Nemdia, Aqualonia, Ophir, Koth, and Argos move to stop us as I speak. They have formed an alliance to stand against me. We will have to crush them, and we will use the power of magic to aid us. Let in the five magicians."

Five robed figures entered the hall. They came around the long table that supported a map of the countries of Hyboria and Hyperboria. Small blocks of wood with flags pined to dowels were spread about.

"I am told by Hyro ben Hasmer that you are worthy wizards— magicians of rare quality," Bailgard said.

None of them spoke.

"You have been told of what you stand to gain if you serve me. You will all be powerful and rich."

"How is it you command such power?" a female voice spoke from the back.

"By my noble birth. You are but shadows of my ability, yet I cannot be everywhere at once. So who better to rule as regents than creatures such as you?" Bailgard asked.

"I am agreed to do your bidding," a man in a red robe said.

All the sorcerers looked at one another, then agreed to the prince's terms.

"Good. I will need all your power in the main assault. Report to Hyro ben Hasmer, it is he you shall take orders from in this fight. With your combined abilities, not even he who calls himself Grimface can stand in my way. In one year, all Hyboria will be mine to command. Your spoils will fill vault after mighty vault with endless wealth, and your extracurricular activities will not be hindered by me."

THE RAIN WAS POURING outside. Grimface came close to the entrance and captured water in his cupped hands. As he drank, his mind and body cried out in unbridled pleasure – for he did not know how dehydrated he had been until he'd taken water unto his lips.

He peered out and saw only forest, rain, and mist all around. Slowly, he climbed out. There was some hesitation in his manner. But he would have to start moving soon. His beasts would need more direction, and he would need their protection until he figured out what action to take next.

Quietly, he climbed from the massive boulders, over the green soft moss, and onto the dark grass. The mist grew thick. Beyond a few paces, shrubs and trees faded from view.

He closed his eyes, then opened them - his vision now showing all things that gave off heat. Which way to go?

The land sloped downward to his right, and he reasoned it must lead to a brook or river. From there he could decide which way might lead from the Pict clans. In the distance, he heard drum beats.

The drumming grew louder. He drew the stolen sword. From the cool distance came immense heat. His vision was blinded by a burst of red. For a moment, he fumbled to raise the blade. Next, he reverted his vision, and looked upon the normal world.

"Ulusk som bor?" a voice said in his ear.

# CHAPTER 19

## Silence of Heart

BEFORE GRIMFACE COULD flee, a black winged creature, blazing hot, came at him. Its gray skin was covered in nodules and two tusks protruded from the monster's mouth.

The beast's claws struck. Grimface raised his sword. The metal blade vibrated violently in Grimface's grip. Pain shot all the way up into his shoulder. From the side came Pict warriors – blades of obsidian at hand, and murderous lust upon their lips.

Grimface stepped back, deflecting two Picts and sidestepping another. The monster closed in again. It batted away the Pict warriors and came at the wizard, who dodged, parried, cut and dodged some more.

Finally, Grimface got a lucky thrust and drove the sword into the creature's gut. The monster strode forward, bellowed, and fell upon the wizard. He was pinned.

Out of the mist came a tall Pict wearing the headdress of a shaman. He walked slowly, as if without a care. On his face, he wore an evil smile that bespoke of cruel intent.

Grimface tried to sing – call upon the power, but nothing would come forth. The very breath within him was being crushed from his lungs by the weight of the monster. The savage approached, then sang a hymn in his guttural language. Grimface felt his throat on fire, and his tongue swell.

The shaman reached down, and with one hand flung the monster from atop the wizard.

"You are mine now, sorcerer," said the shaman in the Aqulonian language. "The prince thought you would be hard to contain, and now you are mine to give as tribute. He shall praise me, and your soul will be mine to torment – one day."

* * *

There was not much cover. Some shallow ditches, a few desert ferns and thorny scrubs; not many places to hide. Benhargan did his best to disappear, and make Kaltopia vanish as well.

He tied the animals to a palm tree, then made for the oasis reservoir; better cover to be had there. No cry of alarm and no challenges came from the tents. The Cimmerian had done his job as ranger, melding with the terrain to gain an advantage.

From the sparse brush, Benhargan watched the men of the black flag visit the water's edge to fill skins and jars. They seemed little interested in anything around them, as they fortified their camp.

None of the tribesmen who were there before were there now, and none of those there now appeared interested in the new comers.

Benhargan found a place to make camp, then ventured back out to secure their horses and donkey. Kaltopia made a fire, and refilled their skins.

The sun was lowering in the west, and the sky came ablaze with dark orange and red. Fires grew bright as jovial voices rose with singing and conversation. From time to time Benhargan eyed the camp of the three triangles; it seemed as ordinary as the others.

As the night wore on, several elders approached Benhargan and invited him and Kaltopia into their camp. Food was laid out, and much feasting was had. The Cimmerian drank little, for his suspicions were growing about all those at the oasis. He slept little too, and kept his sword across his lap, yet no harm befell the two travelers as the night gave way to dawn.

An old man, the caravan leader, approached and sat by Benhargan.

"If you travel alone, you may travel with us. We are going to the city of Muir. There you can find an inn, cool water, and much sport."

Benhargan knew these desert dwellers and their ways. To turn down a clan leader's hospitality could prove dangerous.

"Blessings of Rama be upon you. We accept," Benhargan told the old man.

"Blessings of Rama upon you as well," the old man said. "I am Goh Timran, leader of the Goh. While you are with us, no harm will befall you. Come, make ready. We travel as the sun rises."

THE BONDS WERE TIGHT around his wrists. A loop of tawny rope was placed about his neck and tied to a long wooden pole. The shaman said something in his language, and they began to march through the woods, and to a fate Grimface did not wish to think about.

With every step, he tried to force a sound from between his lips. Nothing would come out. Looking up, he saw the shaman glance back, produce an evil smile, then pat a leather pouch dangling from his side.

They walked for many hours until they emerged into a vast clearing. Lodges were arranged all around - cooking fires blazed, and Pict men, women, and children looked on. In the smoky air was roasting meat, and some intangible smells.

Rust-red mud walls composed the walls of a decorated lodge, and Grimface was shoved inside. The shaman came in and sat at the fire pit. He sat staring at Grimface for some time, then spoke in Aqulonian.

"I now own your voice," he began. "I own your magic. In your eyes is contempt, and you will regret such thoughts." He poked at the fire. "It will do you no good to flee, for my warriors know how to track a deer on a moonless night, under a stormy sky.

"He who calls himself prince wants you. I will deliver you to him myself. But, first I cannot let my clan miss the sport they crave. First you will hear the screams of those soon to feel the fire-reeds against their bare skin. A man and woman we have for that task." The shaman took the stick and poked Grimface twice with it. "This prince did not say you had to be whole when presented to him. You, my city dwelling friend – you will scream the most!" He stood. "Shaka cum!"

In came several muscular warriors who lifted Grimface to his feet.

"Into the stockade you go, wizard. Chi cur cul dorma," he added to the brawny savages.

MUIR WAS NOT FAR NOW. In the distance, the mighty walls that encircled thousands of citizens loomed. In the middle was a hill, topped by a mighty palace made of gleaming white stone. Benhargan had been to Muir twice before with Bulvife. They had stopped there for a few nights before moving south, and before being tricked by Ottin'bar.

"It is a blessing that we fell in with these men from Kush," Kaltopia said.

"The gods work in strange ways. I do not claim to understand them," Benhargan replied.

"But you must admit it is good?"

"I admit only that it was a shame that Bulvife died not in battle."

"It was not your fault," Kaltopia told the Cimmerian.

"No, it was his for being foolish and greedy. He should have left that blade," Benhargan stated.

They were approaching the massive wooden gates of Muir. Soldiers were many here. Dust was heavy in the air as they passed under the lintel and into the city.

They wound their way along narrow streets until they came to an area where warehouses made up the bulk of the structures. Here, Timran dismounted his horse and motioned for Benhargan and Kaltopia to do the same.

"We now part company. May Rama bless you upon your travels and keep you from harm," he said.

"And to you, and your clan, may Rama be with you and keep you," Benhargan replied. He turned to Kaltopia. "Come, follow me."

Benhargan walked his mount to the west gate. Soldiers paced atop the ramparts, bows slung over their shoulders, and twice the number of quivers at their sides. The gate-guards were doubled and armed with blade and pole-arm.

"They are preparing for battle," Benhargan said. "Let us seek out the river port."

Kaltopia and Benhargan wove their way between tight corners deep within the warren of three story tenements. After some time, a vast city square appeared. All about were brightly colored tents and awnings shading baskets of palm-dates, olives, spices, fruits, and roasted nuts. Also, many wares were laid out, such as copper pans and cups, amphorae, ornate lamps, gems, and brass knives.

A cacophony of voices radiated all around them. Dark men wearing various colored robes – white, gray, and tan, pulled at those passing, demanding that they feel their dyed cloth, or the ripeness of their fruit.

The Cimmerian stopped, sniffed the air, then turned ninety degrees.

"The river is this way," Benhargan said.

Kaltopia inhaled twice. "How is it you can smell the river and I cannot?"

"I am Cimmerian. All my life has been forged by the wilds. Even amongst the stench of this city, I can know a river by its scent."

They came to a stone wall parted in the middle by an archway. He ducked under it, and the two found a hundred wooden docks jutting out into a blue river.

"When I came to the cities of the south, I found it hard to remain behind the walls, for the foul air was suffocating. My kind cannot be penned up like common sheep," Benhargan said.

"Why don't you go back to the snow-covered mountains of Cimmeria?" Kaltopia asked.

"Grimface," Benhargan stated.

"That inhuman creature?" Kaltopia said, her voice filled with both respect and fear.

"You are right, he is not like us. His kind are growing few in the realm of mortals. I would not be surprised if he is the only one of his tribe still living," Benhargan said.

Kaltopia grabbed Benhargan by the arm and halted him.

"I did not heed his warning and gazed into the abyss. I remember that voice... it spoke to me, then I was encased in stone and darkness. I am weak because of it, and at times feel my soul slipping from my grasp," she said.

Benhargan looked down into her eyes, smiled, then laughed a very bawdy guffaw. "You have good reason to be worried. Bulvife and I have seen many things unholy and unnatural at Grimface's hand. But I will never question his motives or integrity. In some ways he is father, teacher, and warrior-elite to us all. I fear that when his life is snuffed, there will be a hole left in this world larger than this walled city." Benhargan turned and began walking again.

"Where will we go?" Kaltopia asked.

"Like a leaf in a storm. The gods of Grimface will show us where our path will lead."

They walked down the bank, and from dock to dock. Benhargan would call to a sailor on a craft and ask where the ship was headed. In the middle of the marina, a dark-skinned man with a dark leather eye patch looked up.

"You," he called. "I am Shavrez ben Hotep. I have heard your question from afar and may have good news for you, for I am this day traveling to sea, and toward Argos."

Benhargan turned to Kaltopia. "See, it didn't take long." He turned to Shavrez.

"How much will you charge to take us with you?"

The man narrowed his eyes. "For a man as large as you, and your woman, it will cost an ingot of brass."

"That is far more than I am willing to pay," Benhargan said.

Shavrez rubbed his scruffy chin with his hand as he looked up into the sky. "You will displace cargo and eat supplies. What about ten copper dollops?"

"Ten copper it is," Benhargan said.

"Come aboard and make a place toward the prow between the sacks of grain, the jars of wine. Mind the bow line."

Benhargan left and returned with the donkey and the sacks of treasure it carried. He put the loot into the boat, then sat atop it.

The captain ordered the release of the bow and aft ropes and set the red triangular sail.

Over the course of the day they traveled past palm trees, reed beds, and modest grasslands. At times, they saw the dry and desolate lands beyond. The stale hot air was stifling as the day wore on. As the sun ascended to the middle of the sky, the captain had some sailors erect an awning at the front so Kaltopia might be protected from the harsh heat.

It took many hours to reach the river inlet. Small villages became plentiful, and the shallow draft barges gave way to deep-draft sea going ships.

Once out to sea, the captain came about to starboard and began the journey north. Slowly, the weather changed from sunny cloudless sky, to a heavy white mist, shrouded in gray light.

It took three days to reach Solum Gunor. Once secured to the docks, Benhargan and Kaltopia disembarked and moved directly to the nearest tavern.

Weeks passed, as Benhargan and Kaltopia used their stolen treasure to live a life of debauchery. Fall was coming, the time for war suspended, and those who plied their trade in death, gathered in numbers at every brothel, tavern, and bathhouse. In the weeks that followed, Kaltopia and Benhargan found passion in each other, and fevered excess blurring day into night, and back to day again.

Benhargan staggered to the fire pit, drank down the last of his beer and brooded.

"What burns in your mind, my lustful lord?" Kaltopia asked.

"No word, or sign from Grimface. It is unlike that creature to be absent for so long, while meddling in the lives of mortals," Benhargan replied.

Kaltopia ran her hands over Benhargans chest. "Do not fear – for if he is as powerful as you say, we will hear from him soon."

Benhargan continued to stare into the fire. That feeling he'd had since meeting the wizard was gone. Only anxiety remained in his breast. "Something is wrong," he finally said.

SHAVREZ SAT ON A WOODEN box on the deck of his ship. The sting of a bitter cold wind cut at his lips, ears, nose, and cheeks. As he mulled over going to one of the local taverns along the Taraturn wharf, a large figure wearing a cloak and cowl approached.

"Are you Shavrez Hotep?" the man asked.

Shavrez looked up. "Who wants to know?"

"A man seeking information."

"What business do you have with me?" Shavrez demanded to know.

"An unusually large Cimmerian warrior, and a woman, traveling somewhere north. Did you take them?" the figure more ordered than politely asked.

"I take travelers from time to time. How am I to remember any one of them?" Shavrez countered.

The man stepped over the saxboard and stood tall and menacing on the deck.

"The man was Cimmerian, large, and bold. I doubt you'd forget the likes of him. Did you take him along the coast northward?" From under the dark cloak the figure produced a hand full of dark blue gems, and from the other side a dagger.

Shavrez rubbed his hands together at the sight of the gems, then he looked at the blade. A moment passed as the captain weighed both greed and fear.

"I'm only a merchant." He licked his lips.

"You have two options. One, take what I offer and answer my question, or two, I will cut the answer from you. Choose!"

Shavrez looked at the knife, then at the gems, then back at the knife.

"The treasure?" Shavrez answered a bit unsure he would not be killed anyway.

"That is a good answer. You are a smart man," the figure told him.

"I took such a man and woman up the coast. They put ashore at Solum Gunor many weeks ago, the day of the moon goddess as she traveled in front of the sun-god."

The man handed the shiny gems to the captain. "Tell no one else this information. If I find you did, I will geld you."

Shavrez reached for the stones, then withdrew his hand taking the riches.

"The man said to the woman, they were going to find a tavern; if that helps," Shavrez volunteered.

The man appeared to stare at the captain, as if considering some deep and perhaps dark thought. After a moment, the figure turned, stepped back over the saxboard, and quickly melted back into the darkness.

# CHAPTER 20
# The Great Worm Bites Its Tail

SOLUM GUNOR SUFFERED the churning wrath of the cold-sea that beat against its craggy shore. Up along the rocky bluffs the path through the city zigged this way and that, and cut into the living rock of the cliffs.

The high-gate at the far north-east wall was not busy, and Benhargan found it an easy exit. Not far ahead would be the snowy pass between the two high peaks of Keplan Mountain.

It was a lucky chance that Benhargan found two young, well-bred horses tied up at a road-house. It was easy enough to free them of their bonds, and make better use of them than their masters were doing.

Kaltopia straddled one of the horses; her strong legs clamped around the red and black blanket on the beast's back. Holding herself steady, she looked back at Benhargan who sat erect, looking fierce – eyes searching the horizon,

They traveled for weeks. Few were foolish enough to rattle sabers at them, and even fewer were brave enough to come within reach of Benhargan.

As they stopped at the many towns along the way, much coin was spent on wine and food - and pleasures only known by the most high-born lords. In the air was a hint of the coming snow, and gray clouds dogged their heels for the last few days.

Kaltopia was now every bit as rugged as Benhargan, though she lacked the true will of a Cimmerian. She looked over at him - his sheer raw power, mighty muscles sculpted over bone, and his bronzed skin that spoke of his many years in the wildlands - all of him made her resolve weak before his barbarian ways.

"Dismount," Benhargan ordered. "We walk the rest of the way up."

"In the Pict lands -" she began.

"What of them?" Benhargan asked as his eyes scanned both the trail ahead, and then the flank.

"Your days among the Rangers, do you miss it?"

"What is to miss? Many nights spent eating dried meat and consuming thin-wine from goat-skins? The scores of Picts I've sent to their heathen god? Climbing trees to sleep among the bows? Slitting throats, and leading those brave savages to ambushes? That honest work, I do miss. It is far better than the skullduggery practiced by the magician."

"How did you become associated with Grimface?" Kaltopia asked.

"It was a few winters back. Bulvife and I met a man called Otten'bar. He was of the same make as Grimface – a creature of magic and dark powers. He paid us to steal a scepter from a tomb, and we did. For our troubles, the mage poisoned us, took the item, our money, and left us to die of a curse. Grimface found us – how I am not sure. He too was in search of Otten'bar, for his own reasons. It seemed fitting that we accompany him, and all of us find vengeance with that cur."

"Did you find him?" Kaltopia's voice was thick with curiosity.

"Oh, we did indeed," Benhargan said. "But, those gods of the wizard were not done with us, and Grimface came to lead us from one cause to another. I have a feeling his gods will lead me back to him soon, now that Bulvife is dead."

"You spent many a year with Bulvife?" Kaltopia asked.

"He could not have been more than fourteen seasons when I came across him. I was wandering the narrow streets of the city called Ka'hail. As I remember, I was filled with much wine at the time, and stopped to take a piss. I heard a commotion and approached a long dark street – walled on either side with slum-shanties. There was a large bald man with two war-hounds. All around the boy were men armed with board, club, and chain. As I recall the conversation had to do with sexual favors."

Benhargan's eyes focused far off in the distance as he continued. "I saw the boy was Cimmerian – so I decided to stay back and watch. It is our way to let a man sort out his own affairs. I think it came as a total surprise to those around him when Bulvife rushed the large bald man, tore the chain from his hands, and swung the dogs about like Trabatian maces. I figured he'd run then, but instead, he attacked the others. He preceded to kill two of the bald man's men."

"What did you do?" Kaltopia was leaning from her horse toward the barbarian.

"All fell to Bulvife's fast, and furious attack. It was clear he needed no help from me; he had earned some skill in his travels. In truth, those men had little chance – common street toughs used to their victims complying instead of attacking. So as I laughed at the bloodletting, and the mayhem, I resolved to meet this boy.

"The last to feel the boy's fury was the man. The fat bastard turned to run. Well, I could not let him flee such a well-deserved death, so I extended my sword arm, and the fellow flipped around once and landed on his face. I placed my foot on his back and held him fast. When Bulvife had cut the purses free of each of the corpses, he approached me.

'You let one get the best of you,' I said.

'Your help was not needed!' he said to me. 'Lift your foot and let this cur rise.'

"I had been away from my homeland so long that I'd forgotten about my brethren and our pride of battle. Crom watches us – he knows our efforts. If we are helped, he will piss upon us in the halls of our fathers. A grave slight to be sure," Benhargan said.

"I stepped back and the man climbed to his feet. The boy caught him and beat him to death with his bare fists. Afterward, we went and drank much at a local wine bar. We became drunk – staggered out of the public house, laughing at fools about us, wandering the streets until dawn, trying each other's fighting skills - knocking over carts, and smashing emptied jars upon the street-stones. When neither of us had any energy left, we laughed the harder. For those around us, they thought us quite mad I am sure.

"Before I knew it, a week had passed, and a traveling companion I'd made. If I am Crom's right arm, Bulvife is his left. We have fought enemies, and each other, for nigh on ten winters now..." Benhargan grew quiet. "He is in the Great Hall now, fighting, and roaring with laughter, drinking horn after horn from Crom's personal cauldron of never ending mead – I see him quaffing down so much, that Crom smites him, and the next morning they all battle, feast, and drink again!"

Kaltopia smiled at him. "You loved him," she said.

Benhargan grunted as they came to a massive set of doors blocking their path. A thick stone lintel framed the top of the wooden portals.

Men stood on top of the wall, spears, and bows ready to repel attack. A man with a long black beard peered over the wall.

"Who are you and what is your business here in the city?"

Benhargan casually glanced up. "We're travelers from afar who come for respite, sport, and drink!"

"Respite, sport, and drink?" the man repeated. "What news of the three triangles?"

"Far to the south they are massing an army. We escaped before they took the city of Phisnor. The foe gains conscripts as his forces slither like a snake through the countryside - a snake that would take ten leagues to walk from head to tail-tip."

"Come in and take shelter," the man said, and the door came open.

Kaltopia and Benhargan entered a long narrow hallway – stone walls on either side.

The black bearded man met them inside the passage leading through the thick wall.

"Others have come here too," he said to Benhargan.

"What is the word of your preparations to ward off a siege?" Benhargan asked.

The king has sent runners to the kingdoms within Ophir, Argos, Zingara, Aqualonia, Nemedia, and Corinthia. We are to hold the gates that lead to the northern borders of Argos, and Zingar until spring comes. There is enough food and water here to last three years."

The man looked at Kaltopia, then up at Benhargan. "A Cimmerian, and a Zingaran woman? Warrior companions, or more?"

"When it is important for you to know, I'll be sure to tell you," Benhargan replied.

"Very well, you are admitted into the walled city of Fron. You may be called upon to defend the walls." The man nodded to a soldier at the far end of the hall. The young man flipped up the latch, and let both enter the urban landscape.

Three story adobe buildings were sprawled out like wheel spokes a thousand cubits long, all leading toward a raised stone center. Along these ever-narrowing pathways, cobblestones paved the way to a grand temple. Hundreds of inhabitants moved freely along these access ways.

The two weary warriors followed one such path. At the end, the access led to the Thera Temple – born of white stone, and rising more than five stories into the sky. Benhargan stopped and examined the walls that marked the end of the street and started the temple access. He stretched out his mighty arms and with his fingers fully extended, he touched both sides of the narrowing walls.

"They are clever," he said.

"Who?" Kaltopia asked.

"Those who built this city. These streets lead upward, and funnel an enemy to these choke points where few men can hold at bay hundreds, if not thousands," he said.

"Where do we go from here?"

Benhargan pointed across the temple grounds to hundreds of carts and awnings. The market was bustling with city dwellers seeking luxury goods and freshly picked vegetables of every color. "There we will find an answer to a question," he said.

"What question is that?" Kaltopia asked.

"Where the taverns and wine bars are."

Benhargan sat back and rested his elbow upon the surface of a rough wooden table. He looked along the bench, of which he sat, and examined Kaltopia. He surmised they both could make use of a bathhouse.

He lifted the large drinking bowl to his lips and consumed the rich, red wine. "More!" he called out.

A meek dark-skinned fellow came and poured the libation into his bowl.

"These puny containers will never slack the thirst of a Cimmerian!" Benhargan proclaimed.

Kaltopia put down a still steaming leg of mutton and picked up her own wine – which seemed very large in her dainty hand.

She wiped her mouth with the back of her sleeve and gulped down the libation.

"I have been thinking," she began. "Once we have rested, we should make our way to my homeland. I will have my father make you a commander in our army. Together, we can defeat this enemy who would be lord over Hyboria."

Benhargan smiled, reached over and took the mutton. He tore off a large flap of flesh and consumed it in a ravenous fervor. Again, he consumed a generous portion of wine. "More!" he commanded. "What makes you think your father would make me a commander?. I think you have a naïve view of how these things are decided. In fact, your father probably thinks you were kidnapped by Cimmerians, and perhaps sold into slavery," he added.

She chuckled. "My father would not believe such things. Though I am a princess, I was forged a fighter. My king would not think so little of my recommendations."

"We will see," Benhargan said.

They ate and drank for many hours. Through the small windows that lined the walls, he saw the fire-orange and blood-red of the sun growing old.

"Come," he said, stood and made for the door.

"Shall we try the inn at the far side?" Kaltopia asked.

"That is a very good thought," Benhargan replied. "Then, perhaps we shall visit the bathhouse."

The door came open and they stepped out onto the dark flagstones of the temple square. He raised his hand to shield his vision from the last light of the retreating sun.

"And so, it shall be said that Hyro ben Hasmer cleaned the vermin from the streets of Fron."

Benhargan stopped. In front of him were dark figures surrounded by the blaze of the dying sun. But, the voice he knew.

"If you wish to clean the shit from the streets, then fall upon your swords and be collected!" Benhargan jibbed.

"I will miss that humor... it has served you to the last," Hasmer stated.

From a blinding light came dark shapes. A pair of eyes shone like the fire of the underworld. About Benhargan's chest he felt the coils. In the darkness of his own mind, something told him to close his eyes. His blade came to hand, and he leapt into his enemy.

His ears served him well, for from the side came attackers – sloppy with clanking armament. He spun, cleaved, smashed, and cleaved some more. The welcome sensation of warm blood spattered him, as screams of dying men filled the air.

"I fear your snake-ways not!" shouted Benhargan. "Now, I come for you, magician!"

Singing cut through the sounds of metal and snapping bone. The sound washed over him - a disturbing noise, not at all like Grimface's magic. He spun, looked down at his feet, gained symmetry, and lurched for the singer. His blade vibrated, ringing out like the harmony of a thousand Amazonian lyres.

Hasmer's singing stopped as he back-peddled to avoid the barbarian's attack. A brimstone stench wafted over him, and Benhargan opened his eyes. A monstrous black beast was striking at him with its razor-sharp claws. Two of the implements of death cut through his leather vest and flesh, striking two ribs in the process.

He felt the meat of his chest laid open, and the sensation of his own vital fluids draining down his waist and legs. The creature turned and flew at him again. This time he parried, and with all his strength freed the monster's arm from its shoulder. The thing roared, and fell back.

Behind him, Benhargan realized there was fighting taking place. He turned and raced into the fray. Kaltopia was bloodied, and he made it to her just as her strength failed. Ten armored men had taken their toll on her.

Benhargan kicked one man out of the way, and smashed another with the pommel of his sword. The others came at him, and in his fury, he left none alive. Turning, he saw the green-robed Hasmer with his arms crossed. The sun fell below the buildings and darkness enveloped them.

"You and I have a meeting coming – and I will have your eyes strung like pearls for a necklace when it is done, barbarian!" Hasmer pulled the folds of his robes over himself, a puff of putrid smelling purple smoke filled the air. The magician was gone.

About Benhargan's feet lay many men – or rather pieces of men. He rushed to Kaltopia. Her limbs were limp. He cradled her in his arms. Blood continued to pump from the many lacerations.

Her eyes came open. "Father?" she asked. "Father, I am cold, and afraid."

"You will be fine," Benhargan said. "I am proud of you."

She looked at Benhargan, and a moment of realization appeared in her dimming orbs.

"It is good of you to lie to me," she stated. "Those heralds of death come for me now."

Her sword fell from her right hand, and her dagger from her left. She was alive no more.

BENHARGAN WANDERED the river valleys and lush foothills of Zingara. His eyes were blinded by grief, and his heart heavy. Days were like the strands of a spider's web, all spun together, trapping his very soul.

From afar he saw long lines of soldiers moving south. The beat of the war drum thumped and rumbled in his ears.

As his mind steadily cleared, he knew that there was only one place he could go to find solid ground – the Pict wilderlands. Taking a bearing he headed north-west toward the Aqualonian Frontier.

His travel was swift, for he had regained his mental footing and ranger ways. Many leagues he traveled, day to night, and night to day. Finally, he smelled the scents that he knew far too well – the ranger camps.

The ranger captain seemed less pleased to see him. And, as Benhargan briefed the hardened leader of his travels, the man did not become sympathetic until the barbarian spilled out the last of his treasure onto the captain's desk.

"I have heard that there is a war coming," the captain said.

"A man claiming to be a pure-blood prince of Atlantis," Benhargan added.

"The Picts have stepped up their raids all along the border," the captain replied.

"I can guess whose allegiance they have pledged their warriors too," Benhargan stated.

The captain reached behind himself to a chest, and produced a black flag with gold triangles.

"We have encountered their pay-masters. A fierce foe they are. If you are agreed, I need you to take fifty men up to the Harbanger's Roost. Our scouts have reported that a shaman has been inciting the clans. It is unclear as to how many Picts have rallied to him. Find out what you can, then report back to me."

Benhargan turned to go.

"Wait," the captain said. "That friend of yours..."

"He is dead these many months now."

"While I'm sorry it wasn't you, Bulvife was a good ranger," the captain told him.

"A great ranger," Benhargan stated, then turned and left the tent.

# CHAPTER 21
# Chasing the Blue Dragon

BLOOD OOZED FROM GRIMFACE'S wounds. The deep scratches and punctures all over his body were inflamed and burning from the saturation of sweat. His escape from the briar-walled stockade bore witness to his desperation - by keeping bits of his flesh as souvenir.

The crunch of leaves and branches echoed with each footfall. He willed his stride wider by the moment as his pursuers gained on him. If they were to capture him again, Grimface knew they would do to him what they did to the other captured souls— sandwich them between wicker webs and burn them with rolls of red hot reeds one spot at a time until all the skin was gone.

He shuddered at the thought.

His foot sank into a hole - he tumbled, rolled, and came up running. Behind him, the shouts and war cries of the Picts cascaded from his left, right, and directly at the back. If only he could speak, if only he could sing to summon a protective demon, or raise a mist to hide within - but the Pict shaman had made sure he was mute – a dark spell to deaden his tongue and throat. But now, there was no breath for song. His lungs churned out gulps of air like a mad bellows for one purpose only -to save his life.

He drove headlong into a creek, then up the muddy bank and into a wide meadow. The smell of wildflowers was thick as he dashed on. At the center was two depressions filled with water.

He ran between the black pools and toward the forest fence beyond. His muscles burned, as did his lungs, and as he nearly reached the forest, he stepped into a hole and felt something tear in his leg. His mind cried out as he fell hard into the tall grass. Scrambling up, he hopped on one leg to a stand of trees that demarked the start of the greenwood. He was spent. Here, he'd fight to the last.

I'll not be taken alive, he thought

A hundred Picts poured across the meadow leaping this way and that. At the front was Keochi, the son of the chief shaman. He shook his head like a lion causing the bright, red-feathered headdress to show like a peacock's tail. His face, painted white like death with coal-black around his eyes and along his jaw, showed no pity.

Behind him, sporting many feathers and cockleshell beads, were his followers - hungry for Grimface's flesh. Keochi saw him and slowed. The Pict shouted and all his men laughed loudly. They began to walk toward him, sensing he'd given up and was now easy prey.

Something dropped onto Grimface's shoulder. He didn't move. It slithered down over his chest.

It's over, he thought. A poisonous tree phar – a mercy killing by the goddess, I pray.

He said a silent prayer, but, no bite came, and he cautiously looked up. A hemp rope dangled down, and at the other end was a beast of a man dressed in leathers, and armed with a sturdy bow.

Grimface looked again out into the field. Keochi had removed his obsidian dagger and as he approached, he cocked his head, and his face took on an evil appearance as if to say, I shall maim you so we can have sport later.

They approached, forming a half circle to block his escape.

"Ki cacho, ic ye," Keochi said, but stopped with a look of stunned surprise.

Two arrows were in his chest. He looked up into the trees ahead just as the strum of many bows sent hundreds of arrows into the meadow. In the blink of an eye all of Keochi's men were slain.

Down the rope came the brute. Other ropes descended, and forty-nine other rangers landed on the ground.

"I could not mistake such a face as yours," said Benhargan. He took the mystic by the shoulders and embraced him. "What is wrong, why do you not speak?"

Grimface motioned to his mouth and throat. He shook his head.

Benhargan nodded. "The vile Picts have cut out his tongue! Poor fellow," Benhargan said to his brethren rangers. He turned back to Grimface. "You look much worse for wear. I take it those Picts didn't treat you to honeyed temple prostitutes and horns of wine. No matter. We have enough food in our camp to feed you proper. I must say though that it is an amazing gift of the gods that the wizard who held back a volcano, and traveled through the lands of the dead, stands before me." He chuckled, then grunted. "I will lead you back to the river and across to safety. There at the ranger's camp you will rest and recoup. When you are stronger, I will lead you to Ghe Inote the walled city. The Pict's will bother you no more."

Grimface broke free of Benhargan's grip and hobbled back out into the meadow. He approached the corpse of Keochi and knelt down. He tore an oddly shaped talisman on a thong from the dead man's neck. Taking the Pict's knife, Grimface cut into the man's chest and removed his heart. He stood and hobbled back to Benhargan with the bloody prize in one hand and the ivory carving in the other.

"You thank me in a very strange way," Benhargan said.

Grimface shook his head and pointed at the leather bag at the side of the warrior.

"You want me to put those in here?"

The wizard nodded.

Benhargan shrugged and laughed. "Your mage-ways are always a surprise to me!"

"Cut off their hands, feet, and cocks," commanded a large man with a long blond hair and mustache as he pointed at the dead. "Scatter their parts among the creatures of the forest. That way, those heathens cannot take pleasure in the afterlife."

The rangers moved into the meadow and commenced to do the grisly work.

Benhargan motioned for Grimface to follow, but the wizard's strength failed him and he fell. Slowly he struggled to get up onto his good leg.

Benhargan reached down and hoisted the man up, and onto his back. "Don't worry, old wizard, I'll not leave thee to doom on this peaty ground."

He carried Grimface into the dark woods and the safety of the ranger's encampment far beyond the river.

GRIMFACE TOOK UP A branch and put one end into the fire. He let it catch and burn, then shook it out. He grabbed a white flat stone and on it carefully scribed words in Aquilonian.

Benhargan looked the stone over and shrugged.

"He is dead somewhere near the seasonal rivers in the Kush desert. We heard there was a treasure in an old tomb, but carelessly he triggered a trap. A thick granite slab fell over the door. Bulvife did not emerge, lo we waited many days there. He could not have lived."

Grimface took back the stone, wiped it with some water and laid it by the fire to dry. After a few minutes, he held it and scrawled again. He handed it to his friend.

"She died a warrior's death – a sword in her hand and many slain at her feet. We were ambushed, and though I was occupied with killing, she held the flank from those fiends. I owe a dark magician a slow death for sending her to the lands of the dead," Benhargan said as he lifted a jar of beer to his lips and drank. "We can go to Ghe Inote when you're ready. I've played out my lust for Pict blood in these lands. Have you been inside the walls of Ghe Inote before?"

Nodding, Grimface pointed at the rock. Benhargan nodded and handed it back.

"You are lucky to have escaped the Picts with only your tongue missing. It is well known that they relish the torture of their captives as much as a Cimmerian loves battle."

Grimface scrawled and handed the stone across.

Benhargan examined it. "I see. So, they did not cut out your tongue or scar your throat with a red-hot stick. An evil spell is upon you, and the heart and talisman can be used to reverse it. And, you have a friend who lives in Ghe Inote? This man you call Jup son of Jep can do this?"

Grimface nodded.

"We will find him. If he lives within the city walls!'

Grimface's leg was in pain and he pointed at a jar of wine sitting near the fire pit. Benhargan fetched it and handed it to him. The wizard drank deeply, then set down the vessel and took up the stone and stick again. He handed the rock to the Cimmerian.

"I'll see to it," he said and stood. "It should take a half hour to get the herbs, berries, and mushrooms. The river rocks will take a little less effort. Not to worry, I'll be back before you know it." Benhargan took up his bow and arrows and strode off from the camp and into wilderness.

GRIMFACE PLACED THE cold flat river stones along the inside of his thigh. He'd damaged it, but it would heal. The tonic he created stole away the pain, freeing his mind to wander into ethereal realms.

He watched the flames of the fire glow bright orange with halos of color feathered out into the surrounding air. A voice was deep within his mind, chanting, praying, calling to him from some far-off place.

A wild beast appeared, shrouded in the dark areas beyond the firelight. The shimmering shadows of those spirits that lurked in ancient woods - the old gods, and their servants. Into a deep sleep, he descended - all the while that far-off chanting filled his ears.

Grimface sat up. In the distance, the horizon was filled with a crimson red, as the sun rose. He took up a stone and wrote.

Benhargan approached and knelt, looked at the stone, then shrugged.

Grimface scrawled further. 'I dreamt the goddess spoke to me and said, Allu thulu com alut.'

Benhargan looked over the stone and made a face that expressed sympathy for a man who might be insane. He went to the fire and fetched some meat, then handed it to Grimface and sat back.

"What does it mean?" the barbarian asked.

'Follow to the place where the blue dragon is overhead', Grimface jotted down. He picked up several stones and began to write more, 'It is known by the magi of the desert as the blue dragon. Of all the stars in the sky it comes to visit our world once in three hundred years and bodes tidings of doom, victory, or the coming of a king.'

Benhargan grunted. "So, what of it? An evil prince is loose in the lands of Hyboria, there is much death and war about, and kings are born every day – so, this blue dragon tells us things we already know. Seems useless."

'It is foretelling of the birth of a god-king,' Grimface wrote.

"Just what we need – a god-king in Hyboria," Benhargan said. "Oh well, that means more war, wealth, and valor for those like me."

Grimface smiled. 'I have seen bodies piled high, and two Cimmerians decimating an enemy force at a thousand to one. Then, the vision showed me those warrior-barbarians lost from sight.'

"Ah – a glorious death! Now, that is something that interests me. But, with Bulvife gone, what other Cimmerian is it in your vision?"

'That, I cannot say,' Grimface wrote.

THEY TRAVELED FOR DAYS through thick woods and vast reed-bogs. From time to time they came across a bog-man, black as pitch, floating lifelessly in the dark waters – the shock from his sacrifice etched upon his face as fresh as the day he was slain.

On the fifth day, they came to a rocky hill and began a climb upward. A path and stairwell of stone was hewn from the cliff making for easy travel.

Once over the hill, they saw a valley surrounded by mountain peaks. The mud brick walls of the city Ghe Inote ran for miles forming a hexagonal enclosure. Through the middle ran a clear river of white water that was fed from the distant mountains.

Outside the walls, many miles of fields and green grazing lands stretched to the base of the mountains. Inside the walls, he saw buildings packed closely together, and in the center of the city a palace grew from the rocky terrain.

"By nightfall we will be inside the city," Benhargan said.

Once down from the rocky hills they followed a herdsman's path to a cobblestone road. The traveling was quick and easy and by the time of the setting sun, they had arrived at the gates.

Two guards recognized Benhargan and welcomed him. They opened the doors and both he and Grimface entered the thriving city.

"It is the stench of cities that I cannot abide," Benhargan began as they started down a narrow street. "A man, used to the free air of the woods and mountains, shrivels up within the walls of such a place as this."

Sewage ran down channels cut in the center of the pathway, and from time to time a person would step out of their front door and heave a bucket of filth into the street.

None took notice of the two men as they approached the marketplace. Grimface pulled on Benhargan's shirt sleeve. The brute stopped and turned back.

"What is it?"

Grimface pointed toward a two story, white-walled building. Benhargan narrowed his gaze then shrugged. The wizard frowned, knelt and drew the word for Jup. Benhargan nodded.

The barbarian's meaty fist slammed against the door several times. Above them a window opened, and an old bearded man looked out.

"What is it?"

"Do you know a man called Grimface?" Benhargan asked.

"Who wants to know?" The old man knitted his brow.

"Are you called Jup, son of Jep," Benhargan asked.

"When you answer my question, I'll answer yours," the man replied.

"I am Benhargan, friend and protector of he who calls himself Grimface. And, here," he pointed with his hand, "is Grimface. He bid me to bring him to the house of Jup. Can you help or no?"

"Why does that man not speak for himself?"

"He has been struck dumb by evil magic, and needs the help of a friend who can reverse it," Benhargan told him.

The face above vanished, and moments later the door opened.

"Come in," the old man said. "I am Jup son of Jep, and I do know a man called Grimface."

"You wizards waste much time talking." Benhargan shook his head. "Much wasted time in talk, and little action when called upon!"

# CHAPTER 22
## The Heart of the Matter

JUP MADE TEA. HIS BLACK iron cauldron bubbled and boiled. Taking a ladle, he poured out some of the hot water into cups made of fired pottery. Into those cups, he put a ground powder of herbs and leaves.

"When it is done steeping we shall have a good drink," he said.

For a moment, all was quiet, only the crackle of the fire was heard.

"It is a delicate matter to undo a shaman's magic. But Pict magic I know quite well. You've come to the right place." Jup said. "If Grimface could speak, he would say that my power is strong."

Grimface stood by the fire pit. He warmed his hands for a moment, then presented a wry smile to Benhargan.

Jup came by with a long piece of gray slate and a hunk of white chalk. He motioned for Grimface to write. As the wizard took up the chalk, Jup returned to the cups and brought one over to each man before taking his own and sitting down at the pit.

"How long have you been afflicted?" Jup asked.

Grimface scrawled, 'A month, perhaps a little more'.

"That is all? A magician half as good as I could undo this... that means that even the great Grimface could undo this, if he was not so stricken!" Jup laughed.

Grimface shook his head, and handed over the two items that Benhargan carried for him.

"We are in luck. You've secured an image of their god and a fresh heart – at least somewhat fresh. It should take little time for the effects of this evil magic to be banished," Jup said. He stood, blew into his cup, gingerly tested it with his lips, then drank some down. "You'll be singing in short order my friend." He smiled.

Benhargan sniffed his cup, then put it aside. "Don't you have any drink suitable for men?"

Jup chuckled. "I've never seen a man afraid to drink a tea such as this before."

Taking up the cup, Benhargan growled. "Nor will you this day, but I'd better be compensated with mead, wine, beer, or better to belay this insult."

Grimface handed the slate to Benhargan, whose mood quickly softened. Then, the mute wizard took it back, rubbed the words away and wrote more. These he handed to Jup.

"I see," Jup drank more of his tea. "The blue dragon that travels the heavens is now in the house of Set, a grim and cruel god. We have been seeing the snake markings more and more along the caravan paths of the south. They are markings by the priest and worshipers of Set noting its coming, but I don't think they have read the signs correctly." He looked at Grimface. "I see in your eyes, neither do you."

Benhargan finished his cup of tea and stood.

"If you ply me with no spirits, I will seek them elsewhere," he said.

Jup stood and walked to a wooden shelf hidden behind the stairs. He returned with a jar and handed it to the barbarian.

"Drink this and sit with peace upon your lips."

"What is it?" Benhargan asked.

"Wine brewed from berry, and colliway nectar. I assure you it is unlike any drink you have drunk," Jup replied.

Benhargan tore away the wax lid and sniffed the contents. He raised an eyebrow and put the rim of the jar to his lips. Tipping up the container, he took a fearless drink.

"It fills my limbs with the thought of battle, and passion for a ready woman!" He drank again, but with more commitment. "By Crom, this is a libation that causes a man to soar like an eagle, and dream the music of the Valkyrie, whose breasts heave with lust of battle and coupling!"

The thick red liquid dribbled down his chin and onto his chest. The container rose again, and after quaffing, he set the empty container onto the ground by the fire, and collapsed into a pile of furs.

"Two brass will... so call you to my chamber... in with laurels, and bells, and soaring fables of temple, I take your baked bread..." he mumbled, then fell unconscious.

Jup chuckled. "The lesser beasts are so easily led with treats."

Grimface handed him his slate. Jup looked it over, then looked back at Benhargan.

"You speak the truth; I'd never say as much in front of him." Jup rubbed his hands together. "Now my friend, let us take care of this darkness that engulfs your power, and get you on the path to wake the new born god-king."

He set the talisman on a small dais, then set the blood-black heart on a stone near the fire. Grimface sat opposite the heart, and across from the dais.

In a low guttural tone, Jup began to chant. Smoke swirled from the fire and up though the smoke-hole in the roof. Darker and darker the smoke became until, suspended over the glowing embers, there was a terrible sight. A creature with a hundred eyes looked on them, its fangs dripping venom, and its claws like that of a dire bear.

Jup held the talisman up as he continued to chant, but his tone increased in tempo and soon the room was surrounded by fire and twisting black apparitions. Grimface fell prostrate, as silver lines of crackling power penetrated his body. He twisted like a worm on a hook as blood came from his ears, mouth, nose, and eyes.

Jup stood and approached the black heart. He raised a flint knife, called a strange word loudly, and drove the blade into the mass. Grimface screamed out, and the room fell silent. A stench of brimstone remained as the apparition roared loudly, then faded.

Jup approached the unconscious magician and rolled him face up. Blood was still coming from his nose. He lifted the bleeding man up against the wooden wall and returned to the fire.

The small talisman appeared twisted and deformed. On the stone, the sacrificial heart was black as a cinder. Jup got another jar of wine, approached the unconscious Cimmerian, and sat down. Drinking slowly, he gazed at the fire.

"It is a small thing to free your voice, Grimface," Jup said. "And, when the time is nigh, you will send that son of Atlantis to his forefathers."

Laying back, Jup closed his eyes.

"BENHARGAN," A FAMILIAR voice said.

Benhargan woke and looked about the room. Grimface was sitting cross-legged opposite him.

"I dreamt I had battled Crom!" he began. "And when I defeated him, he offered me a woman. She spoke, and her voice was that of Grimface!" The barbarian rubbed his eyes. He looked over and noticed Jup motionless lying on his back. He looked across the fire at Grimface. "I am glad I'm awake now, for the thought of a woman who sounds like you disturbs the very marrow of my being."

"And disturbing it should be, barbarian," Grimface said.

"You do speak!" Benhargan stood. "Your voice is returned to you! What wonders - that old man is a wizard after all."

"He is a powerful one," Grimface confirmed. "Now that my voice is restored, I have much to tell you."

"If it is a longwinded story, I shall need some beer to fill my gullet." Benhargan turned toward Jup, "What of him?"

"Let him rest. We will seek drink elsewhere, and return when we've had our fill," Grimface said.

Benhargan pushed the door to the tavern open and went in. The inside was lit by lamps and a fire pit. "So, tell more of this plan to fight and kill thousands," he said.

"The goddess has granted me a vision. This is what I surmise from it: We will be in an ancient fortress - walled in on three sides. Thousands of enemy soldiers will fall upon us with fury."

"I like the story so far," Benhargan said. "Your vision is a fanciful image. Two against thousands? Last time the odds were such, you had the god-king's amulet, but now we have only you... you are no magical amulet of a god-king."

"Wit will serve us nearly as well," Grimface stated.

"Tell me of where to find a named blade, imbued with the symbol for blood-letting - now that is a practical thing. Though, I have seen you call upon the dark magic and send many to their deaths. But, you cannot hold out against thousands," Benhargan told him.

Grimface smiled. "All I have to defeat is Bailgard – he is the keystone. Slay him, and the rest will break and flee."

"To view the future only wastes my time." A girl set down a pitcher of beer on the table. Benhargan picked it up and drank, then wiped his mouth with the back of his hand. "You have not mentioned why we would be at this ancient fortress. What is there – treasure? Is it gold, or jewels?"

"Glory," Grimface casually said.

Benhargan sat forward. "Glory? What sort of glory?"

"That which befalls men skilled in the art of war. A statue will be erected of you, to stand testament to your prowess," Grimface told Benhargan.

"Statue? How ridiculous! You babble nonsense now. Know this though, I've grown fond of bathing in mercenary blood," Benhargan stated. "This you have my attention with. How soon?"

"We will need to leave at dawn tomorrow, if we are to make it to the city of Boron."

"Where is this city called Boron?" Benhargan gulped down more beer.

"You know it by another name," Grimface said.

"What name?"

"Carpotinum, in Politain."

"A place filled with temples, greed, and wealth," Benhargan stated. "I could find a purpose there. Many women to bed in the temple-brothels, and much food to feast, and drink to quaff! I will need to stop by my hoard to take some gold with us. It is not far from here."

"Hoard?" Grimface looked surprised.

"Over the years, Bulvife and I have stashed much in the way of treasure. Neither of us has had time to spend it all. Instead of revel, I have spent most of my time following a damn fool wizard and doing his bidding."

"I never suspected!" Grimface laughed.

"One thing you can expect - where I go, death will follow," Benhargan said in a menacing tone.

Grimface smiled. "Of that I'm sure, and am counting on."

GRIMFACE AND BENHARGAN sat at the fire pit in Jup's house. Benhargan put some wood on the coals and waited for the flames to grow large.

He took some meat and impaled it with a skewer, and placed it over the embers. Before long, it was leaking fat and causing the flames to leap and snap.

"Bulvife and I met a princess. She was near a pond where she grappled with some terrible monster... then Bulvife copulated with her."

Grimface sat forward. "The place with the map?"

Benhargan shrugged his massive shoulders. "Yes." He handed Grimface the map.

"Why did you not speak of this before?"

"I was busy thinking of all the things I plan to do in Politain," Benhargan answered. "The princess told Bulvife of a cave below a sacred pool. There we found your note and the room with many scrolls... many, many scrolls – by Crom's hairy balls, the scrolls were endless!"

"Did she have a set of three triangles tattooed upon her back?" Grinface asked.

"She did. A sorceress me thought at the time," Benhargan told the wizard. "Her eyes were golden, and her skin as brown as thistle honey." The Cimmerain folded his arms over his chest.

"The daughter of our foe. She is the princess in my vision," Grimface stated as he unrolled and looked at the map.

The wizard sat back and examined the document. "She told you how to get into the grotto?" Grimface was very serious.

"She did."

"Then she must be an ally," Grinface surmised.

"Why do you say that?" Benhargan's eyes showed curiosity.

"She gave you access to the chamber that contained the key to her father's fortress where she will be held captive." The wizard held up the map. "This is where Bailgard's forces are." He pointed. "And this is where she will be found. On the back side, we find where we will make our stand." He turned the document over and pointed at a map of a savanna plain.

"Looks like the Yeshi Mohan Valley in Shem," Benhargan said.

Grimface paused, looked up at the roof and said, "At last...".

# CHAPTER 23
## The Quest for the God-King

GRIMFACE TURNED TO Jup. "Thank you my friend for saving my life and restoring my voice. Few could have done such."

Jup nodded. "The gods demanded my intervention, how could I refuse? Accomplish your task, Grimface, and I will sing of your accomplishments when you are in the afterlife. The gods and their servants will welcome you into their mighty hall."

Grimface smiled, then took the reins of a horse that Benhargan acquired. "Keep safe, for magicians are growing fewer by the year in this world."

Jup nodded.

The hulking barbarian emerged from the dwelling and secured some bags over the haunches of his own animal. He then secured several large gourds filled with mead, and skins full of wine. Once done, he climbed onto his horse and pulled the reins to direct the beast through the square.

"May you die in a less foul place than this," Benhargan said over his shoulder to Jup.

Jup chuckled. "There are many worse places to die, my giant friend. You may learn this first hand someday." He turned to Grimface. "Do you remember the charm spoken by Suxor to enchant Crispin the hero and make him invulnerable?"

"Of course. It is one of the first ancient spells that were taught to me. Why do you ask?"

"When you are besieged, and the enemy has overcome your defenses – sing it loud."

"That only worked because Suxor had drank the elixir of the gods," Grimface replied.

"Exactly," Jup said.

Grimface climbed atop his steed, his face betraying the puzzlement he felt from Jup's comment. "There will be those who come this way searching for us," Grimface said. "Keep a vigil for them, for they will do you ill."

"I fear little for that nonsense. As my age grows, my patience shortens, and if those of whom you speak come, they will suffer my wrath," Jup retorted.

"Woe be upon the heads of your enemies," Grimface added, as he and his horse vanished into a nearby alley.

It was not a long trip to the gate. As they approached, a man manning the wall shouted down.

"Ranger, where are you off to now?"

"To reap more heads for the wall spikes," Benhargan responded.

The guard laughed and turned back to face the wilds. Two men at the gate opened it, and Grimface and Benhargan rode out onto the northern road.

"Where did you really get these horses?" Grimface asked.

"From the stables of the Lord of Guards himself, Talibach the Clever," Benhargan said.

Grimface laughed. "He'll surely miss the horses at some point."

"He is a fat, pathetic, weak creature; he nearly shat himself when I spoke to him. He will make no fuss."

"Few would," Grimface admitted.

THE NORTHERN ROAD WOUND through dark green pasture lands and low rolling hills. In the distance, they saw a large depression. Benhargan dismounted. Taking the reins, he began to walk the horse.

Grimface did the same and came along side. "That bowl ahead of us is a bog. We must be careful not to end up disturbing the bog-men and other things that linger there. The spirits in that place are easily disquieted."

"Nothing a swift blade and a few arrows won't resolve," the barbarian replied.

Grimface looked deep in thought as he walked. "I have my voice back and can summon protection to watch over us at night," he added.

"Why does your goddess not just protect us?" Benhargan sarcastically asked.

"She is a goddess, and busy with more important celestial things – I'm sure. Does sacred, honest work frighten you, barbarian?"

Benhargan growled. "Do not try my patience wizard with your riddles. Demons or not, if I wished to snap your neck, it could be done before you fill the air with your pretty voice."

Grimface smiled. "The goddess has taken action. She's chosen me because of my faith. She's chosen you because of your lack of faith."

"Lack of faith? I have faith in death. I am filled with the faith that Crom endowed me with - courage to defeat my foes, to take what I want, and die in battle. I have faith that you will challenge me with your magic, and your wizard ways. And I have faith that after death I will climb the sacred mountain where my god dwells, and he will watch as I fight with sword and shield, like my father, and his fathers have done - and do even now."

"You will have faith of a different kind in the end, I am told," Grimface added.

Benhargan stopped and grabbed Grimface's reins. "You say much about me, but tell me little." He looked down at the magician with a scowl. "Tell me one thing; do you see me not drowning you in the bog for your arrogance?"

"Perhaps I should change the subject," Grimface stated, and took his reins back. As he did, he thought he saw the slightest hint of a smile on the brute's face. "These matters seem to upset you."

They walked in silence for hours, until their feet became wet. Benhargan took the lead and maneuvered their way along mossy ridges that protruded from the black and stinking waters.

From time to time they saw the black leathery corpse of a bog-man floating in the dark ponds. There were other things lurking in that water—things looking up from the depths, things that made Benhargan clutch the hilt of his sword.

Grimface felt powerful dread flowing along his spine. If they were not careful, something might come calling on them, and it wouldn't just be the dead men that littered the festering swamp.

By late afternoon, Benhargan maneuvered onto a small island. "We will camp here tonight," he said as he found a place big enough for both, and their horses. "I'll gather firewood, you make the fire."

There were fist-sized rocks strewn about, and Grimface gathered them into a ring. He put some tinder in the middle, stacked dried briar scraps, and ignited it.

As the fire burned, the sun dipped toward the high mountains to the northwest making a long shadow that crept ever closer to them.

He watched Benhargan move along the ridges gathering up chunks of dried wood from the remains left by the stilted, gray, trees. By the time the barbarian returned, he had his two powerful arms full of fuel.

They ate and sat around the fire for several hours. The dried meat and rye biscuits satisfied them, and by the time the moon rose, they had drunk one gourd of honey-wine each.

Grimface asked about Bulvife, and Benhargan asked about Grimface's travels in the afterlife. When the conversation came to its natural end, Grimface stood and took a stick. He traced a large circle around them, put some ash from the fire in it, and then laid on his back.

No sound, save for the fire, filled the air. Grimface's eyes closed and he began humming. Benhargan watched.

Slowly, just beyond the light of the fire, and along the edge of the circle, a shadowy image clawed its way from the damp ground. Twice the height of the Cimmerian, the thing shook its black horns and snorted loudly.

The horses stamped their feet and stumbled about. Benhargan grabbed them both and held them, then turned them away to look out into the western bog-lands.

He checked their hobble-ropes and returned to the fire. Grimface exhaled loudly and lay on his back. It was clear that he was a bit pale from using his magic, and even a little shaken.

"I need to rest. Take the first watch and I will take the second, but for now, I have to close my eyes," Grimface told the barbarian.

"Wizards are frail," Benhargan added, then lay his sword over his lap and looked around. "How you will fight thousands of soldiers with that power, only the gods will tell." He looked out into the swampy waters. "If the bog-men come for you, will this demon-watcher keep you as safe as I?"

"He is not here to protect us from the bog-men," Grimface said.

Benhargan scooted back from the light of the fire. "Not the bog-men?" he asked. "What other than bog-men dwell in this stinking swamp?"

"When it comes, I will tell you," Grimface explained.

Through a misty haze, the moon glowed brightly as an ethereal orb. In the darkness, the sound of water churning came from every direction.

At first Benhargan was not sure if his eyes were playing tricks. There was something moving toward the camp. The sound of sloshing came from within the thickening mist, and it was growing louder.

A stench wafted over him; the stench of decay. He was careful not to move into the light of the fire. If there was going to be a fight, he wanted the element of surprise to be on his side.

The horses were nervous, stamping their hooves, snorting and whinnying. Dark forms shambled just beyond the ability of Benhargan to get a clear view of what they were.

Grimface's demon-guardian looked restless as it craned its head about from side to side.

"It is the Aunk that surrounds us, and its foul minions," Grimface said, as he sat up. "It cannot move beyond the confines of the holy circle and my demon." He stood and walked near the guardian. "It smells our souls. It is drawn to us, and wants to devour that which makes us whole. If we were not so protected, we would be drowned in the bog – made into bog-men."

Benhargan approached with his sword in his hand. "What sort of thing is this Aunk?"

"It is of the old world, worshiped by those who came before men. Once it reigned as a noble lord among the water spirits. But its appetites grew too bold. It was banished to the bogs after raping the daughter of the mountain spirit, and here it has fed upon the likes of all animals, including men. Beware, for it is now a thing with no pity."

"I fear no such creature," Benhargan boasted, brandishing his sword.

"You should. If it lays its tendrils on you, your soul will not arrive in the lands of your god Crom."

Benhargan looked concerned. "If it come for us, I'll take it screaming into the nine hells with me!"

White wisps surrounded them like willow branches hanging over a stream. While the ectoplasmic tentacles flexed and hovered about, they could not touch the two men.

For some time, the dark shapes in the fog moved in circles around the spit of land and its comforting fire. The demon moved from time to time and from side to side keeping the swamp things at bay.

Finally, a faint hint of light appeared in the sky, and the white tendrils recoiled into the mist. The shapeless things retreated, and by the time the sun crested the hills, only a festering bog remained.

Grimface dispelled his demon. "That was a lot of work for one night. We must move into the mountains by next night-fall. Without a solid rest, I will be useless if we are beset upon by anyone wielding the power."

"We'll make it to the mountains," Benhargan assured him. "But it might be close."

They walked their horses all day, and as night came again, they reached the dry incline of the foothills. By the time darkness was fully upon them, the bog lay long behind and shrouded in shadow. Upon the next morning, they entered the forest, and the sounds of animals scurrying about and fowl cawing filled the greenwood.

They traveled further south until the road took an abrupt turn and came to a mountain gate. Several soldiers milled about in front of the narrow pass.

"Halt!" one man wearing the helmet of a Tarantian commanded. "What is your business in Politain?" Benhargan opened his mouth to speak, but Grimface laid his hand on the barbarian's arm.

"We travel to Carpotinium. I have a brother there that needs a blacksmith and a jeweler," Grimface said.

The guard eyed them both with some suspicion. "This Cimmerian is big enough to be four blacksmiths!" His fellow soldiers chuckled. "But, why are his hands free of soot?"

"He has not worked for several weeks since our travels began. He is eager to work, even now his hands flex for a hammer and anvil," Grimface told the soldiers.

"Then enter Politain – if your intentions be supportive of the crown. If you come this way again, bring some extra jars of wine with you, for we who guard this pass live a lonely life."

Grimface nodded and let go of Benhargan's arm. "We will remember your kindness, good soldier," he said, as he moved into the gap.

They walked not more than a mile when several large men approached from the opposite way.

"Your horses, give them to us!" the largest of them demanded.

"You are Zingaran?" Benhargan said.

"What of it?" one of the men with stark white hair asked.

"It is often my experience that Zingarans are dull-witted, and better suited to gathering flowers, or milling grain," Benhargan told him.

The largest of them ground his teeth, eyed Benhargan and Grimface, looked up along the cliffs, then smiled. "Be smart and give us your horses and walk away with your lives."

Benhargan held the horse's head, leaned in, and whispered in the mare's ear. A moment later, he tilted his own ear to the horse's mouth. Turning back to the bandit he shrugged his mighty shoulders.

"My mare says that she declines your offer to copulate with her. It seems that you are more fettered to command the ass end of a goat, or perhaps a dog... she says," Benhargan told the man.

A few of the other men chuckled, but were silenced when the white haired man gave a stern look.

"You ride your tongue like a mindless whore," the man blurted, obviously searching for an adequate response but drawing an empty bucket from his well-of-insults. "Now, give over your horses!"

Benhargan handed Grimface his horse's reins. "Take this and wait to the side," he said. "This won't take long."

Grimface did so. "Don't take all day, remember that we're in a hurry."

The Zingarans took out curved sickle-swords, spread out along the path, and blocked Benhargan's way.

"Now you die," the large one said.

Benhargan did not wait for the man to finish his words, but attacked. The bandit fell back, his guts spilling out onto the dirty path.

The two at the wings rushed in, only to find Benhargan stepping back with a handful of their friend's intestines, pause, then throw the sausage-like entrails over the top of them. One of the men looked up at the gore raining down, and the barbarian beheaded him.

The last Zingaran unwound himself from his comrade's guts and thrust his sword, missed, and stepped back, coming away without an arm at the elbow.

The man missing his arm gripped the stump as blood pumped from the wound. Benhargan slowly walked over and took the man's head, then looked up along the craggy cliffs. Several men with bows drawn, cowered back into the shadows and vanished.

"Quick enough for you, wizard?" he asked.

Grimface nodded. "Seems like you're losing your speed in your old age. Hopefully your sloth was due to our recent hard traveling, and we can hope for improvements before your sword is called for again."

Benhargan let out a growl. "Wizards who standby and do nothing should keep their comments civil."

"Come along! Enough playing of games." Grimface handed Benhargan back his horse. "Mount up and let's make some time."

The two men exited the mountain pass and headed down the hillside. Ahead was one of the bandits, bow in hand, and in full flight.

As Benhargan came alongside, he said, "My advice is that you take up farming; the rough life of the wilds is not for you!" He drove his boot into the man's back.

The Zingaran tumbled into the dirt and rocks. He scrambled to his feet, turned abruptly, and rushed into some brush.

# CHAPTER 24
# Carpotinium

TORCHES ATTACHED TO poles lined the avenue leading to the main gate. As Grimface and Benhargan approached the city, the roads became choked with people, carts, and animals. Among the civilians were city-soldiers, and from time to time a caravan of horses and camels passed ladened with goods. The noise and dust added to the chaos, and by the time they reached the gates, both men were covered in a thick layer of red dust.

"What do you want in the city?" a gate guard asked.

"We're here to ply our trade as jeweler and blacksmith," Grimface stated.

"Move along," another guard shouted. "Keep em moving!"

Benhargan shoved his way through the throng. Grimface stayed close behind the massive barbarian, all the while listening to the passing conversations.

"The king is searching," one man with a herd of goats said to a younger man.

"The magi spoke of the prophecy," a woman with a child commented.

"He's ordered the arrest of any pregnant women," a young man said to his elder.

Grimface latched onto Benhargan's mighty arm and pointed. The Cimmerian nodded, and they made their way toward a wooden building on stilts.

Both climbed up the stairs; Benhargan lifted the latch, and they went inside. Smoke and darkness met their eyes, but the merriment and smell of stale beer and sweet-wine told them all they needed to know.

It took only a moment for their eyes to adjust to the low light, then a room came into focus—filled with bawdy women and inebriated men. Several young boys rushed from group to group filling cups for copper coins.

"Take some of that gold you have and secure us lodgings, food and wine for the night," Grimface instructed as he found an empty table and sat down.

Two dark skinned men approached.

"What is it you want?" Grimface asked.

One with a bent nose and vertical scar running down his chin spoke. "We saw you and your... friend come into the tavern. I'm sure you've heard the king is offering a hundred gold bars as bounty for anyone who can bring to him the pregnant woman carrying the prophecy child. I'd like to know if you'd join my group and we will all share in the profit."

"You know where this girl is?" Grimface asked.

The other fellow looked concerned. "Your Cimmerian friend will come with us, right? He will come in handy I think."

"And?" Grimface looked down at the table, then back up at the two men.

"Well," crooked nose stated, "I know something... of where to look for this woman."

"A Cimmerian is like a hundred normal men," the other man said. "We need his strength."

"What are these flies doing at our table?" Benhargan demanded as he approached.

The two men backed away. For a moment, it looked as if the two would bolt into the crowd.

"What is it you bother us with?" Benhargan barked.

Crooked nose looked down at the floor. "We've come bearing a proposition."

"They want us to join them to recover the woman that the king wants," Grimface repeated.

Benhargan grunted, and nodded. "Four will be better than two."

Grimface looked thoughtful, then motioned for the men to sit, which they promptly did and eyed the large jar of wine Benhargan had brought.

"We all stand to make a lot of money. What is it you know?" Grimface asked.

"No," crooked nose stated. "We cannot start out like that. We will keep our information and lead you to the woman. You two will secure her, and we all will bring her back here to the king."

Grimface looked as if he were in deep thought. "I see. And, we will split the reward in half?."

Crooked nose smiled, four bent teeth showing as his cracked lips parted. "In half? But, we know where she is. We shall keep two-thirds."

"Then, find another Cimmerian," Grimface said.

Crooked nose laughed. "Then, half it is. There is enough wealth to make us all rich as lords. This will be a good partnership. Now let's drink some of your wine to this contract."

Grimface fetched two more earthen cups, and Benhargan broke the seal on the jar. The wine flowed and soon the two swarthy men were slurring, and boasting of their exploits.

Grimface and Benhargan were quiet, listening all the while pouring more wine into the cups of their new companions, and less into their own.

"And, so we were about to lay hands on a gem in the garden of the Grand Vizier, but spied a strange little cage in the fore-yard. I looked in and saw a pair of golden eyes looking back. It was a young woman, supple flesh... oh so soft! She looked as easy and fresh as any I've had in the brothels."

"A slave girl, I'm sure," Benhargan said.

"Her belly was ripe. She turned to hide from my prying eyes, and then I saw it...the mark upon her back." Crooked nose reached across the table for the jar; the further he reached, the lower his head got to the table, until it was planted, and he began snoring.

The other man shook his friend, then smiled at his new companions. "Asiid is a good thief, but he cannot hold his wine. I am called Ka'halem the Nimble."

"What mark?" Grimface pressed.

"Three triangles," said Ka'halem.

"Who were you robbing?" Benhargan asked.

"The Barron, Vomish LeGar, who is the Grand Vizier. He came to town a year ago, and brought much gold and accolades to the king. Now he keeps company with a man of dark arts."

"What is the name of the man who the Barron keeps company with?" Benhargan asked.

"Hyro ben Hasmer," Ka'halem told them.

Grimface looked at Benhargan. "You know this magician?" He gave a knowing nod, then turned his attention to the thieves. "How did you get into his fortress?" Grimface questioned Ka'halem.

"It is not time for you to know. We are not fools. If I tell, you could cut our throats and keep the wealth for yourselves. With such reward offered, many have put aside their good nature, and many a blade has found a back to rest in. If we are to work together, you will have to trust us, and we you. Together, we have a chance of getting her... and the gold." He smiled, but did not grin. "You, this Cimmerian, and we, can bring the girl here, and afterward part rich men."

Benhargan spoke not, but just drank from his cup.

Grimface nodded. "We trust you will not cheat us. You two seem to know more of this business of thieving than we do. After all, we are but a jeweler and a black smith. I gather that you need our muscle and cunning - we will supply you with both. Meet us here tomorrow and we will make plans and travel to this place you know."

Ka'halem nodded. "I, Ka'halem agree." He patted Grimface's shoulder, then looked at Benhargan, but did not touch the man. "We will part company here and see you both tomorrow." Grabbing Asiid under his arms, Ka'halem helped his friend up, and out of the tavern.

Grimface turned to Benhargan. "There is no accounting for luck," he said.

"They are fools!" Benhargan told him. "Hyro ben Hasmer is not a man to take so lightly. It is only by divine powers they were not caught and tortured already."

"Perhaps..." Grimface added. "Perhaps."

THE BARKEEPER DIRECTED them to a thatched roof hut next to the tavern.

"The fire pit in the middle is clean. There is wood stacked in the back, and straw in the stable," said the tavern keeper. "It is never too cold here, so you will not freeze inside. Sleep well, don't die in there and make yourself a burden." He turned and walked back into the tavern.

Grimface made a fire and sat down next to it. He chanted softly. A black mist rose all around the room.

"We can sleep well tonight. Nothing can enter without dire consequences.

"I have a blade for that," Benhargan said.

"No, my friend, we both must gather our strength for the coming storm." Grimface lay back in the dirt, covered his face with his arm and slept.

"What if the danger comes from underneath?" Benhargan asked, but got no response.

He thought for a moment. The ol' wizard has not been wrong too often. He resolved to sleep too. Sleep came slowly, but when it settled in, Benhargan fell into a darkness that time forgot.

"The sun will rise soon. Come and let's meet Asiid and Ka'halem," Grimface said, as he pushed Benhargan on the shoulder with the toe of his boot. "If we're still lucky, they'll lead us to the girl."

Benhargan rose to his feet. He'd slept hard; so hard in fact, he'd drooled all over his shirt. Wiping his mouth, he looked around a bit disoriented.

"Bulvife's girl – the princess?"

"Yes – that's who we're going to steal way with," Grimface affirmed.

The wizard walked to the door and opened it. A cool new morning breeze caught his hair and tussled it. "I smell a storm coming," he said over his shoulder. "Come along, and set your mind to rights, for the way forward will not get any easier."

"Now, that's the first thing you've said in recent days that make any sense," Benhargan told him.

"HOW LONG AGO?" ASKED the man in the dark cowl.

"A few days," said the guard. "One was a jeweler, and the other a blacksmith."

"Anyone else come and ask about them?"

"Just you," said the guard.

"Good..." The man gave the Tarantian soldier a hand full of gold coins – enough wealth to cover his salary for a year. "Speak of this to no one, and know I'll find out if you do. If you do, when I return this way you'll find out what your fellow guard's gonads taste like – before I end your life."

"I will speak of this to none – ever," the guard stated.

"Good," the man said, as he brushed by the soldier and headed toward Carpotinium.

IT WAS NOT LONG BEFORE Asiid and Ka'halem arrived. They gathered the horses and provisions. As they walked their mounts toward the city gates, more and more armored soldiers appeared. By the time they exited, it was clear an army was being assembled.

"Looks as though the King of Carpotinium has eyes on stopping the prince," Benhargan stated.

Grimface made no comment, but followed with a solemn scowl upon his face.

They traveled for many miles into the tree-lined mountains, and across the expansive pasture lands littered with herdsmen. In the distance, stone structures ran up into the hills - ancient structures of the Acheron civilization, crumbling - rotted from within and without.

Benhargan, Asiid and Ka'halem began to head away from the grotesque stone monuments, but Grimface called them back.

"Tonight, we sleep within the walls of Vehal Ta Ahmen, the Vale City of Ahmen," he said.

"That place is cursed. It is said that once the streets ran with blood from human sacrifice," Asiid said.

"There have been screams of the dead heard there. We must not stay, for doom will befall us if we do." Ka'halem had a treble in his voice.

"If the wiz..." Benhargan cleared his throat, "the jeweler says it is where we stay, it is where we will stay." He turned and began trudging up the mountain toward the weathered rock walls.

In the distance a shadow was growing, and the sun was vanishing. They made it to the inverted V shaped gatehouse, and entered.

Moss, grass, and other plants ruptured from every vestibule, on the walls, and all around. A heavy scent of mushrooms and tilled earth was in the air.

Crumbled walls, twenty feet thick, made up much of the structures. Here and there were doorways, and sunken floors, and even empty storerooms.

Grimface seemed to know his way around, and in short-order he found a two-story building with one entrance and no windows. He led his horse in, hobbled it with a rope, and found a large gray stone to sit on. Benhargan did the same, as did their two companions, and soon a fire was made in the large hole at the center of the room.

Smoke wound its way up into the spider webs and bird's nests high in the roof, and finally out through the broken beams and tiles. For some time, they sat around eating provisions and drinking from wineskins.

After a while Asiid walked to the doorway but reeled back, terror in his eyes. "There is an unnatural glow down the passageway. We have made a mistake coming here."

"Calm yourself," Grimface told him. "There are spirits here, but they are not interested in us."

Benhargan grunted. "Good for them, or I would have many a specter sent to the underworld at my hand."

Grimface chuckled. "You can't kill the dead. They dwell here for want of another place to go. They linger for reasons we cannot know."

Benhargan looked at Grimface and shrugged. "No matter, I am sure you have something up your sleeve to remedy any fears our friends may have."

"Not tonight," Grimface said. "That is why I picked this place. Tonight, I sleep like a babe in swaddling cloth." He lay down by the fire, said a few words under his breath, and closed his eyes.

Ka'halem did not see the transformation in Grimface, but Benhargan did. He knew that the wizard would be watching with his demon sight - never completely leaving his life up to the doings of others.

Benhargan sat back and laid his sword over his lap, folded his arms, and drifted off to sleep.

A creature stood at his feet. Benhargan saw its shape - grotesque, misshapen. It snorted, and focused its blood read eyes on him.

"You search for many things, follower of Crom. You have laid waste to men, women, animals, and children. The rivers of blood you've forged flow through many worlds."

It shifted and stood tall in the room, nearly hitting its head on the broken roof beams. Again, it looked at Benhargan and an unknown feeling came over him— fear.

"I have come to deliver a message from a god who sees in you some virtue. A new kingdom of man will grow, and the way will be known to you... for a time."

"Does Bulvife dwell with Crom?" Benhargan asked.

"Bulvife?" The thing laughed. "You are deaf, blind, and lame!" it said to him. It shook its head and then drew in a deep breath, then roared down, toppling Benhargan to the ground.

Benhargan sat up. Sweat was beading up along his brow and face. He looked over to see Grimface in the darkness, watching him.

"What in the name of Crom was that thing?" Benhargan asked.

Grimface tossed some wood on the coals of the fire. A flame erupted, and an orange glow illuminated the room. "What thing?"

"Don't play games with me, wizard. Tell me or I'll wring it from your neck."

"You've had a dream? What was in the dream?" Grimface asked.

"A creature, a messenger from some god. It told me that I have virtue. Now tell me – what was it?"

"A messenger from Crom perhaps?" Grimface asked.

"No, that could not have come from Crom!" Benhargan stood and stepped over the two thieves.

Asiid and Ka'halem sat up, daggers in their hand. They looked around frightened.

"You had a dream or a vision," Grimface said to Benhargan. "The vision is gone. The messenger has seen you, and you have seen him. What that means, only those nebulous beings can tell."

Benhargan sat down. He looked at the thieves with a withering stare. They both remained quiet. The barbarian turned back to Grimface. "Traveling with you has always been trying, now it is most impossible. Why would a god send a messenger to me and not you? It is utter madness," he stated.

"Those gossamer beings visit me quite often," Grimface added.

A shimmering image came to the doorway. A spectral face looked in as if searching for something. It moved away. In the distance were sounds of sobbing and lamenting.

Languages, foreign to all present, reverberated from the walls.

Grimface quietly sat with just a hint of a smile on his face. "The sun will soon be up. We will need to head west. The King of Carpotinium builds his army, and seeks the princess to use her for his own means. Even now his soldiers travel past these ruins on their way to fight Bailgard. But, Bailgard is no fool and even now seeks the right ground in which to ensnare his enemies and make them conscript mercenaries. This day, we will travel well into the woods, as we skirt their ranks."

Asiid looked troubled. "Then how do we collect the money from the King of Carpotinium?"

Grimface shook his head. "There is a rich Sultan to the south who will pay ten times what that king will pay for her. Better to be paid in gold, gems, and myrrh, than to lose one's head coming between two wolves such as the King of Carpotinium and Bailgard. That Sultan may even grant you a harem, and lands."

"A harem?" Ka'halem asked excited.

"More riches and pleasures than you've known, or have known," Grimface added.

"Will you make an oath we will live to see such things?" Asiid asked.

Grimface smiled. "An oath? Of course, an oath it is then."

# CHAPTER 25
# Cunning Bailgard

THE GROUND WAS CHURNED up all along the dirt road leading to Baron LeGar's lands. Once green fields, now looked freshly plowed - and the woods beyond looked as if they'd been trampled by a herd of elephants.

"The army has moved through here without any fear of discovery," Benhargan said.

"Be watchful of rear-guards," Grimface ordered. "Let us travel along the mountain trails for a day and night."

As darkness settled, they saw the fires of the King of Carpotinium's army blazing in the valley.

"I count a thousand fires," Benhargan said.

"Yes, more than six thousand men," Grimface stated. "No doubt he will gather more along his way south. Come, we must make haste to reach the pass at Sultaren. From there we will have a clear view of the next valley."

They traveled hard most of the night. By the time the sliver of a moon was falling, they traversed the pass and came out onto a rocky ledge. In the far valley fires glowed brightly. Benhargan strung his bow and prepared his quiver.

"There are twice as many fires as Carpotinium," Asiid said.

"Yes, and at least two days away," Ka'halem added.

"It is a sizable force," Grimface stated, "but we will travel directly past them, for our prize is in Baron LeGar's fortress."

"Keep up," Benhargan said. "Stay sure-footed and silent. If their scouts discover us, we may be undone." He bolted along the ridge and down the granite rocks into the woods.

Grimface, Asiid, and Ka'halem pursued as best they could, but the ranger was far more deft and swift than they. When dawn broke, they saw him just ahead looking down at something between two large white boulders.

Asiid approached, but stopped short. A pair of bloody legs was protruding from the rocks.

"They were scouts," Benhargan told them, then turned to look at Grimface. "They were easy enough a prey to quell, but where there are two scouts there are more."

"We must keep on task," Grimface added.

"Very well, but these two will be missed soon." Benhargan piled some brush over the bodies.

"He is no blacksmith, and I suspect you are no jeweler," Ka'halem said to Grimface.

"Yes, before we go further, tell us who you truly are," Asiid demanded.

"I am Grimface the magician, and that there," Grimface pointed at Benhargan, "is Benhargan the Cimmerian. By the will of the gods we have been sent to seek out the pregnant woman you now take us to."

"Oh... a wizard and a warrior. What game is it you play here?" Asiid asked. "How is it you've come to be here?"

"I have already told you. The gods have chosen sides, that is how we are involved. This girl is very important. Those who claim ownership of her will one day wield great power," Grimface said.

Asiid looked thoughtful for a moment. "I guess we cannot go against the gods. Nor, can we humble thieves, go against the will of a fierce Cimmerian warrior, or a wizard."

"The gods have seen fit to unite us. It means you were chosen too. Our fate," he nodded to the barbarian, "is interwoven. Once you have shown us the girl, you can flee. At the last moment, I will tell you where a vast treasure is buried, so your time will not be wasted."

"Treasure?" Asiid asked.

"Treasure?" Benhargan repeated, his eyes narrowing.

Grimface spoke, "Ranger, take the lead and move fast. We still have miles to go before we can rest."

"Very well," Benhargan said. He turned and vanished along a deer path.

The sun dipped behind the high mountains. Its dark shadow crept slowly into the valley, until the expanse was filled with smothering darkness.

Benhargan led his companions along a granite path that wound along a high stony hill. At the top, there was an overhang that looked out over a broad valley.

In the distance, fires blazed. Around each were cavalry, infantry, chariots, pike-men, and archers. Atop poles flew the black banner of Bailgard's forces.

Benhargan sniffed the air. "It...it's that smell, that powerful scent that steals minds and souls..."

Grimface inhaled. "Fresh black lotus?"

"Why would the prince provide his soldiers that?" Benhargan mused.

"To keep them from fleeing," Asiid said with a grin as he inhaled deeply and slowly moved closer to the edge of the cliff.

Grimface frowned. "The leaf will draw out those warriors from the King's army, and make them ineffective."

"I wouldn't mind stealing a little," Ka'halem said.

"Good idea... let's," Asiid agreed.

"No," Grimface stated, but the two men began to climb down the ledge. "You fools! Stop before we are all caught and impaled!"

"It is potent! The most I've encountered..." Benhargan's nose led him to the cliff edge, over, and down.

Grimface paused. He looked up into the sky. "So this is it? I had hoped for a little more time. I am prepared, but a little more time would have served me better." He also approached the edge, then slipped over the side.

Driven on by the black-leaf, the two thieves grew reckless. The closer they got to the fires the more the lotus grew in potency – and the more they surrendered caution for bold inclination.

Soon Grimface felt the disconnecting effects of the black-leaf. His mind was fading in thought, and all he knew was the draw of the plant. There was no going back, and he gave in. The dull pleasure - like a tankard of mead, a blazing fire, and a warm blanket on a cold day - soothed every fiber of his being.

The trees were thinning, and he emerged onto a grassy plain where the enemy encamped. As he got closer, he noticed that the soldiers at the fires never moved. For a moment, he had a lucid thought, Perhaps I am on the wrong side of this fight.

He trod over wet sod for a hundred yards, then came to the encampment. Red and black tents were erected all around. Camp fires were burning brightly, and the soldiers were firmly planted at the fireside, or standing by the tents and water barrels.

For Grimface, all thoughts of escape, or fear, or mortality were locked in a white fog inside his mind. Even the soft caress of the goddess could not reach his soul.

He came around a tent. There, in the middle were smudge-pots spewing out white smoke as strange beings fed black lotus leaf into them. There too he saw Benhargan, Asiid, and Ka'halem standing by more than a hundred large amphorae brimming with black lotus. To the sides were tables with large hookahs, men wearing the uniforms of various legions, and spectral beings providing a hose and mouth-tip to each.

Benhargan stood in front of the billowing white smoke, drawing in a deep breath – staggered, then stumbled to one of the tables. Moans of pleasure rose from the hulking Cimmerian as he sucked and chewed the wrinkled end of a hookah hose. His eyes rolled up into his head, and he went down hard.

Asiid and Ka'halem did the same, and so followed Grimface.

Grimace rolled over as he lay on the ground. The muddy grass felt good on his skin. He'd for some reason taken off his talismans and cozied up next to one of the soldiers. He looked up at the armor and wondered why there was no face under the helmet, no flesh under the gauntlets, nor the boots, nor... He knew deep down that he should act, but the leaf, the blessed leaf had him, and he would stay there and die rather than be separated from the lotus.

Spinning lights came to him, dancing like consorts to entertain him with pleasures profound. He heard the clanking of armor and the groans of others.

In the distance, the sound of men and carts came close. Grimface turned his head to see hundreds of Picts milling about, lotus smoke about their heads, and a glazed look in their eyes.

His vision blurred. Several times the sun rose and fell, and just as his vision seemed at the point of darkness and his mind filled with nothing but fog, a host of shadows came and helped him up. The spectral things led him toward a cart with bars.

He remembered being wrapped into a wet blanket. As he realized the lotus was gone, he fought to get free – someone was going to die for separating him from the bliss.

Time had no meaning, and his rage flared for that which he no longer could enjoy. The only thing keeping him from killing those around him and himself was the blanket. Finally, when his head was splitting and his bones ached, his mind fell dark, and he was dead – or so he thought.

Grimface was jolted awake. The sound of wheels rolling over dirt and stone met his ears, and the smell of morning air mixed with urine and sweat was heavy. He clawed his way to a sitting position, then realized he was in a jailor's cart with metal bars. Benhargan was snoring on his left, and Asiid and Ka'halem were standing in the corner with looks of terror in their eyes.

"We are doomed," Ka'halem said.

Grimface stood, bumped his head on the low ceiling, and sat back down. "Where are we?"

"Traveling toward the baron's fortress," Asiid told him.

Benhargan grunted, snorted, and rolled over.

"Wake the giant Cimmerian so he may free us," Ka'halem pleaded.

"Stop your chattering," Grimface scolded. "I have thoughts to gather. The lotus has made my wits dull." He looked out the side and saw the green of the pasturelands passing as the cart jostled up and down over ruts and holes.

"You there, old man, make way. We carry prisoners of Prince Bailgard," a voice called from the top of the cart.

"Prince Bailgard?" called another voice. "How the tides of fate rise and fall."

"Give quarter, or I shall order my escort to remove you and cut off your nose!" said the cart driver.

"Have you seen a tall dark-skinned man with a mustache, and an overly-large Cimmerian of late?".

The cart moved forward.

"No – and you'd be wise to mind your own business," the cart driver threatened.

They passed a man with a walking stick, covered in a heavy brown cloak and cowl. The man looked over, and from beneath the blackness of his hood, he watched the cart pass.

Grimface thought he saw something—a pair of deep blue eyes flash from within the framing darkness of that hood—but the man looked down and walked into the tall grass at the side of the road. He was gone.

The cart trundled on for some time. It turned a corner and passed through into a thick wood. The soldiers driving the cart called out again. "Another old man? You, clear the road or be-"

The thump of arrows driven deep into bone and flesh filled the air. Grimface heard the last breath of several dying men, then the sound of bodies landing hard on the ground.

Footsteps came from the front. The man draped in a cowl approached. He stopped, leaned heavily on his stick, and looked at the locked gate. From under his cloak, he pulled forth a sword and drove it down hard on the locking device. The metal shattered, and he pulled the gate open.

Benhargan woke and sat up, nearly hitting his head on the top of the cart. "What's this?"

The man stepped back as the four prisoners climbed out.

"Who are you?" Grimface demanded to know.

Benhargan climbed out. He looked at the bodies on the ground. "There is only one who shoots his arrows with such precision – only one man that I've seen kill with such skill." He lurched at the man, pulled him to his chest. "Bulvife!" Benhargan said loudly, almost with tears in his eyes.

"By the goddess!" Grimface declared. "It is you!"

Benhargan released the man.

Bulvife pulled off his cowl and laughed. "Traveling these highways in disguise these months has yielded much intelligence, and I have much to tell." He slapped Benhargan on the arm. "I do not blame you for leaving me in that tomb. It was the wise thing to do." Turning to Grimface he smiled. "All along the southern road I've heard tell of Bailgard, and his plans to smash his rivals, and make a kingdom as powerful as Atlantis. There is talk in taverns and brothels that his daughter will bear him an unnatural child that will serve him in his goals. The northern city-states are mobilizing and driving their armies to the south, and linking with armies from Shem, Kush,

Koth and Stygia. They intend to meet the prince upon the field of battle—even as we speak." Bulvife took off his cloak. "Why were you in that jailer's cart?"

Benhargan chuckled. "Stupidity. We were duped by the prince. He is using black lotus to lure his enemies in and capture them. He is very cunning."

"We were on our way to the baron's Keep, to steal the princess," Grimface told him.

"The Keep?" Bulvife sounded surprised. "Your notions of courage haven't changed. To be inside his fortress would mean certain death."

"It is the place the mother of the god-king is. We must rescue her and deliver her to a place where the god-king can be born. Bailgard must be denied such power," Grimface said.

"Then count me in," Bulvife declared while retrieving his arrows. "By the way, who are these two men?"

Benhargan laughed loudly. "I shall tell you while we're on our way. Suffice to say, they are thieves with knowledge of our prey."

"If you were the man we passed earlier, how did you get in front of the cart again?" Asiid asked.

"When I saw Grimface in the cart, I cut through the woods. Your cart moved slowly enough, and it was little effort to get ahead."

"Now what?" Asiid asked.

"We'll take this cart and these horses and make for the fortress," Grimface stated. "The enemy will not stop us, I'm sure."

"Then stop gabbing and let's get to it," Benhargan said.

IT WAS NIGHT FALL WHEN they came across the first guard post. The rutted dirt road stretched out ahead, and the guards took little notice of the jailer-wagon, the prisoners, or the escorts with it. The soldier in charge waved them through. This was repeated all along the way. At the top of a hill, Grimface looked down into a grass-filled plain. A pair of rivers formed black irregular lines winding through tall plateaus of rock that reached hundreds of feet into the heavens.

"There's the baron's citadel," Asiid said pointing at an array of buildings protruding above the miles of mud-brick walls.

"Where is the fortress?" Bulvife asked.

"There," Ka'halem added while pointing at the tallest plateau.

Looking closely Benhargan saw torches and other forms of illumination on the cliffs. "It will be tricky to get up there," he said.

"We know a way," Asiid told them. "Follow and stay quiet."

"Wait," Grimface said while narrowing his gaze at the city. "There is a vast army down there, and something else..."

"Ahead along the road are many impaled bodies," Benhargan said. "A reminder for his conscripts to be loyal; a gift from their master, no doubt."

"We will need to rid ourselves of this cart and horse. From here we must travel on foot," Ka'halem told them.

Benhargan unhitched the horse and let it loose, then the two barbarians pushed the cart into the brush.

Asiid led the way down from the hills and into the valley. They traveled hard and fast. The only ford across the river was held by the enemy, so they had to find another place further upstream to swim across.

Once on the other bank, they made for the city wall and skirted along it toward the north. At the corner, they turned east and moved out into farmland.

In the sky, the blue star with an enormous tail, bright as the absent moon, raced across the heavens. The blazing starlight illuminated the crisscross of irrigation ditches that shimmered with the reflection of the iridescent blue from the celestial body. It was not long before they were at the base of the mighty cliffs.

"This way," Asiid said and led them along a thin path up onto a ledge. From there he moved into a crack in the cliff and into a narrow tunnel. Then he waited.

Once all were within, Asiid struck flint to steel and ignited a candle. Bulvife pulled from under his shirt a piece of metal that glowed a soft yellow. Grimface came close and looked upon the man's face.

"Where did you get that?" he asked.

"When I was trapped in that tomb."

Grimface smiled. "Never doubt a clever goddess."

"Come, or all will be lost and we will be trapped here another day," Ka'halem told them.

Slowly, they made their way down the tunnel as it wound its way around and up a dark core of stone. For a long time, they moved upward. As the path leveled out, a dull orange light came into view. A smell of lilac and jasmine wafted down the tunnel, and a sweet soft sound followed.

# CHAPTER 26
# The Dark Citadel

THERE WAS A VOICE COMING from beyond the light. It was singing...haunting... like the lament of death or a lost love. As they approached the end of the tunnel, they halted.

A heavy metal grate covered the access way. Thick tangles of green vines and dark leaves hung down - lilac, jasmine, myrrh, sandalwood, and rose filled the air.

Asiid motioned for them to come close. "Beyond this grate are the outer-gardens. This is where we saw the girl." He turned and removed a metal tool from a brown pouch at his side. Methodically he used it to liberate several rusted pins from around the covering and make it ajar, just big enough for them to fit through.

Emerging into the garden, Grimface saw the vast expanse of manicured hedges, groves of trees, grass and fountains. Exotic birds moved in the bushes, and in the distance, by a set of wooden double doors, a mandrill was chained and asleep. They moved silently through the grass, around some bushes, and over an arched bridge spanning a babbling brook. On the other side Ka'halem pointed toward a tall stone wall.

"There, the cage," Ka'halem whispered.

Benhargan took the front and Bulvife the rear. They moved behind a hedgerow and along the wall. Grimface listened carefully.

The space widened into a cobblestone pathway that led to a wooden cage on wheels – as one would keep a wild animal in. Asiid motioned toward it. Grimface nodded and laid his hand on Benhargan's arm. He indicated for the massive fighter to wait, as he crept toward the cage. At the edge, Grimface peeked through the bars.

In the corner was a woman dressed in flowing blue robe. Her back was to the opening, and her long hair stretched down to her lower back.

A set of peacocks emerged from the bushes, pecking here and there.

Grimface whispered something to the birds; they turned quietly and went back into the bushes. He looked back at Benhargan, then crept around the front of the cart to where the pinned latch was.

Pressing up on the bottom of the pin, it squeaked as it came out of the metal ring. The birds above started to chatter, and the mandrill snarled somewhere back the way they had come. No one made a move, nor did the girl.

Ka'halem appeared next to Grimface and lifted a small bamboo container of oil up and onto the hinges. He nodded and stepped back. Grimface pulled the door open.

"Princess, we've come to spirit you from this place to safety," said Grimface.

She rustled and turned to reveal a beard and a blade. The man leapt onto Grimface, as armed men came from every direction.

Benhargan loosed his sword, and Bulvife stepped back to unleash his arrows. Both men were covered in a thick cargo net and fell to the sod. Asiid and Ka'halem fell to their knees and began to beg and pray. In a matter of moments, they were all in the hands of Bailgard.

"It was a valiant attempt, truly," a large man dressed in black armor said. "I must say that when I learned that Grimface was searching for the prince's daughter, I was impressed. He who dispatched Otten'bar is no man to be underestimated." He came closer, attended by four armored guardsmen bearing torches.

"Bailgard," Grimface said between clenched teeth.

The prince's golden eyes shimmered in the torch light. "You two, come hither and receive your rewards," he said to Asiid and Ka'halem.

"You've played me well," Grimface admitted.

"You are not an easy man to fool. Much planning was laid, and in truth you had little chance of success. The only reason you still live is that I have plans for you."

"Has not my answer been plain?"

Bailgard stepped closer. "There is little in this world less worthy of living than a man who denies the benefits of his own power. But I am a lord who understands the luxury of mercy. What is it you value, wizard?"

"My service to the goddess," Grimface said.

Chuckling, Bailgard motioned for some men to come forward. They disarmed and put shackles on Grimface, Bulvife, and Benhargan.

"You must understand, Grimface, I will have your power serve me, or no one. I can make it no plainer."

"Yes, I understand. If I do not obey you, you will craft a spell with my true name to undo me." Grimface looked forlorn. "What will become of these my friends—" He pointed at Benhargan and Bulvife.

"They will fight to destroy my enemies, or they will fight in an arena for my amusement. But either way, they will need to be tempered with some pain first. After all, I know I can't trust them to serve me at present – they must be broken. You on the other hand, knowing your true name, I think you will serve me without question," Bailgard said.

"How do I know you possess my name?"

Bailgard came in close, and into Grimface's ear he said something.

Grimface reeled back, forcing the two guards with him. It took a moment for him to gain his calm again. "What of the girl?" he asked after a moment.

"She is inside the palace, kept safe until the birth. After all, she is my daughter and I would care of it if she were to fail in her duty to me." Bailgard motioned for the soldiers to take the men, then noticed Asiid and Ka'halem standing there. "Ah, yes... you two. You have done well. I have treasure for you; all you can carry in gold, silver and gems."

Benhargan and Bulvife came past Grimface.

"Now what, wizard?" Benhargan asked. "Next time, shall we save our enemies the trouble and just cut our own throats?"

They filed past the snarling mandrill and through a pair of large double doors. The corridor was carved from the living speckled rock, and the floor tiled.

Behind, Grimface heard Bailgard say, "Close the doors and release the mandrill. Once the beast has made sport of those dupes, send out some men to seal up that grate."

The door closed and the screams of Asiid and Ka'halem echoed in the distance. The prince came alongside Grimface.

"In two years, I shall have command over all the kingdoms between Cimmeria and Stygia, and in ten years the Black Kingdoms to the Hyraknian Mountains I shall have too. I need men with such power as you to keep and enforce my will. Consider being the overlord over Hyraknia, standing poised to take Vendhya in the south when I so command it."

"Your Atlantean lust for conquest will serve you ill," Grimface said. "Hunger for destruction and power blinds you. Your daughter's son will not do your will? He will have a mind of his own, and powers you never dreamt of. I think he will have your guts tied in knots for his pleasure, and not the other way around."

Bailgard laughed. "You do not understand that my grandson will do my bidding. The god that I worship will see to it. If I think he is disloyal, I will dispel him as easily as I can do you. My own power is nothing to mock, and far greater than you will ever wielded."

The prince advanced ahead of Grimface and spoke to one of the soldiers. "Put them in adjoining cells. Their scheming means little at this point. I'll come check on this one tomorrow." He pointed at Grimface. "Let the jailer know not to be duped by him. He has powerful magic in his voice."

They came to a place where the passage diverged, one going up and one going down. Grimface broke free of the guards and lunged at Bailgard, slugging the man in the mouth and knocking him to the side. Two soldiers pulled the wizard away.

"You cannot win in your plans!" Grimface shouted.

Bailgard wiped the blood from his mouth, then turned to Grimface; his eyes narrowed. "Don't make me have you chained to the wall and your mouth sewn shut." He wagged his finger at the man, then touched his bloody lip. "Sloppy – such a sloppy and foolish act. I expected far more from you than that unhinged act of blind rage. You have become more barbarian from your cavorting with those beasts than you know. Get your head together. I will visit you soon."

Bailgard turned and went up along the passage, and Grimface, Benhargan, and Bulvife down into the bowels of the fortress.

At the bottom of the passage the floor leveled out. Thick wooden doors appeared, fitted into the walls along the tunnel. Candles were placed in alcoves near each door, and at the far end was another door that led deeper into the dungeon.

Standing there was a slender man dressed in a leather tunic fastened with a black leather belt. From one side hung a short sword, and the other side a ring with pins. He approached.

The lead soldier provided instruction and Benhargan was placed in one cell, Bulvife in another, and Grimface into yet another. The door of each was shut, and a pin placed in an iron loop to secure it.

Grimface listened as the footsteps of the soldiers vanished. After some time – and hearing no sound from the jailer— he sat down on the cold stone floor. From around his neck he produced a crystal, said a few words and the room came awash with light.

He saw straw piled in the corner, a bucket for bodily waste, and nothing else in the room. He took off his shirt, turned it inside out, and removed a needle he'd hidden there. Next, he untied the threads that formed a hidden pouch and removed the contents.

"Bailgard, you may have my true name, but your wits are as dull as a grindstone," he softly said.

Swiftly he laid out the cloth, and gathered straw into it. Taking the needle and thread, he began to work. Lastly, he wiped Bailgard's blood from his hand onto the cloth.

"There will be many surprises to come for you Bailgard, but this one will be your undoing," Grimface said.

BENHARGAN BOLDLY STEPPED out into the oval arena. His hands were chained, and the bright light of the sun beat down upon his head as if it were a war drum. Ahead of him came a man in black armor and a Zamorian helmet.

"We meet again, Cimmerian. I am tasked with breaking you. The prince believes you will make a mighty commander – if you can be made to serve. I see such in you too. But, you are wild like a stallion – and need to be broken - to know your place."

Benhargan looked at the man. "Then begin, if you dare. After what that wizard Grimface has pained me with, your torments will seem sedate. In fact, I might even join your army just so I can take the head of Grimface for my lodge pole."

The man seemed taken back, then laughed. "You are full of surprises, Cimmerian. Forgive me for not fully believing you. Now when you crawl across this arena floor, upon your hands and knees, and ask permission to join the army, I will believe."

"What is your name – black heart? Benhargan asked.

"I am called Leonitus of Ostrogoth, Baron of Corinthia Karpashuet, and captain of the prince's mercenary army known as the Bloddolk Foe."

"It will read well upon a stone when I have planted you," Benhargan told him.

Leonitus grimly smiled and nodded his head. "If it be the will of the gods, then so be it."

THERE WERE FOOTSTEPS coming. Grimface listened at the door. He concentrated on the pin just outside. He felt it, and slowly it moved upward. A clack filled the air as the pin hit the stone floor. He pushed the door open.

Standing there was a beautiful flaxen-haired woman in a purple gown. She didn't smile, but narrowed her gaze as she bent down and picked up the pin.

"You are the wind that will scourge Bailgard from the world," she told him.

Grimface looked down and realized the woman was with child. "Princess?"

"I am Mirida, daughter of Bailgard the Acrimonious. You are Grimface, a name you took after your family, people, and lands were destroyed by Otten'bar," she said. "And you have come with two Cimmerians to take me to a place to bear my son. Kings fear my unborn child, for in him they see the sewn seeds of their doom. You and I know that once they stop fighting Bailgard, they will come to kill my child."

"Your words are true. We've come to bring you to the east to make a kingdom all your own," Grimface said to her, as he moved down the hall to both Bulvife's and Benhargan's cells. The doors were open and the chambers empty. "Where are the men from these cells?"

"Through there." She pointed down to the door at the end of the hall. "The torture chamber lies beyond. They are probably in there."

Grimface quickly went to the door and opened it. He traversed down the hallway until it opened into a wide and tall chamber.

Bulvife was hung by his arms from a gallows post. Below him, a blazing fire. Two guards stood by, and as Grimface entered, they all turned to look at him.

"You two fall upon your swords!" Grimface commanded. Without hesitation, the guards did as they were told and died instantly. "You, torturer, douse that fire, then move aside and lower that man," he furthered.

The torturer retrieved an iron caldron, soaked the fire with the contents, then lowered Bulvife.

"Cut his bonds and kneel," the wizard said.

The man did.

Bulvife rubbed his wrists and then took a blade from one of the dead soldiers and cut off the torture's head.

"Why didn't you do this when we were captured?" Bulvife demanded.

"Cimmerian, the way mortal's battle is well known to you, but the ways of wizards are almost unknown. I needed something from Bailgard if we are to succeed in our task. Trust me when I tell you he would not have given it to me willingly. So, I had to find a way to take it. Now we're ready to leave this place."

"Where to?" Bulvife asked.

"First to collect Benhargan, and then south east to a bog."

"A bog?" Bulvife looked bemused.

"Indeed!" Grimface laughed. "And then, on to Shem."

The hallway was mostly dark, illuminated by candles in alcoves every twenty paces. At an intersection, Grimface waited. It was not long before the sound of men came towards them. A young soldier dressed in black scale armor was leading. He turned the corner and stopped.

Grimface stood there barring his path.

"Who are you?" the young soldier asked out of reflex, just as a cry came from the back of his party, he turned mystified at what was happening. The young soldier was garroted by Grimface for his trouble.

Bulvife came from among the enemy bodies, blood dripping from his sword. "At the end of the hall is a door, and beyond I hear the clash of arms," Bulvife said.

"Benhargan, no doubt. Let's have a look," Grimface told him.

The door came open, and an arena, formed from the remains of a crater was visible. The stands were clear, but there was much chaos in the middle. Skilled men with weapons were battling one lone Cimmerian. Some held long red-hot, iron tipped poles, others carried more traditional weapons such as spear, sword and shield. It appeared to the wizard that Benhargan was leisurely fending off the attacks.

One large, pale-skinned man carried a sickle-sword, a darker-skinned fellow carried a trident. Benhargan yawned and strolled toward them. His bravado caused the men to step back.

The Cimmerian eyed the group. He growled, cocked his neck to the left side, then the right, and focused on a group of three men with shields. He charged, stopped and came around, rolled, kicked away a branding pole, leapt, grabbed a shield, and then spun the man into the air. The fellow slammed into several others, causing them to fall back.

Bulvife turned to Grimface. "He's doing rather well," he said.

"Enough of this – we have too much to do to waste time," Grimface said, then began to sing.

Benhargan stood there as each of his attackers were seized at the ankles and dragged below the ground by spectral hands.

"Not him!" shouted Benhargan, as the man in black armor looked on. "By Crom – you shall not kill him – he is mine to kill!"

Grimface stopped. He looked somewhat irritated by Benhargan's declaration, but knew that a line had been drawn by the Cimmerian that he could not cross.

"Very well, get on with it!" Grimface shouted.

Benhargan turned to Leonitus. "You wanted to test me in single combat – now is your day," he said.

"Then know this, barbarian, I will meet you with sword and shield. Prepare yourself, and I shall do the same." Leonitus picked up a fallen shield and drew his own sword. He knelt and prayed for a few moments, then stood up. "I am ready."

Benhargan picked up the same, then looked up at the sky. "Crom, watch as I send this worthy soul to his god. Then, when I come to your mountain, prepare a feast, and drink, and I will beat YOU in single battle!" He bent slightly at the knees and advanced on Leonitus.

There was much maneuvering to begin with. Benhargan seemed to have abandoned his typical bold attack style. The two men came together, shields clashed, and swords bit into each other, then they fell back and maneuvered again.

The air was charged with anxiety, as each man looked for an opening. Benhargan advanced, and Leonitus fell back, then the reverse. They came together, broke apart, shield upon shield, sword against sword. Many times, this occurred, as Grimface grew impatient.

Benhargan bellowed loudly, charged, bent down, scooped up some sand with his shield, and threw it at Leonitus. The man failed to protect his face, and the dirt and sand smashed into him. It formed a gray cloud all around.

A moment passed, the sound of vicious battle filled the air, and as the dust settled, Leonitus stood with a shocked expression written upon his face.

"You... you cheated," said the stunned warrior.

"In battle, there are two types of warriors. One that wins, and the other that is dead," Benhargan said. "I will make a sacrifice to your god. Know that few men have posed a challenge to me, and now you will be counted among them. Rest - off to your god with you." Benhargan withdrew his sword and let Leonitus collapse to the ground – his blood pooling below his body.

Grimface shouted to Benhargan, "If you are quite done wasting my time, let us be off to the task we've come to do!" He motioned for Mirida to come forward, then turned to Bulvife. "Keep her safe. Now, to the garden where the mandrill dwells."

They vanished into the dark passage. Grimface led the way.

Benhargan stood poised at the garden door. Grimface came and opened it.

"Wait here until I tell you to come," the wizard said, then went out. A moment later he called, "Come, but do not linger. Go to the grate and pry it open."

Benhargan went through. Turning, he looked on in surprise, for Grimface had the mandrill at his side, petting it softly, and whispering in its ear.

The barbarian shook his head, turned and made for the grate. Once at the tunnel he grabbed the bars with his meaty hands, tore it from the rock, and tossed it aside.

Grimface came, stopped at the cave, and spoke a few words, then entered. He produced the crystal from under his shirt; the radiance of it filled the tunnel with white light. At the end, he dispelled the light, then looked out into the valley.

"I did not account for this," Grimface said over his shoulder.

Benhargan came alongside. "More sheep for the slaughter?"

Thousands of campfires were lit all along the valley floor. Sounds of soldiers, horses, and equipment moving about were everywhere.

Grimface waited only a moment, then led them down the path and along a dark shadow that cut through the enemy ranks. They moved silently and swiftly for many hours, until they reached the mountains and the safety of the woods. That's when Bulvife noticed the Picts.

# CHAPTER 27
# Path to Damnation

BULVIFE TUGGED AT GRIMFACE'S sleeve. "Picts are to the west of us and on our trail. How do you want to proceed?"

The ground shook, and in the distance powerful thunder rose. Grimface turned to look at the fortress. A massive number of torches came spewing out of the stronghold and moved like a serpent into the army's ranks. More torches were lit and those soldiers moved out along the base of the mountain.

"They've discovered we're missing," Grimface whispered. He looked up the hill. "Higher up we will go over these mountains and skip the pass."

Grimface began to climb. Benhargan took the front, Mirida behind him, followed by Grimface and Bulvife.

Slowly they scaled up along the broken granite cliffs, following the paths made by the mountain sheep.

As the sun came overhead, they saw the valley below and the madness of the search. Soldiers on horseback were probing along the woods, while men on foot looked all around the base of the fortress. Closer to them, Bulvife spotted a band of Picts; it seemed they had the scent of the fleeing captives and were in full pursuit.

A hundred yards below, a Pict appeared and looked up at them. He howled and a dozen more came forth. They began climbing, nimbly scaling the rock walls like a Cimmerian youth.

"Quickly, to the summit! It is only another sixty feet," Grimface said.

They scaled the rough stone, finding toe holds and places to grasp infrequent. Halfway along, Benhargan reached down and grabbed Mirida under her arms and pulled her up to a ledge he'd found.

"Climb onto my back," he told her.

"I will not. I can climb as well as you," she told him.

"You'll get us killed with your slow pace is what you'll do," Benhargan chided her, then put his back to her and forced her feet off the ledge.

She let out a shriek, then fanatically clung to his back.

"That's better," Benhargan said as he began to climb hand over hand, until he vanished over the stone lip at the top.

Grimface made it next, then came Bulvife. Looking down, Grimface saw the red and blue painted faces of the Picts as they clawed their way up the rock. Benhargan appeared next to him, and dropped a large tree stump over the side. The first four Pics were smashed and plummeted down into the rocky shale and dirt a hundred feet below. Angry words in Pictish filtered up as the surviving savages continued to climb.

"They've no doubt sent a messenger to Bailgard," Grimface said. "They will be joining in the hunt soon! We must keep moving."

"This way," Bulvife said, as he took the lead along the ridgeline.

The sound of battle horns came from afar. They echoed in the valley, then were repeated. Grimface stopped and looked out over the scene of chaos.

"They've called back the searchers," the wizard said.

Bulvife looked on. "And look!" He pointed at the far end of the valley. "They're mobilizing, and heading out."

"It has begun," Grimace stated. "They will move south – the last of the great wars is in motion."

"Then they have called back the pursuers?" Mirida asked.

Grimface shook his head. "No. Your father has sent a force to find you and kill us. Even now they make their way through the woods below. The Picts will tell them of our direction, and they will follow."

"Shall Bulvife and I thin out their ranks?" Benhargan asked.

"No! We are now in a foot race to make it to the Yeshi Mohan Valley in Shem!" said Grimface. "We stick together, all the way there."

They traveled for hours – charging down rushing streams, over alpine boulders, and past scrub-pines. At a switchback, instead of taking the path, Bulvife took them down the side.

Scrub brush and rope like vines made their descent easy, and once down to the base of the valley, they found a swift moving mountain brook to take a moments respite. As they drank, Grimface instructed them on their next step.

"A days' travel from here is a swampy bog. Once we get there we have to get across in one day."

"The ancient ones?" asked Mirida.

"There are things in that bog that we do not want to meet with," Benhargan said and shuddered. "Horrors that live in the wake of the wizard."

"If we travel hard, we can make it by first light tomorrow," Grimface told them.

Once they'd sated their thirst, Bulvife looked up toward the trail of the mountain. "There is movement above us. I smell Picts, and... perfume," the Cimmerian told them. "It will be a short time before they find where we leapt from the path. They are no fools."

"Use all of your ranger skills to get us to the bog-lands by daybreak tomorrow," Grimface told both Bulvife and Benhargan. "Our very survival depends on it now."

The traveling was hard, and over many miles of uneven land. They traversed two rivers and bypassed several towns. By the time the day was spent, they were all in need of some rest.

Benhargan found a cave. Grimface illuminated the space with his crystal and explored a bit.

"We'll rest for a few hours, but then we must continue," the wizard said.

"I'll take the first watch," Bulvife volunteered.

"No, we all will sleep. I will weave a mist to hide us for now," Grimface told them, then sat at the head of the cavern and sung a tune.

In the distance, among the woods and brush, a fog rose from the ground. It swirled and twisted as it approached the cave. In some places it glowed, and in others dark shapes moved. When Grimface stopped, the white vale hung so thick, they saw no sign of the ground just outside the opening.

Lying back, he closed his eyes and crossed his arms. "I will come awake in a short while, and we will go then. Try and get some rest now."

Grimface woke. He looked around and noticed Mirida watching the opening. She turned and came to him. Laying her hands on his chest, she said a word in a foreign language.

"It is the old word, the true word for rest," she said. "Though I had learned it as a child, I did not know how much it could do until now. Before we go, I just want to say, thank you for liberating me."

Grimface smiled. "There is much I don't know about the world, but what I do know is that a kind word from a lovely young woman is worth all the rest a man could want."

Bulvife and Benhargan approached.

"Is it time?" Benhargan asked.

"It is," Grimface affirmed.

"Then let's get to that bog," Bulvife said.

THE FOG FADED BACK into the ground. Darkness lay upon the woods like a blanket, yet all four of the travelers followed each other with perfect precision. They traveled for hours, weaving this way and that, through brambles and thickets. In the middle of a clearing Bulvife stopped and motioned toward the dark line of the forest fence ahead of them.

Picts came from the woods. They rushed at them from two directions.

Grimface shielded Mirida from the attack, while Bulvife and Benhargan engaged the wild men. The fighting was hard - as bloody as any battle can be. A scream came from behind, and a savage ran at Grimface. The wizard pulled forth his sword, parried, sidestepped and cut into the savage's spine. The creature did not cry out, but instead quivered, then lay still.

In the chaos, the remaining Picts broke and ran. Bulvife and Benhargan, infused with blood lust, pursued the creatures into the forest.

"Wait!" shouted Grimface, but it was too late. His two Cimmerians were lost in the darkness. "Curse those thick-headed brutes," he scolded. "Stay close to me, there may be more."

A few moments passed while he looked about the clearing. A sound like a melon hitting the ground caught his attention, and Grimface turned to see something round roll up to his feet.

It was a severed head of a Pict. Benhargan emerged from the brush, all the while chuckling. He approached Grimface.

"There will be no reports back to Bailgard from this group," the barbarian said.

"Where's Bulvife?" Grimface asked.

"He will be along in a moment." Benhargan pointed across from them. "He was in pursuit of three when I caught up to the other five."

A rustling caught their attention, and they all turned to look at Bulvife.

He was covered in blood and stopped, bent down, and wiped dirt over the fresh, red liquid that covered him.

"They struggled," he said, "and it got messy."

"Most likely there are more out there," Benhargan added.

"We can't go easy now, not if we're to make the bog by dawn," Grimface told them.

"Then I have very good news," Bulvife stated. "The bog is not far in this direction." He led the way through the woods for less than an hour until he came to where solid ground became a soupy mess.

The stench of bog was ripe, and in the distance Grimface saw the shimmering of shapes that skulked about in search of warm, living things to defile. There too, was the glow from that ancient corrupted spirit that dwelled within.

"Okay, rest up. As soon as dawn is upon the field, we move across. We can't stop for any reason," Grimface told them.

THEY CLIMBED A LOW hill in the middle of the bog. A thunderous roar cracked the air. Grimface glanced back. In the distance, he saw horses, men, and dogs flooding into the bog. The sun was at midday, and there was much more bog to travel.

"The hunters are upon our heels," Grimface declared. "If ever your ranger blood was keen, let it be today!"

There was no time for food or drink or stopping as they moved as quickly as a savanna leopard toward its prey. The high-ground at the swamp's end was in sight. By the time the sun had reached the western foothills, and the long shadow of night was reaching across the wetlands, Bulvife landed his foot onto solid, dry land.

"We've made it. Up the hill and to a better vantage point!" Bulivife called as he took the lead.

Once they were a hundred yards away from the ancient swamp, Grimface turned to look. Bailgard's soldiers were halfway across. Some men had set torches alight. A cool breeze came from the north as the mist rose from the bog and steadily moved toward the doomed men.

"Once they realize their mistake it will be too late – all will be dead men. If Bailgard sends more to pursue us, they will have to circumvent the bog or wait for day to cross," Grimface said. He stopped and stared off into the night sky for a moment. "Ah, the prince is now at the head of his army, and travels toward Kush... some of his soldiers have loaded on ships, and others by foot to scourge the land and sow confusion among the allied kingdoms."

"What is the strength of the prince's forces?" Benhargan asked.

Grimface looked at both men. "I will not lie to you. With all his troops – mercenaries and allies, his forces number more than two hundred thousand. And worse, he has a cohort of magicians with him too. Their power is tremendous," he added.

"His enemies possess magic too," said Mirida. "There is hope still that he will be defeated. The great commander Huro von Xiver and his sub-commanders have gathered forces from the south, and once combined with the north, will come close to the number of soldiers in my father's forces. The fight is not lost – not yet."

"Come, let us climb higher. Those things in the swamp – we should leave them far behind," Benhargan told them.

At last, the blood-red hue of the setting sun vanished. In the valley, the fog reached the enemy forces. Grimface, Mirida, Bulvife, and Benhargan saw it engulf the torchlights. Shortly after, they heard the screams of those unlucky souls.

Grimface exhaled an almost lamenting sound, then turned to a look at Bulvife.

"Take us to Malkaltuia."

Bulvife nodded. "There's at least seven leagues to travel if we rest little."

"There was never a choice in the matter," Grimface said.

"Then let us seek out some horses and maybe a cart," Benhargan suggested.

"Now, that is good thinking barbarian! Very good thinking indeed," Grimface added.

Two days later, they found an unattended cart in a village. In the next town they found a horse to pull the cart. This was a great relief to Benhargan and Bulvife who had the unlucky task of pulling the wheeled vehicle. In yet another town, they freed a mercant's purse-of-coins from his unconscious body – a task that Bulvife found distasteful, but did anyway.

At Malkaltuia along the Argos coast, they paid passage aboard a ship sailing for Shem. Three days it took to make port at Asgalum. Benhargan paid for horses, a cart and donkey.

They found a market to buy food and drink, and headed out along the Bengal river road.

Late on the eve of the seventh day, the band arrived at the base of a hill surrounded by broken mud brick walls, mounds of pottery shards, a dry moat, and crumbled ruins. All around the hill were dry grasslands and herds of white rhino and black oxen.

They climbed up through an area where the city gates had been, and wove their way through debris to the ancient fortress center. A well was still there, cut through the tan bedrock deep into the hill.

Bulvife stood at the edge and hauled up a sack of water. "At last, a cool drink."

Grimface turned to the Cimmerians. "Drink up, barbarians. Soon I will have need for you to climb into that well, and bring forth armor and weapons you will find in a hidden tomb there. Both, you and Benhargan must go, if we are to have sufficient time to prepare."

# CHAPTER 28
## The Innumerable Foe

BENHARGAN GATHERED up some large wooden beams. Grimface made a contraption that sat over the well.

A rope was retrieved from the back of the cart, looped over a post suspended between the beams, and fed down the hole. Bulvife secured the other end of the rope to the base of an ancient statue. Grimface gave them his crystal light, and the two barbarians descended into the darkness.

At the bottom, Benhargna and Bulvife dropped into knee-deep cold water.

"Which way did the wizard say?" Benhargan asked.

Bulvife pointed. "That way - upstream."

They sloshed their way through the crystal clear water for quite a long time. The illumination revealed much of the tunnel, and Bulvife saw the finely laid stone work that formed the arched aqueduct.

After a while a golden glow appeared in the distance. The clear, white water, flowed past a ledge, and beyond that ledge was another tunnel leading into the rock. Next to the opening was a bright, glowing, metal loop embedded in the stone.

Bulvife climbed up. "Look! The chain that holds the gem that Grimface gave us – it too is glowing!" He pointed.

"Weapons of war interest me now. Not trinkets," Benhargan said.

"When I was trapped in that tomb, I found a gem the size of your fist. It will make a fine gift for a princess," Bulvife stated.

Benhargan grunted. "You're a ranger, and not a man who stays put. What do you think will happen when she wants you to settle down with her and be a king? It will drive you mad. No, my friend, you are a creature of the greenwood, and if you think anything other – you are a fool."

"Why do you say such things?" Bulvife asked.

"I thought it was obvious... Like treasure, and life, all tangible possessions are fleeting – thus you are fleeting. You'd be better off visiting many different ladies at the temple than destroying that princess's belief that you'll be a faithful lover."

Bulvife stopped, turned, and looked back at Benhargan. "I've never heard you speak thusly," he said. "What possesses you so?"

Benhargan shrugged. "I'm just telling you that afflictions of the heart are far more damaging than blade, fist, or bow."

"Now, I'm worried about what the walled cities have done to you!" Bulvife turned and continued into the warren of tunnels.

The two men wound their way through the halls. They came to a large open chamber filled with brightly glowing items. Across the room was another doorway, and beyond that, darkness.

"Let's make a litter to carry as much as we can," Benhargan suggested.

"There are two polearms we can use, and we can strap these rugs to the poles," Bulvife said. "After that, we can load it up with whatever we need."

It took a short while to make the stretcher and load it with the armor and weapons. When the two Cimmerians lifted it, the poles bowed dramatically, but did not break.

The last item to be taken was the crown from the head of a mummy, of which Benhagan put upon his own head with a chuckle. They made their way back toward the underground river.

BULVIFE AND BENHARGAN were gone an entire day and night. Grimface had done his best to secure the perimeter, though it would be impossible to keep those determined from entering.

As the night of the second day began to fall, he saw the rope jiggle.

"Tie the items to the rope and I'll pull them up," Grimface told them.

One by one the items came up to the surface. Once all was stacked to the side, Benhargan and Bulvife emerged from the well.

"Now what, wizard?" Benhargan asked.

"Go and look from the crumbling battlements. We are not alone," Grimface softly added.

Benhargan went directly to the askew mud brick tower. All around the ancient fortress were fires. He returned. "A hundred thousand men – or more," he said, as if detached from his thoughts.

"But who are they?" Grimface asked. "Are they the advanced forces of Bailgard's army? Are they soldiers from the alliance set against him? Or are they others?"

"What others?" Bulvife asked.

"'We'll know in the morning, for they will send scouts and a herald to see who we are."

Grimface took one of the glowing rugs retrieved from the well and laid it out. He helped Mirida to lie down on it. Afterward, he sat at her feet and sang of such pleasure and happiness - and all wept.

Upon completion of his song, dark and baleful creatures roamed the ramparts, their red and glowing eyes watching for all who might approach the fort.

The magician fell back, gasping for breath. Mirida sat up and laid her hands on his chest; she said some words, and Grimface seemed invigorated once again.

She turned to the barbarians. "Take your rest as you can. I fear that tomorrow, all the forces of Hyboria will fall upon this little heap of earth." She lay back and closed her golden eyes.

AT DAWN, GRIMFACE WAS up. He was standing near the path that led from the ancient gatehouse. Five groups of men stood just outside, each of their banners held by men in armor, and all were different liveries.

They had taken to arguing with each other when Grimface approached. Benhargan and Bulvife were at his side as he spoke.

"What brings you to the ruins of Terar Chul Remod?"

"Who are you?" demanded a man with a white horse on his standard.

"I am he who is called Grimface, the maker of lords, the destroyer of kings."

A man whose banner shown a yellow sun spoke. "Do you ally with the usurper or with us?"

Mirida appeared from the ruins and came down. The men looked on with suspicion.

"Who is this girl?" demanded white horse.

"I am Mirida, daughter of Bailgard, and mother to a god!" she said.

"Give her to us – we will keep her safe," suggested yellow sun.

Grimface laughed. "Such little thought went into that request, that I dismiss it out of hand. I know full well the girl will not last ten paces before you slit her throat. Do not play me the fool! So, listen closely. In a few hours, that blackest of princes, Bailgard, will come from the north with an army the size of which none of you can survive alone. Go now, and strengthen your alliances, send word for reinforcements, and gather all those who practice magic, for if you don't, Bailgard will crush you all and take your lands. When the dust of battle settles, the victor can come negotiate for the girl. Now go, for you have much to discuss in the ways of war in a short amount of time."

The men looked at each other, then at Grimface. It appeared as if they'd make independent tries at taking her, but Grimface raised his hands and said a word, and the sands under them shook.

They turned and ran from the hill and made straight for their camps. Grimface turned to Benhargan and Bulvife.

"Arm yourselves with that armor you found. Take up the swords and shields, and place the pole arms around the well facing outward at an incline. I will do what I can to thin their ranks when they come. By nightfall tomorrow, this land will be covered in severed heads, arms, and legs, and you, my barbarian friends, will be knee-deep in blood and gore. I suppose that pleases you both?" He looked at Bulvife and Benhargan with a grin.

"More than you will know," Bulvife lamented.

"I'm glad that talk is at an end, and the thieving and skulking is finished. Now is time for action, time to release the rage, and bring all those who come this way to death!" Benhargan declared.

GRIMFACE WATCHED FROM the fallen tower. He saw the banners of those who challenged Bailgard going back and forth from camp to camp. He knew that there would be much parley over who would get what for acquiescing to which demands.

While the kings of those banners schemed, Bailgard took to the field. His men poured into the valley, set up camp and lit their campfires.

It was this moment that Grimface counted on - the time where those disorganized fools saw the true danger – for Bailgard's army outnumbered them twenty to one.

The morning would bring a battle the likes of which Hyboria had not seen since the age of Atlantis, and it would all focus right in the middle of the ancient Kush prairielands.

Grimface already knew that the Atlantean Prince would come to see him at the ancient fortress. There was no doubt that the man would sweep his enemies from the field. The true question was, did he suspect Grimface could – and would – undo him.

"The men who wore this armor must have been dwarves!" Benhargan said angrily, as he tried to patch together some scale, plate, and braided armor. He could find little that fit him. He could make a pair of greaves work, and a cuirass, and a helmet, but none of the breastplates would fit.

Bulvife on the other hand found plenty to fit, and even found several re-curved bows with a wire-like string. He brandished sword, shield, dagger, javelin, and spear.

They spent the night placing weapons about, in a fallback strategy, all converging on the well. Around the fallen walls, they dug traps, and placed spikes, and briars.

By dawn the next day, the rumbling of thousands of hobnailed boots striking the ground shook the walls. The battle had begun. From a collapsed space in the ancient wall, Grimface and the others watched it unfold.

The various banners lined up against Bailgard's forces: infantry with pikes in the front, javelin throwers behind, and the archers behind them.

Chariots were on the far-right wing, and cavalry on the other. Dog-men were spread out; their snarling war-beasts ready to attack. The drummers, trumpeters, and flag-men were near the rear where the generals and the kings were. The trumpets blared, and the combined army of the alliance began moving forward.

Bailgard's forces were moving toward their enemy. Among the forces under the black banner of Bailgard were Picts and Aqualonians, Opharians, Kothian, Zamorians, and many others. The rhythmic beat of the two converging armies made the ground quake, as thousands of men closed the distance.

In the sky, vultures, ravens, and every manner of carrion bird appeared. On the ground, the carnivorous beast of the wild began to gather. And still the ground quaked.

Bailgrad's army stopped. In the gap between the armies, thousands of black shapes came forth from the ground and attacked the alliance.

In the rear, where the alliance kings sat, men with robes wove magic, and lightning fell from the sky, as did hail and fire – all the while the alliance troops continued to move forward, until their front line of spearmen smashed into Bailgard's pikes and collapsed.

Smoke from burnt flesh and cries of anguish filled the air. The clash of armor and arms were like a roar from some inhuman horror.

Grimface watched with the intensity of a backgammon master. Some troops fell here, some fell there, some were moved to fill the gaps - it was the art of war.

The two front lines merged and ten thousand men fell dead. Bailgard was on a rolling platform in the back, and he stood tall as he began to sing. A creature the likes that no man has seen came from the ground.

It was larger than ten elephants, and stood taller than an Aqualonian siege engine. It had a long tail with a barbed point, and four massive legs with claws that looked like spears. The beast reared back and trampled a hundred men, then let loose a blast of fire that incinerated a hundred more.

The monster was biting, chewing, and clawing as it thrashed against the spears and arrows that were loosed upon it, then it was gone. It vanished in a puff of purple smoke that settled over the alliance forces, choking out hundreds more.

Bailgard's men gave a tremendous battle cry and charged. Man-to-man, the battle ensued. Bodies were hacked, and impaled, and the moans and prayers filled the air as readily as the arrows and spears.

As the light began to fail, the defeated Alliance retreated. Bailgard's army was a third of its original size, but still formidable. The whole of his forces turned now toward the ancient fort, and Grimface's army of three.

The wizard came to the well. "They come for us now. We will be battling in the dark, though your armor and weapons will provide sufficient light for fighting. Stand to my sides at first, for you will be my wings in this fight. I shall sing the ancient song, and no weapon forged by man shall molest you. When the time comes, I will silence Bailgard and his army will fall to our wrath. Mirida, it is time you descended into the well."

She came to him and laid her hands upon his arms. "I give you the blessing of my god, you will not falter, and his power flows to you." She turned and walked to the well and vanished.

Grimface sat down and chanted for a few moments, then he began to sing. His voice shook the ground.

From the earth came misshapen forms that carried blazing weapons and armor. The sounds of the enemy's drums were growing closer, and then dark clouds shut out the sky and lighting struck all around the fort with such burning force as to make a billion spots of sand glow white-hot.

Many of the approaching men were struck down. The ones that made it to the crumbling walls were met with Grimface's horrors. The creatures shrieked and lashed out. Grimface's battle had begun in earnest.

Burnt flesh, and screaming men filled the night air. Blasts of fire and lightning illuminated the sky. Bailgard's voice came from overhead as he ordered his men over the walls.

Those who got past the traps at the ramparts were met by Benhargan and Bulvife, whose blades cleaved bone and flesh. And yet, more came.

Grimface changed his tune, and the skin of the two Cimmerians glowed a mighty golden color. As arrow, spear tip, or sword blade struck them, no wound formed.

Picts came to the square, and the two Cimmerians waded in. Enemy arrows and spears drew no blood, nor slowed the Cimmerians in their blood lust. As Benhargan swung his sword, it passed through his enemy's blade, armor, flesh and bone as if passing through a thin vale of water.

Like a scythe through grass, the two barbarians cut down the enemy, until Bailgard appeared at the gates.

"Where is he who calls himself Grimface? I have come to teach him that magic is not for children," he called loudly.

# CHAPTER 29
# Blasted Heath

"YOUR VALUE IS SPENT. I have no further use for you. I will take back my daughter, and in the aftermath of this battle be raised to the level of king and own Hyboria by will of force alone," Bailgard shouted.

"Come forth and meet your doom, he who claims Hyboria for himself!" Grimface shouted back. "Your Atlantean blood will make this ground fertile in years to come!"

More soldiers poured over the walls and it was clear that Benhargan and Bulvife would soon be overwhelmed. Over his shoulder, Grimface shouted, "To the well, it is now time for us to part ways!"

The barbarians fell back. Their blades hummed, as arms, legs, and heads fell to their mad fighting. The bodies were piling, and the gore intensifying. The furious flood of deranged and battle-mad men seemed without end.

Grimface closed his eyes. Fire erupted from the ground and followed a wide path out into the valley. Soldiers were consumed. In the distance, horrors battled other horrors and black-winged things swooped and tore men limb from limb.

"Goodbye, beasts," Grimface called back. "You shall never set eyes upon Grimface again!"

From somewhere deep within him, a powerful energy frothed to the surface. Grimface moved and raised his hands. Fire was all around and everything combustible within the fort burst into flames.

A buzz rose in the air and a hot wind lay everyone beyond the gate flat. He walked past the fallen soldiers, until he'd left the safety of the mound. Bailgard's men fell by the thousands.

In the distance, the hint of dawn was coming. Grimface turned to face Bailgard, who was climbing to his feet.

The Atlantean's face was red with rage, and his clothes were smoking. He came and stood. "Noct et tu come foe deli tomb..." he began.

Grimface knew the words well, though he'd used them on rare occasion himself. Bailgard was going to undo his soul from the fabric of the universe, and there was nothing that would bring him back. Consignment to oblivion was going to be Bailgard's final act against Grimface – a fate that anyone possessing the power truly feared.

Just as Bailgaurd reached the part to insert Grimface's name, the wizard produced the doll and held it high. He pulled some loose strings that laced the doll's mouth, shutting it tightly.

Bailgard's mouth closed and did not reopen. He clawed at his tightly drawn lips, fully confused, then looked at Grimface and realized his mistake.

"Your henchmen sought to silence my voice – I credit them with the idea," Grimface mocked the prince.

Without hesitation, the prince drew his sword and launched himself at Grimface. Behind them the fires of Terar Chul Remod burned with incredible intensity.

Grimface took his sword and parried Bailgard's attack. The two men locked blades in single combat as they thrust and slashed at each other with fevered abandon.

Blood was falling all about as each man took wounds. Grimface fell over a crumpled body, hit the ground hard, blocked Bailgard, and rolled back to his feet.

The sun crested the far hills and all around the fortress from where the lighting had landed, a blast of bright light shown in the face of Bailgard's army, and the prince. It was as if millions of tiny mirrors all over the ground blazed with the morning sun. Bailgard raised his arm to protect his eyes. Grimface rushed at him.

The large man in black armor looked down - his chest open, and his beating heart exposed. A grin grew across his sealed mouth, as he saw his own sword buried deeply in Grimface's body.

The prince reached for the doll still in Grimface's hand, but the man held it fast. He pulled at Gimface, then fell to his knees and onto his side.

Bailgard, the last Prince of Atlantis was felled. Grimface removed Bailgard's hand from the hilt of the sword and staggered back. The blade was through his vital organs. He knew there was little time.

Falling to his knees, he took the doll threw it into a burning pile of wood not far from him. The wizard drew the sword from his own flesh and let it fall beside him. Blood pumped from his wound - bubbling gobs of red cascading to the ground. He looked behind him. The battle was still alive – men dying, and dark smoke swirling.

A bright light engulfed Grimface and he saw the battlefield—thousands of dispossessed souls wandering aimlessly about. A white fog was coming from afar.

Grimface stood up from his torn body and walked back up to the fortress. The Cimmerians were fighting – Bailgard's men flowing over the walls. The Cimmerians were in nirvana, covered from head to foot in the think dark blood that once gave life to their enemies.

He watched as the dark prince's forces pressed in, though they now climbed over the corpses of their comrades to reach the barbarians. A few more deaths, and the two barbarians were lost from sight behind a wall of dead bodies.

A light touch fell onto Grimface's shoulder, and he spun around. The fog had wiped clean the battlefield and there stood Chali his sister.

"Your family awaits you," she said with a gentle smile.

Grimface stared, his mouth open.

"Close your mouth brother, for a hawk may take your tongue!" Chali said, then laughed with such mirth that the wizard smiled.

He laid his arms around her shoulders and crushed her to him. "This is all that I've wanted since the fall of our people!"

"Welcome home, my brother. Come, see your children and wife – they wait," Chali said, and led him by the hand into the mist. There, in the distance, music filled with love came to his ears, and heart. At last, he was at peace.

Benhargan stepped back, as he roared with mad laughter – cloaked in the delight of battle. His foot found no ground for which to stand, only mangled flesh. He looked up, and a flash of light filled the sky. In the dazzling brilliance, the form of a person appeared. As it moved forward, he saw it was Kaltopia, a vision of white light, with a shimmering blade of brilliant polished metal in her hand. She was clad in shiny armor, and only for the briefest of moments looked down upon the Cimmerian with a smile.

She fell upon the enemy, and shocked screams rose. Somewhere, beyond the pile of the dead, she was laying waste to those who came to make war against her lover.

In his surprise at seeing her, Benhargan slipped in the thick blood, fell back, grasped for the rope, and plummeted into the well. He hit the water, knocking the wind from his lungs, then was hit from above by Bulvife.

There was another flash of fire, a hot blast into the hole, then piles of lifeless bodies of their foe collapsed and buried the top of the well. The sky was gone from view. The two barbarians got to their feet.

Benhargan's battle-mania faded. "What by the gods happened! Some treachery meist thinks has sent us tumbling into this well!"

Bulvife splashed the ice cold water over his face and hair. "I am on fire with battle lust!" he said.

Benhargan nodded toward the tomb. "Let us walk back toward the caverns."

It took only a few minutes until they found Mirida sitting on the ledge with her feet in the water.

She looked up with an almost expectant smile, then a melancholy came over her. "Are they all dead?"

"I don't know," Bulvife said.

"Your friend has traveled over. He, you will not see again," she said to them.

Benhargan grunted. "Ha! We have thought such before, and have been rebuked when that wizard has turned up again.

"He is gone," Mirida reassured him. "He will not return now."

Benhargan shook his head. "I'll believe it when I lay dying, and he has not shown his face." He looked up and down the channel. "We have to find a way out and back up, so I can finish this battle."

"Any ideas?" Bulvife asked.

"I guess if there was one well, there will be another," Mirida said to them.

"Okay, we'll follow the stream down-river," Benhargan suggested.

"Agreed," Bulvife stated.

They followed along the waterway in single file.

Benhargan stopped.

"So, somehow you killed the prince? I see that you flee with the girl," a voice said from the darkness.

"Hasmer," Benhargan said. "I owe you a messy death."

Ahead, the burnt and mangled body of the sorcerer stood. His robes were torn and bloody, and one of his hands missing, wrapped with a crimson cloth.

"I am going to enjoy hearing you two barbarians plead with me for death!" Hasmer began to sing.

But, before he could get out much of a tune, he clutched his throat. Benhargan had, somehow, leapt to within a few feet of the magician, and had sent his sword through the sorcerer's neck. Hasmer moved his lips – a fearful manic stare in his eyes.

"Trust me -," Benhargan said. "I would have loved to stretch this out, and flayed you alive, but I don't have the time."

Hyro ben Hasmer took two steps, then fell into the water, and was washed down stream.

"Who was that?" Bulvife asked.

"Just one more for my body count, nothing more," Benhargan said over his shoulder. "Now, let us be out of this estuary and back to the fighting!"

Ahead, Bulvife heard a confluence of two streams.

The tunnel met with another equally well wrought aqueduct and they continued. It took quite some time to find another opening, but finally, ahead, a light met their eyes.

A wooden grate was over the mouth of the tunnel. Bulvife took his sword and cut it away and stepped out into the bright sunlight. Men and women looked on as the two Cimmerians and the princess came out into a streambed. In the distance, there was a pillar of black smoke.

"We traveled a pretty distance," Bulvife said to Mirida.

"We did indeed, if that is the place from which we came," she replied.

"There was a mighty battle to be sure," an old man commented. "My son and I went to watch. There was much fire, death, and things that cause a man to question his own mind. Even now, two days after, the beasts clean up the remains."

"Two days?" Benhargan asked. "What trick is this, Crom? Underhanded, even for you to snatch such a glorious death from me!" He began walking toward the smoke.

"Wait!" said an old man. "We will all come too. We wish to see what is left. Maybe those armies have left treasure."

It took half the day to reach the battlefield, and another two hours to reach the blackened hill fort. All around the ruins, were scattered bones, shards of glass, torn armor and weapons. Near the fallen gatehouse Benhargan found Grimface's body, bloated from the heat, and eaten in places by wild beasts.

He walked up the hill; now only a blackened heath of melted brick, and swirling ash. In the middle, where the well once lay, was a mass of charred bodies formed into a solid charcoal dome.

Mirida pulled at Bulvife's arm. "We should go. The east calls to me, and I know that my child will be born there. Come with me, and together we shall found a new civilization. Be my king, and I will be your queen-wife." Her voice was sincere, filled with passion and longing.

Benhargan returned and harrumphed. "There are no soldiers left. The war is over!" he said disappointed.

Bulvife looked over the place again, then chuckled. "So, the wizard is really gone? I, for one, will drink much beer and mead to his memory, until my time comes to meet him in the lands of the dead. Come brother, we shall go to the east, and see this lady to her destination. There will be more wars to fight – I am sure of it. We will fight them together and die with blade in hand," Bulvife added.

"It galls me – that the magician has died a hero's death! Come, before we go, we must build a pyre, and see his remains sent to the gods. After all, as frustrating as he was, he was an honorable man."

"Very well. After, we will go east," Bulvife said.

"If the wind shall blow us that way!" Benhargan laughed.

Bulvife took Mirida by the hand and led her from the gates. There he saw hundreds of villagers standing about with blank expressions on their faces.

"I am Bulvife," he began, "Cimmerian, ranger, and warrior! We have lived to tell the tale of this epic battle! And, you will remember the name of

Bulvife, Benhargan, and Grimface. You shall bring wood for a pyre and food and drink for sacrifice. This war has ended, and your lives spared."

Benhargan spoke up. "In these ashes, you shall erect three statues! I will oversee your work. This ground is sacred, and you will provide sacrifice here until the stars fall from the sky." He walked toward the old man. "Do this and your days will not be falsely spent," he told him.

"We will do as you ask. Come, you will take respite with my family in our village. I think such work will take until the harvest. Thanks to these soldiers, we will reap much grain from these fields for many years to come... I think."

They left Terar Chul Remod and walked to the village. There Benhargan oversaw the work of the statues. Forged from limestone and brass, the likeness of the two Cimmerians, and the one wizard took shape.

In time, Mirida's belly grew, and something within her womb shifted and undulated. As the Blue Dragon was cresting the horizon, and the smell of rain wafted upon the air, Mirida took Bulvife by the arm. "It is time for us to take our leave. In five months' time my child will be born, and a new age will rise in the east."

"Benhargan, how goes the shrine?" Bulvife asked.

"It is all but complete. Paint and an eternal fire is all to be done and set."

"Then we can go," Bulvife said. "Come brother – conquest calls us, and our art is in demand. Away to the Seria Mountains and on toward Zamora and the green forests of the northern frontier."

As they prepared to leave, a string of ponies and three riding mounts in hand, Bulvife looked back at the small temple to Mitra where their likeness was erected.

"I'll be back," Bulvife said, as he walked into the shrine and looked up at the image of Grimface. "There is something strange that you brought to us, wizard. It was not your magic, or your wisdom... though both were telling of your many years. I speak of something you taught Benhargan and I – that there is more to living than dying – and there is more to making life than taking it. You cunning old magician – if I knew better, I'd say this you knew too, that we'd learn this lesson from you – and be all the richer for it."

"Come you sentimental fool! "chided Benhargan. "I have women to take, battles to fight, and drink to consume – and you are delaying me!"

Bulvife chuckled. "So it appears that I alone learned from you. Farewell my friend, and I hope you've found your family and peace where you've gone." He turned and strolled back to the caravan. Taking his horses reins, he began to walk.

"Tomorrow is the last day of the Blue Dragon," Mirida began. "Let us make good time if we are to get over the mountains before the snows fall."

Bulvife smiled and nodded. Benhargan shrugged his massive shoulders.

And, so it came to pass, that upon the dawn of the last day of the Blue Dragon Star, the three survivors from the war made by the last prince of Atlantis, vanished into the wilderness toward the east.

THE CIMMERIAN LOOKED at the thief who was nearly as drunk as he.

"So, why did you bring me here to this place?" His smoldering blue bail-fire eyes bore into the Khemite.

"I thought you might find it interesting. This place has been hallowed since long before you were born. Long before that god of yours, Crom was a child. It is said that a great battle was fought here, and three men stood against thousands. It is said that two of those men were Cimmerians, like you." The thief pointed at the marble gates that led into the courtyard of the temple. "Through those gates are the three statues."

The Cimmerian brushed back his cropped black hair and grunted. "Wait here, I will return."

He walked into the old temple and found his way to the courtyard. There in the middle were three statues, ruined with age. He looked upon their worn features and gazed at the faded inscriptions at the base. He nodded his head and walked back out.

"Did you see? There was one as large as you! He was probably your great, great, great grandfather," the thief said.

"Shut up," the Cimmerian chided. "We've wasted enough time on foolish errands. We will go back to the city, and I will take a woman, and we shall drink more beer and wine. Afterward, you will show me where this Tower of the Elephant is."

# ABOUT THE AUTHOR

The author Lawrence BoarerPitchford has penned more than seven novels. He has created tales of fantasy often with dark overtones and flawed anti-heroes. Along with fantasy, he has written novels of historical fiction, and science fiction, all providing the reader with vivid settings and relatable characters sure to titillate the avid reader.

If you liked The Last Atlantean Prince, you may also like some of his other works. They can be found at Amazon Books.

**CLASSIC FANTASY**
 **The Lantern of Dern Blackhammer**
 **In the World of Hyboria**
 **The Last Atlantian Prince**
 **Steampunk/SciFi**
 **Harrow's Gate**
 **Jake and the Solomon Lake Treasure**
 **Historical Fiction**
 **Sawbones.**
 **Thadius**
 *Horror/Mystery/Detective*
 **The Cox Head Horror**

# Don't miss out!

Visit the website below and you can sign up to receive emails whenever Lawrence BoarerPitchford publishes a new book. There's no charge and no obligation.

https://books2read.com/r/B-A-MRTR-YKVVB

**BOOKS 2 READ**

Connecting independent readers to independent writers.